The Englisher

BEVERLY LEWIS

Doubleday Large Print
Home Library Edition

BETHANYHOUSE
MINNEAPOLIS, MINNESOTA

The Englisher
Copyright © 2006
Beverly Lewis

Cover design by Dan Thornberg

Published by Bethany House Publishers
11400 Hampshire Avenue South
Bloomington, Minnesota 55438

Bethany House Publishers is a division of
Baker Publishing Group, Grand Rapids, Michigan.

ISBN 13: 978-0-7394-6811-1
ISBN 10: 0-7394-6811-1

Printed in the United States of America

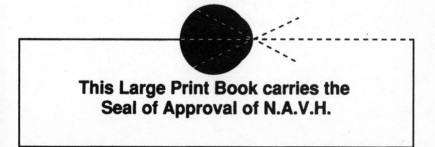

**This Large Print Book carries the
Seal of Approval of N.A.V.H.**

Dedication

To
David and Janet Buchwalter,
my cherished cousins.

By Beverly Lewis

ABRAM'S DAUGHTERS
The Covenant
The Betrayal
The Sacrifice
The Prodigal
The Revelation

THE HERITAGE OF LANCASTER COUNTY
The Shunning
The Confession
The Reckoning

ANNIE'S PEOPLE
The Preacher's Daughter
The Englisher

The Postcard • *The Crossroad*

The Redemption of Sarah Cain
October Song • *Sanctuary**
The Sunroom

The Beverly Lewis Amish Heritage Cookbook

*with David Lewis

BEVERLY LEWIS, born in the heart of Pennsylvania Dutch country, fondly recalls her growing-up years. A keen interest in her mother's Plain family heritage has led Beverly to set many of her popular stories in Lancaster County.

A former schoolteacher and accomplished pianist, Beverly is a member of the National League of American Pen Women (the Pikes Peak branch). She is the 2003 recipient of the Distinguished Alumnus Award at Evangel University, Springfield, Missouri. Her blockbuster novels *The Shunning*, *The Confession*, *The Reckoning*, and *The Covenant* have each received the Gold Book Award. Her bestselling novel *October Song* won the Silver Seal in the Benjamin Franklin Awards, and *The Postcard* and *Sanctuary* (a collaboration with her husband, David) received Silver Angel Awards, as did her delightful picture book for all ages, *Annika's Secret Wish*. Beverly and her husband make their home in the Colorado foothills.

Circles of sunlight dappled the side of the old covered bridge and the rushing creek below. On the treed slope to the west of the bridge, two children gripped the long rope in a jumble of fear and delight, swinging double. Their hands smelled of twisted hemp and sweat, but neither minded. The warm breeze on their faces, the "tickle in their tummies," as the little girl often said when swinging fast, were enough. That, and playing here in this enthralling place, where their older brothers caught pollywogs in the creek, jabbering in Pennsylvania Dutch and nibbling on soft pretzels all the while.

"I won't let you fall," the boy said.

"You're sure?" the girl asked.

"Here, I'll show ya how." He crisscrossed his black suspenders over the smaller girl and then snapped them onto his britches again. They began swinging high and higher as the sky opened its arms wide.

Prologue

Creative redirection. That's what my English friend Louisa says I need, though she says it ever so gently. Which is a right fancy way of saying I must be vigilant in finding acceptable ways to express my art . . . my very soul. She and I both know I belong here with the People, so I continually stifle the part of me that once gave me such joy. My never-ending urge to draw and paint.

It must be hard for Louisa to witness this grief of mine, especially as we are ever so close, like sister-cousins. She, too, mourns what she's abandoned, for the time being— her fashionable life in Denver, the modern world that weighed her down. She lives each day to see the beauty in all things Amish, *the art of being*, as she calls the simplicity of our lives here in Paradise, in the thick of buggies, social gatherings, and cookie-making frolics. And Louisa Stratford has experienced a broken engagement, as have I.

It's odd, but nearly the minute I had promised my preacher father I would turn my back on my artistic passions for a full six months, right then, all kinds of new temptations popped into my head like never before. I find myself tracing a design with my finger on my dress, or squinting and eyeing the shape of the cast-iron bell *Mamm* rings for supper. It's as if the drive to create cannot be squelched, neither from within nor without. But I hope, for the good of my word and for the good of my family, I can suppress it long enough to join church. By then surely I will have learned to obey. Without Lou's loving support, though, I can't imagine succeeding.

Nearly as strong as the tug to express myself on paper or canvas is my eagerness to see Ben Martin again. This befuddles me. An *Englischer*? Just as I am free of Rudy

Esh, in every way, I am determined to forget about this boy who can be nothing but trouble to my goal of joining church.

Yesterday, out on the road, we happened to run into each other when I was bringing the horse and sleigh home from an errand. Lo and behold if I wasn't alone, which is mighty unusual, as Luke or Yonie, two of my younger brothers, or *Mamm* regularly accompany me.

There he was. Tall and blond, just strolling along in the cold, his strong arms swinging at his sides, his head turned to gaze at distant snowy hills. Well, I didn't even think twice about whether or not to stop the horse—I did so straightaway, sitting alone in my father's buggy, risking being caught talking to Ben in afternoon's brash light.

I felt downright peculiar listening to him talk about his "hope," as he put it. *Jah*, he's determined to change my mind about turning him down for coffee—"we wouldn't be gone but an hour," he coaxed.

Of course, I couldn't even begin to ponder such a thing, and I managed to steer the conversation to something else altogether—the menfolk's local championship game of checkers over at the Gordonville Fire Hall.

Ben's eyes brightened and not surprisingly. I've learned that most men perk up at the mention of games: corner ball, baseball, volleyball, and whatnot. So I was glad to have diverted his thinking away from me, at least for a time. Now, if only I can stop thinking of *him*.

We must've talked for a good quarter hour. And without considering the consequences of being caught, I fed his obvious hope, slipping out from beneath my warm lap robe and climbing down from the carriage to talk with him. Right there along the road in the frosty air, where ofttimes I walked in the warmth of a summertime night, breathing in the sweetness of honeysuckle while cornstalks creaked in the field. On such evenings I liked to stare up at the stars, bemused at just how many the Lord God created. Right there, where it struck me anew that if the almighty One had taken time to form all those stars in the vast heavens, then did He also have time to heed a sparrow's fall and the number of hairs tucked under my white prayer *Kapp*?

I stood there and visited with Ben, where any one of the People could have witnessed the intriguing intent in his eyes. I can only guess what my own face—my too-readable eyes—communicated back to him, because my heart was saying some fearsome things to *me*. Things I don't recall feeling toward another man, not even my former beau, Rudy. And if it's true that the Lord God sees everything, He must never again see me with Ben.

Oh, such ill timing! On the heels of my handshake-agreement with *Daed*, yet. First, the pull of art on me, and now suddenly another issue weighs so heavily. *What on earth can I do about Ben?*

Honestly, I find myself sighing loudly whenever I think of this most recent encounter. That and dear friend Lou's kind admonition. *Creative redirection, indeed.*

Fair seedtime had my soul,
and I grew up
Fostered alike by beauty and by fear.
—William Wordsworth

Chapter 1

A half dozen blackbirds perched themselves on the makeshift scarecrow on the
edge of the snowy garden. The figure wore
Preacher Jesse Zook's own black trousers
and green shirt, which had already seen
better days when twenty-year-old Annie
had snatched them up, rescuing them from
the rag bag. The long shirtsleeves had been
rolled up months before to reveal the straw
man's upper appendages. Now the old felt
hat and wind-tattered clothing were quite
frozen, unyielding in February's blustery
gale.

The stark white clapboard farmhouse

was a welcoming sight in the fading light as Jesse made his way to the back porch. Stomping his snow-caked boots against the steps before making his way indoors, he was immediately aware of a tantalizing aroma.

Barbara's zesty veal loaf.

He hurried to the sink to wash up. "Smells wonderful-good, love."

"It's just us tonight," his wife said from the cookstove, her black apron barely spanning her fleshy middle.

"Oh? And where are the boys and Annie . . . and Louisa?"

Barbara Zook straightened, her face pink from the heat of the old stove. "Well, our sons were each wearin' their *for good* clothes, headed for some business in town."

Jesse nodded and gave a breathy chuckle. "Which means they each have themselves a girl. And Annie? Where's she keepin' herself this Saturday night?"

Barbara explained that a friend of Louisa's was flying in from Denver. "Annie hired one of the Mennonite drivers to take her and Louisa to the Harrisburg airport."

Another Englischer coming yet, Jesse thought. There had been nothing smart about his permitting Annie's fancy friend to stay *this* long, either. And now there would be two of them?

Since Louisa Stratford's arrival, Jesse regularly tossed in bed, wishing he had done things differently back when he might've changed the outcome of all the foolishness between Annie and her long-time pen pal, who was, more often than not, referred to as Lou by not only Annie but now Omar, Luke, and Yonie, his three teenaged sons. A young woman with a masculine nickname—downright peculiar.

Even so, this Lou had kept Annie here amongst the People. She seemed to be something of a balm to his daughter's soul, as well. For that, he was obliged.

He dried his hands on the towel and dropped into his chair at the head of the table. He considered his daughter's promise to refrain from painting pictures such as the one on the cover of last month's *Farm and Home Journal,* which he had prudently hidden away in the barn. When Annie set her mind to do something, she generally followed through. The difficulty was in knowing whether or not she'd been sincere when she gave her word to him some days back.

He recalled the time he'd caught his only daughter drawing in the barn as a wee girl, and her promising never to do it again. Some offspring were mighty easy to know, to have a real, firm connection with—and he certainly had this with his sons. But Annie? Well, they had the typical family rapport, but she was different . . . which was to be expected, he guessed. After all, she was a daughter.

Put aside your sin and give obedience a chance, he'd told her. And she had shaken his hand on it.

Now his present appetite for food quelled the jumble in his head, and he was pleased to see Barbara bringing the meat platter to the table and setting it down near him. She returned to the counter for a bowl of creamy scalloped potatoes sprinkled with bacon bits, and there were serving dishes of buttered red beets and of snow peas. When she'd seated herself to his right, he bowed for a silent prayer.

Afterward they ate without speaking, for the most part. No need for his wife to be made privy to those things that caused him continual irritation.

Truth be known, it wasn't just Annie's

worldly pen pal that concerned him so much. No, his grim memories of an impromptu burial—the remains of one Isaac Hochstetler, too young to die—also kept him awake at night. Jesse had been the one to handle the small knit of bones while the bishop gingerly pointed the flashlight over the hole as Jesse dug. Then he placed the skeleton in a clean burlap bag, laying it to rest back a ways from the cemetery itself. The knowledge of the lad's remains lying in the undisclosed grave gave him the willies . . . as though he and the bishop had done something altogether deplorable.

With the bishop's agreement, he had told Zeke where Isaac had been laid to rest. Zeke's response had been troubling.

Now Barbara spoke up suddenly as she served a piece of pumpkin pie with a dollop of whipped cream. "I guess Louisa's friend won't be stayin' with us."

Jesse grunted. "Why's that?"

"Evidently Courtney Engelman turned up her nose, according to Annie. Wanted electricity, I guess."

He felt the hair on the back of his neck prickle out. "This one's a *gut* friend of Louisa's, ya say?"

"Well, she must be, 'cause she was goin' to be in Louisa's wedding back last fall."

"So where's *this* Englischer stayin'?"

"That perty Maple Lane Farm guest-house, over yonder." Barbara forced a smile. She looked down at her generous slice of pie, not speaking for the longest time. "I . . . uh, I've been meaning to tell ya something," she said, meeting his gaze.

He touched her arm. "What is it, dear? You look all peaked."

"Well, jah, I s'pose I am," she said softly. "I've been having dreams—the same one— for a week now. 'Tis awful strange. Isaac Hochstetler's back in Paradise . . . like nothing ever happened to him." Tears filled her eyes and she reached up her dress sleeve and pulled out a small handkerchief, her lower lip quivering.

"Ach, Barbara . . ." He did not know what to say to comfort her. He couldn't just come out with the fact that Isaac could never, ever simply return. His bones were the final proof, although scarcely a soul was aware of them, aside from the bishop, himself, and Zeke. "I'm sorry your dreams are so troubled," he managed to say, stroking Barbara's hand.

Jesse retired to his rocking chair, mentally adding his wife's woes to his own while sitting near the fire. After a time, once Barbara was finished with her kitchen duties and had turned her attention to her needlework, he got up and donned his old work coat, carrying his uncertainties silently to the barn. He went straight for the rolled-up magazine cover, tucked away in the haymow in a safe and out-of-the-way place, where he had also hidden the old rope swing. He'd thought of turning it over to Zeke years ago but could never bring himself to relinquish it. More recently he had thought of simply burning it in a bonfire.

He sat on an old willow chair—his "thinking chair," he liked to call it. His father, a sage if ever there was one, had crafted the now ragged-looking chair in a hodgepodge sort of symmetry. Jesse had helped gather the willow sticks in early spring, when the sap was running, he recalled.

Now he looked at the cover art—Annie's own—holding it in his callused hands for at least the hundredth time, so mesmerizing it was.

Why would she choose to paint this?

He huddled against the cold, breathing in the pungent scents of manure and feed.

Comforted by the presence of the livestock, he pondered Annie's odd decision to paint the very place where Isaac had been abducted.

How could she possibly remember him yet? Does Isaac haunt her dreams, as well?

———

Louisa and Annie stood near the baggage claim area, across from the rental car counters, waiting for Courtney's arrival. Terribly fidgety, Louisa adjusted her head covering, then went to check the monitor for the second time. "Looks like her plane's late," she told Annie, returning.

"Hope everything's all right." Annie frowned slightly. "But you know more 'bout all this. . . ."

"Oh, it won't be much longer."

Annie excused herself, asking Louisa to "stay put," then headed toward the ladies' room.

Louisa hoped Annie wouldn't have any trouble finding her way back again. But then she realized how easy it would be to spot Annie here in this rather smallish airport with not another Amish person anywhere in sight.

In a few minutes, Courtney came gliding down the escalator, lanky as a model, her carry-on bag slung over her shoulder. Louisa gave a little wave when Courtney got closer, but Courtney kept walking.

"Court?" she called after her, very aware of how pretty her friend's shiny brown hair looked swinging loose around her shoulders. A slight twinge of envy nagged her, but Louisa pushed it away, keeping an eye out for Annie. "Courtney?" she called again.

Turning, Courtney stared at her. Really stared. "Louisa?" She literally gawked, her sea green eyes wide. Then, as if to shrug off her surprise, she said, "Well . . . hey, look at *you*." Courtney held her at arm's length, still studying her while Louisa wondered how she might explain her Plain attire to her longtime friend.

She felt terribly out of place, wishing Annie would hurry back from the rest room. "How was your flight?"

"Fine . . . just fine, thanks." Courtney scrutinized Louisa with a droll expression. "You said you were trying to fit in here, but . . . I had no idea you'd come out in public like this." At once she laughed as if making a joke.

Louisa was instantly glad Annie wasn't near. "You know what they say: 'When in Rome . . .' "

Courtney still looked a bit shocked. And she was speechless now, which was a good thing, especially because Louisa turned and spotted Annie walking toward them. "There's my pen pal, Annie—the one I told you about."

"So that's your famous Amish friend," Courtney said. "I can't wait to meet her."

Annie was smiling as she hurried to Louisa's side.

"Courtney, I'd like you to meet Annie Zook. And, Annie, this is Courtney Engelman."

Annie smiled, nodded. "Welcome. Nice to meet you."

"Thanks," Courtney said, looking Annie over, obviously unable to suppress her interest. "Same here."

When the luggage from the flight arrived, Louisa went with Courtney to pick up her second bag—*with five more pairs of shoes, no doubt*—wondering if it was such a good idea for Courtney to have come after all.

"How long have you been dressing . . . uh, like this?" Courtney asked quietly while they waited at the carousel.

"Since day one. But that's a long story."

"Oh?"

"I'll tell you all about it, Court."

When Courtney spotted her bag, she excused herself, waded through the other passengers and snatched it up.

Together, they returned to join Annie, who waited demurely near the luggage carts in her plum-colored dress, her long wool coat draped over her arm. "We're all set," Louisa said, and the three of them walked out to the curb where their driver was waiting.

"I wish you would have let me in on the dress code before I came, Louisa," Courtney whispered. "I hope you don't expect me to go around like that."

Louisa grimaced.

While they placed the luggage in the trunk, Louisa wished she hadn't said a word about filling Courtney in on her reason for dressing Plain. Suddenly, she felt it was flat none of her business.

———

Annie sat quietly in a white wicker chair in the upstairs bedroom at the Maple Lane Farm B&B while Courtney got herself settled. Situated in the midst of a wide meadow, near a winding brook, the colonial inn was only a short walk to Amish neighbors, one an accomplished quilter Annie knew.

Courtney gabbed up a storm with Louisa as she plugged in her portable computer and then rustled about to find a place in the empty bureau drawers to put away her clothing.

"How's it going with your roommate?" asked Lou.

"Oh, I've got two now . . . one's a guy," Courtney said, lowering her voice and glancing at Annie.

"Well, when did that happen?" Lou seemed very interested.

Courtney's eyes twinkled. "It's not what you think. We're just sharing a house. And Jared's terrific in the kitchen."

"He cooks?"

"Bakes bread, too." Courtney again glanced at Annie.

Lou mentioned a dozen or more other names Annie had never heard her say before, as Annie curiously observed Lou's interaction with her English friend. It was fairly clear Lou was hungry for information about the outside world, and Courtney seemed

more than willing to respond to the many in-
quiries, filling Lou in on the life she'd so
abruptly left behind.

Annie soon began to feel like a fifth wheel
but did her best to show interest. Courtney
paused from the chore of unpacking and
perched herself on the high canopy bed,
patting the rust red and white homemade
quilt.

Lou glanced sheepishly at Annie, then
stared pensively at Courtney's makeup bag.
Saying nothing, Lou reached up to run her
fingers across the delicate edge of the lacy
ecru canopy.

Courtney let herself fall back on the bed,
staring up at the underside of the canopy.
"Now *this* is elegant stuff," she muttered,
looking again at Lou's plum-colored dress
and black full apron, which matched Annie's. Courtney's pretty eyes drifted to Lou's
white head covering and lingered at the
middle part in Lou's hair.

Lou must have sensed the scrutiny and
resumed her chatter, asking about Courtney's plans following graduation. Annie felt
increasingly awkward, listening in on their
banter like a moth on the stenciled wall.

At one point, Lou glanced at her watch.

"We need to get going, over to Zooks'," she said.

Courtney frowned. "I should freshen up."

"Ach, you're just fine," Annie said.

"Yeah, let's go," Lou said. "Annie's mom's the best pie baker in the civilized world."

Courtney's eyebrows rose at that.

"Let's not keep her waiting," Lou urged.

Courtney shook her head. "Really, Louisa. I need time to unwind. I feel like I'm still flying. I'll join you tomorrow."

Lou gave in. "All right, I suppose you *do* look like you could use a bubble bath." The way she said it, Annie guessed she might long for one herself. "Glad you're here safely, Courtney. I guess Annie and I'll head home."

"Home?" Courtney gave Lou a curious look.

Annie wondered what her friend would say, but Lou only winked as if revealing a private joke. "You know . . . home for now."

Courtney nodded, then reached to feel Lou's dress sleeve, grimacing as if she'd touched a hot burner. "What sort of fabric is this, anyway?" Lou looked sheepish again, but Courtney's expression turned animated. "I think we've got a lot of catching up to do."

Lou's smile returned.

Annie spoke up, offering to return for Courtney with the horse and buggy first thing in the morning.

Courtney shook her head. "Maybe if I had directions, I could walk over."

"Too far. But if it's any consolation, I'll bring the team over myself," Lou offered.

"You?"

"Sure. I know how to manage a horse."

Courtney raised her eyebrows as if to say, *Now, that's interesting.*

Lou seemed momentarily pleased. "Welcome to Amish country," she said. "Loosen up. Have some fun!"

Annie was surprised by Lou's sudden offhand approach.

"So what time is breakfast?" Courtney asked.

"Six-thirty."

Courtney's mouth fell open. "You're kidding, right?"

"Too early?" Annie asked, stifling a grin.

"And don't forget," Lou added, "church is right afterward."

Courtney groaned. "Uh, that's a really long ordeal, right?"

Annie and Lou exchanged glances.

"C'mon, Court," Lou said. "We talked about this. You'll have a front-row seat."

Courtney sighed audibly. "Fine. A three-hour history lesson."

"Yeah, that's the spirit," Lou said.

"Cool. See ya," said Courtney.

They said their good-byes, but Annie could not shake her unsettled feeling. Not because she wasn't somewhat accustomed to worldly folk but because Courtney seemed to have something up her sleeve. Surely she wasn't here simply to tour the countryside or to visit an old friend.

Why'd she come here really?

Years ago Jesse had learned everything he would ever need to know about cows and milking procedures. The practical aspects and the shortcuts allowed by the bishops, including the use of an air compressor to keep fresh milk cooling and stirring in a bulk milk tank, powered by a diesel engine.

But this night, with lantern in hand, he heard only the mooing of Holsteins chained to their wooden stanchions. Milk cows were such an enormous part of his family's livelihood.

The memory of lowing cattle had been planted in his mind for nearly two decades now, since the fateful evening he'd met with Isaac's stubborn father, Daniel, in the Hochstetlers' barn. *"You are God's anointed."* Jesse had been adamant, cautioning Daniel of the dire situation at hand. *"You've rejected almighty God, don't you know? It is imperative that you take up the office of preacher as ordered by the drawing of the divine lot."*

Imperative. The word had pounded in Jesse's brain even then. Alas, Daniel had chosen that dark and different path, against the angels of heaven. The first-chosen of the Lord God had stated his decision, slapping his black hat against his thigh for emphasis. *"The deed's done. I've made my bed. Now I'll lie in it,"* Daniel had told him.

Jesse wandered outside, making his way through the snow, strangely drawn to the tall scarecrow over yonder. He stared at it, gritting his teeth. No need to protect a sleeping garden against the boldest of birds in winter, and spring was months away. One look at the arctic gray sky and anyone could see that.

Anger, long suppressed, rose in him and overflowed in one hasty gesture. Marching forward, he set down his lantern and began to dismantle the straw man, first tearing away the cold-hardened shirt to reveal the straw body, then the worn black britches. His gloved hands fumbled repeatedly as he breathed in icy air.

Helpless Isaac, his life snuffed out like a wee candle. Barbara's dreams fraught with empty hope, when the reality is in the buried truth.

Jesse thought of his daughter, welcoming yet another worldly outsider into their midst. *Where will it end?*

His disturbing thoughts pushed Jesse beyond the brink of good sense.

The old hat was next to go, and the wooden crossbeam. When Jesse was done, the pieces lay on the desolate ground.

He piled up the scraps of clothing, along with the wooden structure itself. He carried the whole of it to the refuse pile behind the barn, conscious of a pounding in his temples and heat on his neck.

The raucous cawing from the backyard

willow made him stop and look up as he made his way toward the house. In the moonlight, he saw half a dozen blackbirds perched boldly on the uppermost branches.

Predators will come no matter. . . .

Chapter 2

Ben Martin had a hankering for a turkey sandwich on toasted rye. He clicked out of the Churchill Downs Web site, having navigated around each location on the site for a solid hour. Stomach growling, he headed to the small galley-style kitchen and opened the fridge and the see-through vegetable drawer for some lettuce and half a tomato. Then several slices of smoked turkey, the all-important mayo, and two pieces of dark rye.

He dropped a handful of ice into the largest glass mug in the cupboard—a gift he'd received for being a groomsman for his good buddy's wedding last year. *Back before everything broke loose. . . .*

When he'd finished making the sandwich, he cut it in half diagonally, as his mother always did. He remembered as a boy lifting the lid on his Aladdin lunch box and finding the sandwiches halved. One of Mom's trademarks. That and the cored whole apple, wrapped in aluminum foil. Why she didn't quarter it and cut out the seeds like his classmates' mothers did, he'd never known.

While eating his lunch, he flipped through his mail, spying an overnight letter from his mom, which included his Social Security card. *Finally,* he thought. He was one step closer to acquiring a Pennsylvania driver's license.

Weeks ago he'd asked her to mail his birth certificate as well, since due to 9/11 Homeland Security measures, two additional forms of ID, along with his Kentucky license, were required. Unfortunately, his mother hadn't had time to unearth it, having moved important files to the attic when their basement partially flooded during a severe storm in mid-November last year. Although she was rather apologetic, it didn't seem she was trying all that hard, most likely hoping Ben would give up this nonsense and return home, upsetting as all this had been to her.

Not wanting to wait any longer, and tired of asking for it only to realize he was rubbing salt in the wound of his leaving, he had decided to apply directly to the Office of Vital Statistics in Frankfort, Kentucky, for another official copy.

Finishing off his sandwich, he began to fill out the application, recalling a long-ago exchange between himself and his sisters. And one mouthy cousin.

He had been trying to get his mom to find some baby pictures for his "Guess Who?" project at school. But his mother had been busy cooking and entertaining their relatives from Iowa at the time. One of the cousins and his sisters had ganged up on him, teasing him mercilessly. "Well, maybe you're adopted," his cousin had said, sporting a mischievous grin.

"Yeah, ever think of that?" said his sister Patrice.

Yet another sister, Sherri, had joined in on the fun at his expense, holding up a mirror to his face. She made a scrutinizing frown. "Here, take a look and see."

He had kidded them back. "Cool! You're not really my sisters then, right?" He eyed the obnoxious cousin, too. "And . . . you? Well, figure it out, cuz."

"Wait a minute," Patrice had declared with seeming disappointment, still holding the mirror. "Your eyebrows have the same arch as Dad's."

"Huh?"

"And you have Mom's nose."

Sherri piped up. "You inherited Daddy's funky annoying laugh, too!"

"Don't forget Mom's morning breath," Patrice added.

"Okay, that does it." He began chasing them around the house, catching Patrice and holding her upside down over the toilet, threatening to douse her, head first.

"I'm gonna die . . . and it'll be . . . your fault," she screamed. "Mom!"

Diana, his youngest sister, had sat in the corner, clapping and egging him on that day. He thought of all four of his sisters now, missing them. He wondered what they would think of Annie if they ever had an opportunity to meet her. But that was a slam dunk. They'd like her all right. *A lot.*

He put down his pen and twiddled it between his fingers. "So . . . have I stumbled onto the girl for me?"

Putting both destiny and love in the same breath was foolish, wasn't it?

Annie was not only Amish, but of the strictest order. He knew this from hearing his employer, Irvin Ranck, speak of Preacher Zook and his family, who were cousins to Irvin. Ben had no business seeking out such a girl. How well did he know Annie, anyway? Sure, he'd enjoyed talking with her on the road the other day, and she kept showing up at the same places as he did. But, hey, this wasn't a metropolis. People were bound to run into each other here.

But love?

He dismissed his mood as relating to homesickness. After all, he sometimes felt disconnected from his family, living here instead of in his native Kentucky, having rarely left his hometown—until recently. He spent hours on email and instant messaging each week, keeping in touch with his family.

Still, there was no denying he was captivated by the Plain culture as a whole and always had been. Even the infrequent times he had bumped into a few "horse and buggy" people in Kentucky.

He leaned his head back and reclined against the exceptionally comfortable chair, pleased to have stumbled onto it at a local estate sale. *A great find.* He congratulated himself once more on having negotiated the price down. *Another trait I inherited from Dad.* He chuckled, the correlation leading him to think of a whole list of other qualities the two of them shared.

He cut loose with a nervous laugh in the stillness of his living room, but it did not keep him from pondering, for the umpteenth time, the mystery that had brought him here to Pennsylvania's Amish country.

———

Daybreak came all too quickly, and Ben stumbled over his boots on his way to the shower. *Too short a night,* he thought, wondering why to this day he wasn't one to sleep in, even as tired as he felt this quiet Sunday morning.

He took his time shaving, combing through his hair, and dressing, all the while considering Irvin Ranck's standing invitation to attend church. But Ben had put him off this long—why change his mind today?

He made enough scrambled eggs to satisfy his enormous appetite, recalling Zeke Hochstetler's recent visit. He, too, had mentioned this Sunday was to be a preaching day.

Does everyone attend church around here?

Ben forked into the soufflé-light eggs on his plate, enjoying his meal, thinking about his growing friendship with Zeke. He was one uptight fellow but seemed to enjoy hanging around the tack shop several times a week. It was from Zeke and a few others like him that Ben had learned a great deal about the Amish in a short amount of time, and it didn't take much to imagine a whole group of them assembled at a long table for breakfast.

But fleeting images of such a gathering came almost too easily, as if he could taste the eggs, like the ones on his plate, only with diced green peppers, onions, and bits of ham. He shook it off as he had other mental images since arriving here. He wasn't the only outsider who'd experienced an obsession with these people, strangely set apart, and their staid, family-oriented culture.

He glanced at the digital stove clock. *I'm working too many hours,* he concluded, forcing himself to switch gears, pondering how to win a yes from Annie on coffee or dinner.

Inhaling deeply, he recalled how silent, even obstinate, she had been at the outset of their first meeting. The second time they'd met, too. Or had she been merely cautious? She must have had a safety antenna up her whole life, around strangers at least. *Englishers,* Irvin said was the name the Amish assigned to the likes of him.

How many Englishers does Annie know? He thought of Louisa, who was the most mysterious case of all. *What sort of person dresses Plain when she isn't?*

He used his fork to get every morsel and had the last bite of jellied toast. When he was finished, he carried the plate and coffee mug to the sink.

In no way was he interested in attending church today. But he *was* eager for a drive deep into Amish country. . . .

Chapter 3

Louisa had gotten up extra early to help Annie hitch up the team, and before leaving to pick up Courtney and bring her back for breakfast at the Zooks', she turned on her smart phone—her Palm—to see if she had any messages from London . . . namely, from Trey Douglas.

Sure enough there was one, but as she listened she detected a new urgency in his tone. He said he had "the perfect idea" and wanted to discuss it with her.

After speed-dialing his number, she hurried back to the house to warm up. She stood in the enclosed porch, out of earshot.

"What's up, Trey?" she asked when he answered.

"Hey, Louisa! Great to hear your voice."

He sounded eager, almost too confident, and the more he talked, the more she sensed something big was up his sleeve.

"You said you had an idea?" she prompted. "What is it?"

"Well, for starters, I thought maybe you'd consider flying over to see me. Spend a long weekend here soon . . . I could show you around. It'd be terrific, Louisa." He paused. "You might even think about staying. . . ."

"Well, that sounds like fun."

Then she swallowed, hard. *Staying?*

"So, you ready to pack your bags? Abandon your Amish lifestyle for the glamour of London?"

I hope he's kidding, she thought, feeling oddly resistant. She wasn't sure why she wasn't ready to jump at the chance to travel . . . to see Trey again, face-to-face. *Have I changed so much?*

"Louisa?"

"Yep?"

"I really hope you'll think about it."

She sighed. Until just this moment, she

hadn't fully come to grips with her feelings. There was no way she could return to their former relationship. Sure, he was nice. Charming . . . and really wonderful, too. He treated her like a lady in public and loved to pick up the tab . . . show her off. But he had no clue about the happiness in something as simple as feeding peacocks or walking beneath a noonday sun, soaking in its warmth on an otherwise brisk day. No, he couldn't begin to understand how it felt to pull on crusty old work boots—too big, so she stuffed in rolled-up socks—to help clean out the manure ditches, holding her breath but getting a real kick out of the earthiness of country living.

"I'd like to pick up where we left off," she heard Trey saying. "I should never have walked away. . . ."

She wrinkled her nose at the thought of getting too intimately involved, especially distasteful after having broken off her engagement to Michael not so long ago. *I wish he wouldn't pressure me.*

"I don't know," she said, suddenly dreading the notion of spending time with Trey. This came as a surprise because she had been enjoying his attention since coming here to Paradise, had even been attracted to him. But now?

His voice was softer now, almost irresistible. "Sure you know, Louisa. Trust me, you'll love London."

She inhaled, slow and long. "No, Trey. It's nice of you to ask, but I'm staying here."

He didn't challenge her but promised to keep in touch. Then, quickly, she said goodbye and hung up.

She smiled to herself when she began to ponder maybe it wasn't only her love of simplicity that had prompted her to refuse Trey's invitation. Maybe it had more to do with Sam. . . .

She hadn't told Annie, but she had exchanged a few *hellos* with one of the young Amish men at the Preaching services recently—Samuel Glick, who went by the nickname Sam. It wasn't that she had a crush on him in the typical sense of the word. But she found herself strangely intrigued by him.

Heading out the back door, she called to Annie, who came running out of the barn to catch up. Then, raising her skirt, Louisa climbed into the right side of the carriage, still finding it amazing she could get in and out dressed like this . . . not to mention handle a horse.

When she and Annie arrived at the inn on Paradise Lane, they found the front door unlocked, and since it was so early, they simply tiptoed upstairs to Courtney's room. There they discovered her sound asleep. They stood at the foot of the canopy bed, observing the mound of covers and the beautiful quilt.

"She's out cold," Louisa whispered. "No way she'll be ready now for breakfast or Preaching. . . ."

"I say we shake her good—that'll get her up," Annie said jokingly.

Louisa considered Annie's suggestion. She wished they could let Courtney sleep off her jet lag, but if so, they would not see her again until much later in the day.

Gingerly she sat on the edge of the bed and whispered Courtney's name.

Zero response.

She jiggled against the bed slightly, but again nothing.

Finally she jostled Courtney's arm. Her friend awakened, but it wasn't pretty.

"Hmm? Oh, hey, Louisa. Is it morning already? I had trouble sleeping." She raised her head slightly off the pillow. "I took a sleeping pill around two o'clock."

Yikes, thought Louisa, pulling the covers higher in an attempt to tuck her friend back in. "I'll skip Preaching service and come back for you in a few hours," she offered.

Courtney's eyes drooped shut. "Nah, you go ahead. I'll have to sleep this off . . . past noon or so."

Louisa rose, still looking down at her friend. "This afternoon, then?"

Courtney gave no response.

"She's out but good," Annie said softly. "Ain't so keen on church, I take it."

Neither was I at first, Louisa realized.

———

On the way back from the B&B, Louisa hurried the horse, Betsy, enjoying the feel of the reins even more since talking to Trey. The morning was sunny but freezing cold, and she embraced the familiarity of Annie's companionship.

"Too bad Courtney didn't get a good night's sleep," Annie said.

"Yeah, not many people have the chance

to attend an Amish Preaching service—and she snoozes it."

"Oh, she isn't the first person to snooze through a preaching," Annie said, grinning.

Louisa giggled, surprised at Annie's joke.

"She might've enjoyed it," Annie continued wryly. "Or at least found some humor, ya know. All the Plain costumes crammed into one room."

Louisa snorted. "She'll get over it . . . jah?"

Annie poked her playfully. "You and your *jahs*."

"It's just so much fun."

Annie leaned forward. "Are you enjoying your time here, really?"

"Well, sure." Louisa looked away, not sure she was ready to share too much. Fact was, as much as she loved Amish country, just seeing Courtney again had made her homesick. It reminded her, too, that she hadn't heard from her parents in the longest time. *Maybe they've given up on me.*

"Nobody's keeping you here, ya know," Annie said, as if reading her. "I wouldn't blame you one bit if you wanted to follow Courtney home. It's been so much fun just havin' you—"

Again, she thought of Trey's sudden invitation. "Annie? Listen to me . . . I'm not going anywhere, unless you're tired of me."

"Oh, you. How could that be?" Annie was quiet for a moment. "And I understand, too . . . how it feels to be lonesome."

Louisa nodded, her thoughts wandering now to Michael.

"I mean to say, no matter how peaceful it seems here, no matter where you grew up, home is always home. I'm sure Ben Martin misses Kentucky, too." Annie gasped and clapped her hand over her own mouth.

"Wha-at?" Louisa giggled. "Where did *that* come from?"

Annie mumbled through her hand. " 'Tis hard to say."

"You can't fool me. You like him, so what's wrong with admitting it?"

"Just everything, really."

Louisa jerked her head in a nod. "But why? Maybe it's time you got to know him. Find out if there's any potential there."

"Ach, for goodness' sake . . . potential for what?" Annie shook her head. "You can't be serious."

The Zooks' lane came into view, and

Louisa pulled hard on the rein. "I guess it's something you'll never know, then."

Annie smiled. "I have no intention of knowin'. Ben's not for me. End of story."

"Fine. Don't find out. That's cool."

They looked at each other—the sort of knowing glance between close friends—and burst into laughter.

———

Following the common meal on Sunday, Louisa noticed Sam Glick walking around the long table, heading toward her.

Annie was off chatting with two of her sisters-in-law and several other young women, so Louisa didn't feel quite as uneasy as she might have when he leaned down and asked, "How're you today, Louisa?"

She looked up, aware of the confidence in his gaze, the way his eyes drew her.

"Wanna go for a walk?" His voice was low.

Doesn't he know who I am?

She looked around to see if anyone was observing them. Surely Sam knew she wasn't one of them. "Well, if you think it's a good idea . . . I mean—"

"Seems like a nice day for a walk, jah."

She wouldn't laugh. The day was bitterly cold and no one in their right mind would want to go walking in this weather. Yet she found herself saying yes."

Annie couldn't help but notice what a striking pair they made: Lou wrapped in a heavy woolen shawl over her dark blue cape dress and white apron, and Sam, one of Jesse Jr.'s best friends. Sam was taller than Annie had realized till now, looking downright handsome, his broad shoulders filling out his black split-tail frock coat. Still unhitched at twenty-three, Sam was clean-shaven and wearing newly pressed black broadfall trousers. Dark hair clean and shiny as can be, his bangs peeked out from beneath his winter hat as he strolled with Louisa through the slush and snow.

Ach, interesting . . .

Louisa had never mentioned Sam during their long nightly chats. Annie *had* noticed, however, that following the last Sunday singing, Sam had sought Louisa out. Just as he had today.

Now Annie watched as they trudged out onto the narrow farm road that led to the

vast whiteness of the dormant cornfield behind Deacon Byler's farmhouse.

Best not to interfere. Annie stood at the
kitchen window, observing Sam's long gait
and Louisa's ladylike pace. *I wonder what
they're talking about.* . . .

Lest she become too curious, she turned
to search for her friend, Esther Hochstetler,
and found her rocking infant Essie Ann near
the wood stove at the far end of the kitchen.

"How're you and the children makin' out
over at Julia's?" asked Annie softly, still
thinking how peculiar it was for Lou to go off
with Sam like that.

Esther smiled prettily, her blue eyes
brighter than Annie had seen them in some
time. "This here babe's my big reason for getting up in the mornin'." She went on to talk
about Essie's first real smile, the "precious little cooing," and "so many dear, wee things,"
as if Esther were a brand-new mother. Then,
quickly, she spoke of Laura, Zach, and little
John. "The children miss their father somethin' awful," she confided in a whisper.

"I'm sure you miss Zeke, too." Annie
glanced about her to see if they were being
overheard.

"I best be talkin' with you 'bout that here before too long." Esther blinked back the tears.

Annie patted her hand. "I 'spect you're confused . . . understandably so."

Esther sighed. "I miss seein' you. We don't have enough time to, well . . . talk plainly when you come to Julia's to work." Esther lifted the baby onto her shoulder. "I also don't want to wear out my welcome at the Rancks', ya know."

"I doubt that's possible," Annie said, knowing her cousin Julia as she did. "You're mighty welcome to stay as long as need be, and that's the truth. My cousin has said so repeatedly."

"Well . . . I sometimes worry 'bout that. Zeke wanted to visit last evening, but he was so belligerent Irvin had to take him aside, Julia told me later. She said he'd have to be seein' Irvin for coffee every couple of days— for a good long while—before they'd consider letting him spend time with me alone."

Annie reached over to touch Essie's tiny rosy cheek. She thought of the colors necessary to paint such a sweet face, if she were allowed. "You mean to say Zeke hasn't even laid eyes on this little one yet?"

"Sadly, *nee*—no." Esther looked away, as if to deny more tears. "'Tis his own fault, I daresay."

"Such a hard time it is for you."

Esther nodded her head slowly. "Oh, Annie . . . more than you know."

Annie pulled up a chair. "Well, if Irvin's decided to take Zeke under his guidance, so to speak, that's a wonderful-good thing."

Esther dabbed a hankie at her eyes with her free hand. "I know 'tis . . . jah, for sure. It's just that . . . well, I do miss him quite a lot. In spite of everything." She blinked fast, still struggling. "And to make matters worse, I've got me a bad case of the baby blues."

"Aw, Essie . . ."

Esther's lower lip trembled uncontrollably.

"My sister-in-law says there are good herbal teas to help with that."

"Oh, jah, I forgot. I know just which one I'll brew up."

"Well, I'm glad we talked today."

Esther nodded; then she looked up at her. "I would also like to know what's good for a broken heart. . . ." Her words hung in the air.

"S'posin' if I knew that, I'd be quick to tell

you." Truth be known, making Ben's acquaintance had somehow begun to soothe Annie's own brittle heart, strange as it seemed.

Louisa was surprised when she realized how far they had walked into the silent field. Caught up in interesting conversation with this country boy who insisted on calling her *Freind*—Pennsylvania Dutch for "friend"— she had lost track of time. And her good sense, she feared.

"I'm glad we had this chance to get alone . . . if only for a bit." He looked over his shoulder at the distant Byler farmhouse. "Can I talk you into comin' over to the barn singing at my father's place tonight?"

What's he thinking, asking me out? She wondered what Courtney would want to do tonight, as well. *Having her here complicates things even more.*

She tried to guess what he might be thinking behind his spectacular green eyes. "I hope you aren't fooled by my Plain dress," she said. "I have no intention of becoming Amish . . . I only wear Annie's dresses and aprons so I'll fit in here for the time being. Don't want to cause trouble for the preacher's daughter."

He smiled and tilted his head to shade it from the afternoon sun. "Seems to me Annie finds trouble a-plenty as it is. All the fellas are still scratchin' their heads over her—well, her and Rudy Esh. 'Course, now he's married to Susie, but Annie really hurt him by lettin' him go and all."

She wasn't about to say she knew much of anything about that. It was not her place and none of his business, and she was fairly sure he would respect that. Maybe he'd brought her out here, far from the homestead, to see what he could get her to say about Annie. "Sometimes it's best if relationships fail. That's all. Rudy looks very happy with his bride." She found that saying *bride* reminded her, once again, of how she'd nearly made it to the bridal altar herself. And she thought again of Trey, how his pushing, even though it was long-distance and via voice mail, really annoyed her.

"That Annie Zook's one fine catch, but no one seems to be able to get her attention much." Sam was still smiling broadly, but it was clear to Louisa that Annie wasn't the girl he was most interested in at the moment.

He told her of his surreptitious stint at

Harrisburg Area Community College, on the Old Philadelphia Pike, and Louisa was shocked at his openness. "I had no idea," she said, wondering how he ever would've fit in.

"I didn't dress Plain, mind you. I did my best not to stick out, just as you are doin' here, Louisa."

"What did you study?"

"Business, and I got what I was after. I finished up all my courses . . . graduated with a three-point-eight, but only a few know. The brethren weren't so happy with me, but they figured I was in *rumschpringe*. You know about that?"

She said she'd heard of the tradition from Annie. "How will you put your studies to good use?"

"Still workin' on that."

They walked a ways farther in comfortable silence.

After a time, she said, "How hard is it for a person to figure out what they really want in life?"

He paused as if pondering her question. "I s'pose it can be easier said than done."

"That's the truth. I can't count the times I

thought I was right on with something . . . only to realize I was following the wrong path."

"Things tend to come more easily for some than others," he replied. "My brothers, for example . . . things just fall into their laps. The oddest thing."

She agreed that life's struggles came and went.

He paused briefly. "Would ya want to head on back?"

"Sure, if you do." She couldn't believe such an appeasing remark had popped out of her mouth.

"Well, if it were up to me, I would stand right here and continue talking to you," he admitted.

She tried not to smile. He was so honestly outspoken. Certainly countrified, but smart, too. His interest in higher education was a real no-no, from what Annie had told her, but Sam was anything but pretentious. She knew clearly where he stood on everything from raising chickens to butchering hogs to conservative politics, such as they were, and even how many strapping sons he hoped to have one day. Louisa believed she was forging a bona fide friendship with Samuel R. Glick—no game playing, no pressure. He knew she wasn't staying in Paradise. They were just walking and talking and having fun in this moment.

"What's the *R* in your name stand for?" she asked boldly.

"Family name. But not your typical Amish." He explained it stood for Ranck, commonly a Mennonite name. "There's an interesting story that goes with that."

"I know some Rancks," she said. "Cousins of Annie Zook's father."

"I heard that, too." He pushed his hat forward a bit on his head. "My connection to the Rancks comes from three generations back, is what my father says. My great-grandfather fell in love with an Amish girl and married her. That's how I came to be Amish, too."

Non-Amish marrying into a cloistered group? How weird is that?

"I've never heard of that . . . where someone from the outside comes in and joins."

"It's rare, but it happens."

Louisa and Sam turned to walk back toward the deacon's big stone house.

"I hear some of the youth are callin' you Lou," he said suddenly. "But you seem more like a Louisa to me."

"Oh, that's Annie's and her brother's idea. I doubt it'll stick."

"Well, I sure hope not. You're much too perty for a tomboy name."

She felt the flame of embarrassment in her cheeks. "Uh, I think Annie will wonder where I've disappeared to."

"Oh, I'd say she's smarter than that."

"You know what?" she said suddenly, surprising even herself. "I think I might go to the singing tonight."

His eyes lit up. "So I'll be askin' ya to ride home in my courting buggy, then?"

Not to let on . . . and not to be stupid, either, she said, "That's very nice of you, Sam. I hope you won't mind if I think about it, though."

"If you're coming to singing, you've gotta get home somehow, jah?" He smiled broadly.

"I suppose that's true." She left it at that. One small problem, of course. Courtney would *not* be interested in attending a barn singing. Even if she surprised them and agreed to go, there was no way it could possibly work unless Louisa talked *her* into abandoning her fancy clothes and slipping on one of Annie's cape dresses.

Yeah, like that'll happen!

Chapter 4

Not only was Courtney gone from the B&B when Louisa and Annie arrived back at the colonial inn later, but she had taped a note on her door.

Hey, Louisa!
All that sleeping made me hungry, so I'm out for a late lunch. I figured you and Annie had someplace to be, since it's Sunday. I'll catch you later.
I've got wheels—I called for a cab!
See ya!
Courtney

Louisa slipped the note deep into her dress pocket, and she and Annie made their way down the long staircase. They turned and waved to the smiling owner and headed back outside to the waiting horse and buggy.

"She must've slept in really late," Louisa said, checking her watch. "It's already three-thirty. Guess it was my fault . . . that long walk with Sam."

"You could ask to use the phone here, maybe."

Louisa agreed it was a good idea. They hurried back up the walkway and into the house. After requesting permission, they were led into the large sitting room, near the open kitchen, where she dialed Courtney's cell number. She got the voice mail, left a short message, and hung up. Courtney was probably talking to one of her college pals back home. *But she has call waiting*, Louisa remembered. So Courtney would have known Louisa was trying to get through. *No, of course not . . . she wouldn't have recognized the inn's ID.*

Once they were outside again, Annie hopped into the driver's seat. "You'll see her later," Annie said. "Don't fret. Maybe she'll try callin' you soon." She picked up the reins, smiling.

"Well, I guess if I brought my Palm along sometimes that might help." Louisa laughed at herself, realizing that on some level, at least, she had actually begun to dismiss the outside modern world—if only occasionally.

They rode along, crows heckling overhead in the icy air as Louisa settled into the front seat of the enclosed gray buggy for the ride back to the Zooks' farmhouse. Looking over the stretch of drifted white cornfields, she was aware once again of the way the fields literally ran up to the People's front yards. *As if the Plain and the fancy are somehow interwoven, in spite of their differences*, she decided, realizing inwardly that she, too, was an odd part of this intermingling, at least for the present. *A modern woman's soul dressed in Amish garb. The strangest thing I've ever done*. She recalled again Courtney's reaction at the airport.

"Are you planning to go to the singing tonight, Annie?" She hadn't intended to ask quite so abruptly. The question was out, nevertheless.

"Why, no. I just assumed Courtney was comin' for supper." Annie glanced at her,

eyes revealing a surprised glint. "Any particular reason why *you'd* want to go tonight,
Lou?"

Not wanting to stir up unnecessary suspi-
cion, Louisa simply said, "Just wondered."

"Well, if we did happen to go . . . and we
took along your friend, she might cause a
stir if she showed up in her trousers, ya
know!"

No kidding, Louisa thought. Just then it
occurred to her—"I hope you didn't worry
about *my* coming here. You certainly had no
idea I would do my best to blend in. Not be-
forehand, at least."

Annie shook her head. "Ach, no, your
visit was long overdue. Don't think another
thing 'bout it."

She found it interesting how accepting
Annie had been even from the earliest days
of their letter writing. She recalled Annie's
prompt replies with Amish sayings printed
on a separate page along with sketches of a
one-room schoolhouse, Annie's father's
black buggy, and other childish drawings.
Never had there been any hint that Annie
was doing something inappropriate by having an English pen pal, or that she should be
careful about what she wrote. No indication,

either, that Annie had any problem with Louisa's being "worldly" and Annie, herself, as Plain as can be.

"I say we plan on goin' tonight," Annie said, bringing Louisa out of her reverie.

"You do?"

"Sure, but first let's see what happens with Courtney's plans—whatever they are—before we decide." Annie smiled. "There's been some quiet talk of a square dance."

Oh, great. Sam didn't say anything about that.

Louisa's Palm was in the top drawer of the bureau in the Dawdi Haus. She wondered how long before Courtney might actually call. "If we dress her up Plain—" she laughed out loud—"she might end up riding home with a cute Amish boy! Who knows?"

Annie cast a knowing glance her way. "Cute, jah?"

"Well, you know." And she was fairly sure Annie caught her meaning.

"A raw day for a walk, jah?" Jesse said after the common meal when he saw Zel coming back from the outhouse.

Zeke nodded, his face drawn, his black hat pulled low on his forehead.

Jesse waited for Zeke to get closer before saying what was really on his mind. "S'pose you made it over to the graveyard all right, then?"

Zeke's bearded chin trembled momentarily. He slapped his gloved hands on his arms. "Can't seem to get myself over there, now that I know where you and the bishop buried him."

"Well, no one's sayin' you have to go, Zeke. Maybe it's for the best if you don't." Jesse put a hand on his shoulder. "You've been through some rough waters."

"Jah, my life's out of kilter."

Rightfully so. A man needs a wife—an bedient *one* . . . "How's the missus?" sse asked. "You've visited her and the ldren over at Irvin's, no doubt?"

Well, I stopped by there, but my tem-
fierce. Awful hard for me to control it
ore." Zeke paused, breathing loudly.
still, Irvin's keepin' me from my wife
ildren."

d   ld you want me to speak to my
e   n that?"

"No . . . no. 'Tis best, prob'ly, that Irvin do things his way, since he's the one givin' my family shelter for now."

For now. . . .

Jesse wondered, indeed, if the Rancks were getting their grip on Zeke's wife . . . would the People *ever* get her back? Especially with all her talk of saving grace and whatnot. "If she's not back home in a week—and hasn't repented of her pride— we'll have to be talkin', you and I."

"A sorry situation all round. If she'd just stayed home, 'stead of seeking out that Mennonite friend." Zeke scratched his face, looking down at his toes. "I have yet to see my youngest up close."

"A baby girl, I hear," Jesse offered, hoping to raise Zeke's spirits.

"Named after my Esther. And your daughter."

"Oh?"

"Essie Ann's the full name."

Jesse and Zeke turned and walked together, not saying any more as Jesse pulled a cigar from his frock coat. He offered it to the downtrodden new father, who, even though he was known to dislike the smooth, sweet aroma, accepted it gratefully.

Ben had been driving in broad circles around the vicinity of Annie's house for more than an hour, enjoying the wintry countryside, lost in reverie. He decided to drive down Route 30, stopping long enough for lunch at a Bob Evans restaurant.

Resuming his aimless driving, he listened to WDRE, 103.9, out of Philly, all the while stopping frequently on the most deserted roads to take digital pictures of various snowscapes—an old corncrib and wooden windmill, and outbuildings where snow clung to rugged stone structures.

But it was the virtually never-ending fields, stretching away from the road on either side—corn and tobacco fields dormant beneath a foot of snow—that reminded him of home. *I'll give Mom and Dad a call tonight*, he decided.

Having made it a point to know precisely where Annie Zook and her family resided, Ben had driven past the tall farmhouse several times in the space of a few days. A slow-moving peahen wandering onto the slushy road had intrigued him. He had stopped the car to watch the large bird strut in slow motion.

Annie raises peacocks, he thought, recalling the interesting tidbits he'd gathered while having supper at Irvin and Julia Ranck's. *Not chickens or pigs, but peahens and their young.*

Now he found himself watching an Amish father pull four small children on a long wooden sled, mesmerized by the man and his plump wife as they picked their way over the plowed roadside, bundled up in their black garb, including the mother's winter hat, a candlesnuffer style he'd seen in parts of Kentucky, as well.

They must be headed home for milking.

Later he went in search of the area's historic bridges. He had done some initial checking on the Internet and had printed out a listing of Lancaster County covered bridges, complete with colorful pictures and descriptions of each. There was the picturesque Pinetown covered bridge built in the late 1800s northeast of Landis Valley on Bridge Road, as well as the Hunsecker Mill Bridge on Hunsecker Road, damaged due to a tractor-trailer hitting the overhead support beam and steel rods, leaving a splintered mess of wood and twisted metal in its wake. Originally constructed in the mid-1800s but rebuilt after Hurricane Agnes destroyed it in 1972, the bridge had been fraught with troubles. Several of his tack shop customers had told hush-hush stories about vandals attempting to cut up the bridge and carry it away. It was the longest single-span covered bridge in Pennsylvania, as well as one of the newest, and was featured on the cover of the state's transportation map, attracting many tourists.

But it was not the folklore of just any bridge Ben was after, nor the fact that it was the two hundredth anniversary of the nation's covered bridges that spurred him on. He believed in his gut he would know the one bridge he had come in search of when he saw it.

Creeping along on Belmont Road, past the weathered wood siding of the Progressive Shoe Store on the right, he slowed the car as a stately covered bridge came into view. He pulled off the road and set the brake. Slowly he surveyed the long expanse of the bridge with barn-red planked sides, spanning Pequea Creek. *A kissing bridge* popped into his mind, and he wondered where *that* had come from.

He reached into his jeans pocket and pulled out his wallet, then removed a folded picture. He opened it and compared it to the landscape before him—the gray stone abutments and the wide creek, now frozen, beneath the wooden bridge. He was also very aware of the stark black grove of trees to the left of the bridge, down along an embankment, although he was uncertain as to why. Everything matched the picture he held in his hands. A picture he'd stared at so often, he actually felt as if he had been here before.

Getting out of the car, he stood with his hand on the door. Then he walked closer and paused in what might have been the shadow of the bridge had a cloud not blown across the face of the sun.

This is it, he realized.

He scanned the sloping area to the west of the road, then turned to look into the distance, seeing Queen Road to his left. Quickly he returned to the car and snatched up his Lancaster County map from the seat. He was able to locate the road, *this* bridge—a small icon set on a thick blue line defining the creek—and he decided he had indeed found the match.

He checked and double-checked. Not a question in his mind. This was undeniably the landscape captured in the striking picture he had carried with him ever since first seeing it last Christmas. . . .

He had gone to hang out with a friend at a printshop in Marion, Kentucky, one miserably cold afternoon. The place was so unpretentious no one ever would have guessed a slick-looking magazine was being created on the premises.

"Hey, wanna see how we lay out our cover art?" the pudgy designer asked, motioning for Ben to have a look.

At his first glance at what was to become a magazine cover, Ben felt something of a fist growing in the pit of his stomach. The featured painting, titled "Obsession," rattled him as he observed a reddish covered bridge and a grove of trees bursting with autumn colors. From one of the trees hung a long rope swing.

What jolted him even more was the sunbeam highlighting something unlikely on the

wooden seat of the swing—a peach stone—
that sent a wicked shiver down his spine.

"Can you make a copy of this for me?" he
had asked the designer.

"Sure," his friend said. "This picture happens to be the winner of our first-ever art
contest." The man went to print a full-color
copy.

Ben hadn't thought to ask who the artist
was, only to inquire of the location of the
painting.

"Well, I believe it's Lancaster County,
Pennsylvania" was the reply.

"Nothing more specific?"

The guy nodded. "Someplace in Paradise. How's that for a name of a town?"

As Ben stared at the painting, he'd felt his
friend's curious gaze.

"We've got a few Plain groups around
here," the designer continued. "Sure is hard
not to gawk at people who look so out of
place in the twenty-first century."

Ben had agreed. But how did that explain
his fascination with the painting? No Amish
folk in it anywhere . . . just an old covered
bridge, the stream, and a cluster of trees at
peak foliage.

There has to be a logical explanation, he thought.

Still, Ben had not told anyone how captivating he found the painting to be, nor that the picture had stirred up a world of visions in him.

Now he stood on the brink of the actual bridge, staring at the frozen creek below. Turning away from the stone abutment, where he had leaned hard for fear he might become ill, he faced the dark tunnel.

The sound of footsteps echoed, and he looked but saw nothing. No one.

An inexplicable sense of danger registered in his brain.

Turn back! Run!

Ben's hands were suddenly cold. He had lost all feeling in his fingers. They were as strangely numb as his soul.

What's happening to me?

Chapter 5

Louisa led Courtney up the stairs in the Dawdi Haus to get her dressed for the barn singing. "Annie and I hang out here," Louisa said, opening the door.

Courtney stepped inside and cautiously looked around the stark bedroom. "So this is where you've been holed up," she said.

"Yep," Louisa replied simply, stunned that Courtney would agree to dress Plain. Or that she would consider attending the singing at all.

"Cool," Courtney had whispered so only Louisa could hear. "I'll just pretend it's Halloween."

Annie brought over a royal blue dress and a black apron from the wall pegs, and Courtney rolled her eyes as she slipped into the skirt part of the cape dress.

When Annie ran across the hall to borrow a few more pins from Mammi Zook, Courtney looked at Louisa and shrugged. "How bad can it be? A barn singing, right? Like hillbilly night at summer camp. Remember, Louisa?"

But this is the real thing.

Courtney screwed up her face when Annie suggested pulling her thick locks into a low, tight bun. "Is this necessary?" she asked Annie, who was quick to nod.

"Oh, jah, ever so important," Annie attempted to explain. "Without the Kapp, the rest of it is all for naught."

But for bangle-loving Courtney the bottom line was curiosity, most likely. Despite her aversion to the Plain attire, and the fact that her layered hair kept slipping out from the twisted sides and low hair bun, Courtney said she wasn't going to miss out on a "rare chance" to be eyewitness to an Amish barn gathering, especially after sleeping through Preaching service earlier.

Louisa couldn't help wondering what

Courtney's true motivation was for going tonight. She suspected it had much more to do with checking up on her, especially in the guy department.

All during the ride to the singing, Courtney kept commenting on how incredibly slow they were moving. Omar, at the reins, said nothing, but Louisa noticed his mouth tighten. Louisa had become accustomed to and now relished the slower pace of things but couldn't imagine Courtney ever giving up *her* wheels. Not to mention her lipstick, mascara, and eye shadow, all of which she was wearing even now beneath her black bonnet. *A peahen dress with a peacock face,* Louisa thought wryly, and grinned.

And riding in a buggy without a heater in the cold—the bone-chilling kind—wasn't something a girl like Courtney would ever forget. Nope. She'd go straight home and tell Louisa's mother how crazy her daughter was . . . living like she was on a Lewis and Clark expedition or something.

When they arrived at the Glicks' home, Omar took care of the horse while Annie led Louisa and Courtney up the slope to the barn, pushing their boots through the snow. The night air was plenty nippy, as Annie

might say, and Louisa saw that a large bonfire had been built in the side yard.

"Come along," Annie said, as they went
up the snow-covered earthen bridge that
led to the upper level of the two-story bank
barn. Louisa helped Annie push open the
heavy wooden door to reveal a large haymow swept clean enough to see the wide
wood planks of the vast floor in the center.
Bales of hay had been stacked high on either side.

The young men stood in clusters, their
black hats straight on their heads. Some of
the shy ones ran thumb and pointer fingers
up and down their suspenders, while the
girls were prim in below-the-knee-length
dresses of blue, green, violet, and burgundy
all along the opposite wall. Gas heaters were
scattered here and there to ward off the chill.
But nervous tension, Louisa suspected, was
partly responsible for the frosty atmosphere.

Courtney turned to Louisa. "How do I
look?"

"Like a woman on the prowl," Louisa
whispered, then laughed.

Courtney poked her in the arm as they
stood on the threshold. "I'm in over my
head here, aren't I?"

"Just do what Annie does," Louisa offered, hoping that was sound advice.

"Jah, and say what I say, too," Annie added, grinning.

"I'll just say 'jah' all night," Courtney agreed.

"Yeah, and get yourself a ride home with a handsome feller," Louisa teased.

"How exciting," Courtney replied, batting her eyes.

Louisa felt strange encouraging Courtney to come along, even though she herself was still very much on the fringe of this alien society. *Which is where I need to stay*, she thought as she caught a glimpse of tall and smiling Sam Glick. The notion that Courtney might witness firsthand Sam's obvious interest made Louisa uneasy.

Is it too much to hope she won't notice?

She sighed, imagining the fallout.

It was past suppertime when Ben called home. His mother answered on the third ring. "Oh, it's good to hear from you. I hope you've changed your mind about staying there."

"Well, I'm not calling about coming home."

An awkward pause ensued.

"You okay, son?"

"Wanted to check in . . . see how you and Dad are doing."

"You have sisters, too, you know."

"Oh yeah. I keep trying to forget," he quipped.

His mom laughed a little, and then he inquired of his dad's health.

"Oh, your father just never quits. Can't get him to rest much at all."

"So he's working long hours?"

"Always."

"How does Patrice like KSU *this* semester?"

"Fine . . . a new start for her. She wants to know when she can hook up with you on instant messaging. She calls here on her cell quite a lot."

Then she can call me herself and ask. . . .

Immediately he thought better of suggesting it. He knew if Patrice called, she would ask incessant questions.

He asked about his high-school-age sister. "Is Sherri doing all right?"

"She's standing right here, grabbing for the phone . . . wanna talk to her?"

Well, no, he really didn't, because then Sherri would feel they should pass the phone around the whole family and he wasn't up to that. But he was polite and said, "Sure."

Sherri had frivolous things on her mind, and he wondered why she wasn't blabbing the boy-girl stuff to one of her girlfriends instead. "Hey, I miss you, bro," she said. "When're you ever coming home again?"

"Are you kidding? I've got a good job here. I've moved on . . . in another month I won't even remember your name."

Sherri giggled. "You *better* remember. I've got algebra tests soon, and you're my ticket to an A, don't forget."

"Got my own apartment, sis."

She groaned. "Don't rub it in."

"Come visit sometime," he said, just to see what she'd say.

"Yeah, like Mom'll say yes to that. Well, speaking of homework, Mom's giving me the eye. Better go."

"See ya, needle nose."

"Whatever."

Mom got right back on the phone. "Say, Ben, I read in the paper about a serial killer admitting to some crimes in Lancaster County. Have you heard anything?"

He resisted the urge to groan. Mom had an obsession with true crime stories, gravitating to dubious newspaper articles and TV drivel. Anything sensational.

"Amish farmland has evidently been used by killers before," she continued.

"Oh, Mom. C'mon!"

"No, seriously. I should send you the article."

Ben sighed, ready for a topic change.

"Some folk are saying it must be sacred ground."

"What is?"

"Amish soil . . . where the victims are buried."

"Yeah. Mom? I gotta go."

"When are you coming home, Ben?"

"Mom—"

"All right, fine. But be careful, please?"

"Sure, Mom." He wished Dad were home more often, spending time with her.

She was clucking into the phone. "It's so nice of you to call. We all miss you terribly."

He was ready to say good-bye when he spied the picture of the Pequea Creek bridge on his kitchen table. "Hey, have we ever been to Pennsylvania before?"

A short pause ensued. "Hmm . . . once when you were in grade school."

No wonder I remember.

"We came home early from that vacation, though. Got tired of all the people—not the Amish, but the tourists."

He smiled. "The place *is* hopping with sightseers, people dying for a glimpse of the horse-and-buggy folk."

"Well, speaking of dying, you be very careful, dear."

"Hey, did you find my birth certificate yet?"

"Still looking," she replied.

"I needed it weeks ago . . . will you put it at the top of your to-do list, please?"

She agreed to.

"Good-bye. I'll call you next week," he said and hung up.

Serial killers dumping bodies in Amish farmland? Give me a break!

Louisa recalled instantly what it was that had first forged her friendship with Courtney back in middle school. This girl had magnetic draw. She wore a perpetual winning smile, and she could put a person at ease, make them laugh . . . even disarm them, if

necessary. And she was doing it now, min-
gling, along with Louisa, meeting one
cousin or friend of Annie's after another.

Louisa figured the boys were somewhat
leery, having met one too many fancy girls
clothed by the preacher's daughter. For this
she was relieved, glad Courtney would have
no interaction with Sam. *I'm off the hook,* she
thought. But she wondered how it would go
if she didn't end up riding home with Annie.
Even so, she wouldn't worry away the night.
**Courtney will only be here for another
day or so. . . .**

Some time later, two boys were brave
enough to walk over and talk to Courtney,
one blushing perfect circles of red on each
cheek.

But when someone started playing a
guitar, the talkative guy, one Annie quickly
informed her was a cousin "once removed," asked Courtney if she wanted to
join several other couples in the square.
Courtney flashed a look that said, "What're
we waiting for?" and followed willingly.
Surprised, Louisa would've lost her socks,
that is, if she weren't wearing heavy black
hose.

Just then Louisa saw Sam making his

way through the crowd toward her. She willed herself to breathe, more than happy to see Courtney so well occupied.

"Hullo, Louisa . . . you're way over here? And why's that?" he asked, smiling down at her.

She looked for Annie, who had suddenly disappeared. "I, well . . . Annie and I brought along a guest."

"The made-up girl?" asked Sam, his eyes still on her. "Not from round here, that's certain."

Louisa shook her head. "You're right about that."

Sam did not turn to look at the couples, nor did he show any more interest in asking about Courtney. He leaned near and whispered, "Would ya like to square dance with me?"

Pausing, she wondered if this was such a good idea. *Why did I show up here?* She felt almost shy as he stood beside her, the sleeve of his white dress shirt brushing against her arm.

Would Sam be this interesting if he were dressed like any modern guy? she wondered.

Even so, she did not step away from him, wondering what to do with her feelings.

Then, when the music stopped and more couples joined in, the blond teenage boy caller hoisted himself onto a square bale of hay and announced, "Stir the Bucket," which brought a big round of applause and a few hoots from the boys.

"Now's our turn," Sam said, reaching for her hand. "All right?"

She lifted her hand, surprised how his touch made her blush. *Does he notice?*

Her heart complicated things, too, doing a weird sort of beat. *I can't let this happen.* Even so, she was walking with him, in step, following.

What'll Courtney say if she sees me?

Just that quickly, Sam let go, and she got in the line with the other girls. She wanted to shield her hand in her dress pocket, wanting to remember the feel of her hand in his at least for the rest of the evening.

The guitar strumming started again and the caller began the intros with a bit of patter chatter. He called the corner folk to come up to the middle and then back to their places, called "home."

Someone hollered, "Swing your own, 'n' leave mine alone!" which was followed by a long string of Dutch and a burst of laughter by the group.

Yee-haw, thought Louisa, glancing up the line and noticing Courtney doing the do-si-do with her own Amish partner. *Too funny! Who would've thought?*

When it was time to meet Sam, lined up across from her with the other guys, she smiled freely, wondering if he might hold her hand again tonight, and not just during the barn dance.

Shaking off the thought, she realized what a fool she was. *What am I thinking?*

———

After learning many new square dance moves, Louisa and Sam sat side by side in his enclosed carriage. Sam did much of the talking, for some reason wanting to explain that many of the more settled, baptized young men were no longer buying open buggies for courting. They were purchasing the enclosed gray buggies, skipping over the reckless time of youth, planning for their future as husbands and fathers. But he made it clear to her that he had no plans to join the church.

It was as if her reluctance to say much encouraged him to fill in the gaps. And talk he did. So much so that Louisa wondered if he talked the ears off other girls. Well, other *Amish* girls.

But there was a side to him she found incredibly appealing. The way he drew her into his private circle, his sphere of reality. And when she talked of her family living in Colorado, he wanted to know as much about them as she would share. Unlike Trey Douglas, who, though he continued to send email, did not seem to take much pleasure in her family-related remarks. As for Michael, the only one of her relatives *he'd* shown much interest in, besides her, of course, was her father.

But Sam's focus was nearly entirely on family—his ancestry, the present family tree, and the all-important future one. Yet she wasn't put off by his attempts to woo her, as she clearly knew he was doing. Or trying to.

Would Annie be freaked if she knew?

Maybe Annie did know. And maybe she wasn't saying much because she was crossing her fingers . . . as Sam might be, as well.

"That's one fancy friend you've got," he said, sitting on the driver's side. "Courtney sure doesn't look as Plain as you do."

She hoped that was a compliment.

"*Auslenner*, she is," he continued, "decidedly so."

"Uh, back up, Sam."

"Ach, there I go forgettin' you don't know Dutch." He took off his hat. "Your friend's a foreigner. Doesn't much fit in here."

And I do? Now, that's scary.

"Well, about now, I think Courtney might be really ticked off at me," she admitted.

"Courtney's upset 'cause I brought you home?" Sam asked. "She and Annie got stuck riding back to Zooks' with Omar and his girl? Is that it?"

She laughed, breathing in the cold air. *That and more*. "Yeah, I'll catch it tomorrow."

"Why's she visiting, anyway?" he asked.

I wonder, too.

He smiled. "She's not comin' to talk you into returnin' home, is she?"

Louisa thought she noticed a worried look flicker across his face. "She wants to connect. We haven't stayed in touch much since I came here."

He leaned back in the seat, reins in only one hand. "Why'd *you* come to Amish country?" he asked.

She hadn't told anyone how close she had always felt to Annie, having been pen pals for so many years. She wondered if she ought to tell Sam—test his loyalty. "If I told you something, would you keep it quiet?" She felt suddenly compelled to step out of her comfort zone.

"You've got a secret, I take it?" Sam looked at her curiously.

"Annie and I both do." She forged ahead, explaining their letter-writing relationship. "I'd always wondered what it might be like to spend time with my good friend." *There's so much more to it, but I won't bore him.*

"You weren't runnin' away from anything, then? Just wanted to see Annie in person?"

Well, not entirely true. . . .

"I craved a simpler life."

He was silent for a moment. Then he said, "A love gone sour?"

Man—this guy's good!

If she changed the subject quickly, Sam would know the truth. If she made up something, she'd be ticked at herself. "Maybe it's best not to talk about where I've been and who I was . . . back then."

Back then? Who am I kidding?

"Well, I know you live somewhere near Denver . . . and you were Louisa Stratford then, same as now." He looked at her with serious eyes. "But what're you hidin'?"

Let it go already, she wanted to say, but bit her tongue.

He reached for her gloved hand. "Your beau—your man—is he waiting for you to find your way? Is that why you're here for the time bein'?"

She shook her head. "No one's waiting. And I guess I could say I had lost my way. But not anymore."

"*Des gut,* then," he said too quickly. "That's just right fine with me."

Yikes . . . Louisa sat back against the seat as the realization hit her full force. *He's falling for me.*

Chapter 6

On Monday morning, Courtney arrived early enough to join the Zooks for breakfast. Annie observed her reaction to Mamm's overflowing platters: eggs, bacon, and sausage, along with homemade waffles and cornmeal mush, all laid out in a neat row in the center of the table. Or maybe it was not the variety of food that caught *this* Englischer's attention. Still, Courtney's soft green eyes were wide with something that looked like wonder, and she had little to say during the meal, as if she had many more thoughts than words.

Omar and Yonie were exceedingly

friendly, almost too much so, Annie thought, asking Courtney about Colorado weather and suchlike. Luke eyed Courtney suspiciously, though, and held back, as was his usual way.

My brothers must wonder how many worldly women I'm going to invite into the house! Daed and Mamm must be wondering, too, thought Annie, hoping Courtney's stay wouldn't ruffle too many feathers. Her arrival in Paradise had already raised Mamm's eyebrows, beginning with Courtney's staying at the B&B rather than at the Zooks' home. Still, Mamm had cordially welcomed Courtney this morning, though Annie noted her parents were not overly friendly. Even Mammi and Dawdi were quieter than usual.

Daed's stern words of rebuke were still floating in Annie's head. Goodness knows she was not interested in yet another straight talk from her father. In no uncertain terms Daed had let it be known that her sinning days were to be a thing of the past. And she felt his eyes on her too often.

Six months is a long time to stay far from my art, she thought. *But, then, so is forever.* She contemplated the life vow she was expected to make to the church come next fall, feeling she had little choice as each day passed. She also knew that her promise to her father would be up in mid-July.

"Pass the bacon, Annie," Daed spoke up.

Quickly she reached for the large plate and passed it to her right, to Luke, who then handed it on. "Would ya like some sausage, too?" She leaned forward, able to see Daed sitting at his usual spot at the head of the table.

"Jah, sausage. *Es gut.*" Her father's gaze caught hers briefly. He wore his black work suspenders and a bright green shirt. "And more coffee, Mamm."

Her mother jumped to her feet. Courtney looked shocked, as if she'd never before seen a woman wait on a man.

Well, won't she be surprised all round?

Annie's thoughts flitted back to the first few weeks of Lou's visit, back last November when she'd arrived here in a yellow taxi cab. Late into the night, the first several weeks, they had whispered about the vast differences between the Plain life and the fancy. The role of husbands and wives being one of the bigger discussions, she recalled. According to Lou, worldly men often catered and even kowtowed to their women. And English women, more often than not, were eager to be the boss of the house. Eager, too, to run things in general. *The empowered female,* Lou had kept saying, as if that were the right way to do things.

Annie still found such a thing fascinating, although she had no way of relating to it, mainly because she'd only known one English fellow her whole life. Well, Cousin Irvin was English, too, but he was as conservative a Mennonite as there ever was, so he didn't really count.

But Cousin Irvin's tack shop employee and *her* new friend, Ben Martin, was mighty fancy. No question about that! Even so, Ben had shown no indication of such namby-pamby behavior toward her or Lou, who had often been on hand to witness the interaction between the Englischer and Annie. Lou had been a sort of safety net, but one that Annie was beginning to feel she no longer needed.

"More raspberry jam for anyone?" Mamm asked, reaching for the pint jar.

"I'll have some," Luke spoke up for the first time this meal.

Omar reached over, after Luke had scarcely dipped his table knife into the jam, and snatched it out of his hand.

"Ach, boys . . ." Mamm said, a twinkle in her eye.

"Say, here, we've got ourselves company." Daed's was a more serious tone.

Annie glanced at Courtney, her long and thick eyelashes blinking quickly as she observed the rather ordinary interplay between the boys. *Guess she's never seen home-made preserves, either,* Annie thought, trying not to smile too much.

"Please pass the raspberry jam," Courtney said suddenly.

Annie didn't think she'd ever heard anyone Amish say *please* at the table. Such a fancy sort of word it was, used by the English, which was maybe the reason the People didn't say it, as a rule of thumb. Was their snippy English guest trying to teach *them* manners?

———

To say they were much too far from home was not an exaggeration. Annie was still scratching her head, trying to figure out how Lou had managed to get Mamm to say Annie could go along to the Rockvale Square Outlet mall, with its 120-plus shops to choose from. *Sugar talk was part of it*, she realized. Goodness, but Lou had even talked Mamm into allowing Annie to skip eating at home so the three of them could go to a restaurant at noon. Annie enjoyed every minute of it, even though the place Lou chose ironically had been the same establishment where Rudy Esh had sometimes taken Annie during their long courtship. *Maybe it was a good thing for me to eat here again,* she thought, taking in everything around her, relieved and grateful she felt no remnants of sadness.

Has Ben so completely captured my thoughts?

She hurried to catch up with Lou and Courtney, who were eyeing a pair of blue jeans with an accompanying long-sleeved jacket. "One sweet-looking outfit," Courtney called it. Lou, on the other hand, seemed more interested in the pure white lace blouse beneath the jacket. For Annie, though, the pretty lace and the blue denim didn't go together.

But what do I know about worldly clothes? She wondered if the blending of the simple look of the jeans with the fancy lace was likewise how the outlet shoppers must be viewing her and Lou in their Amish dresses and shawls, with Courtney in her tight tan stretch pants and black leather jacket. *Like we somehow don't quite belong together.*

Once again, Ben came to mind. *Unequally yoked,* that's what she'd be if ever she were to give in and go on a date with him. It was as far from being Amish as the modern mannequin Courtney was now pointing to in the shop window. There was simply no middle ground.

"Hey, check out that cool sweater," Courtney said, her gaze on a bright yellow V-neck top.

Lou pulled her black shawl around her more closely, looking over at Annie as if to see how she was doing, exploring this too-modern environment.

"We can go into any store you wish," Annie offered. She did not want to stand in the way of Courtney's desire to *shop till she dropped.* Or Lou's, for that matter.

Annie had made up her mind to enjoy herself, even if it meant haphazardly showing the slightest interest in the modern clothing and whatnot. Even if it meant denying the images of color and design stirred up by surrounding herself with this aspect of the modern English world. Simply stepping foot into a store like Liz Claiborne Shoes was yet another factor in whetting her appetite. It did not serve to discourage her thoughts of worldly Ben either.

I must hold fast to the Old Ways, she told herself, following Lou and Courtney into the store. *As best as I can!*

Ben had decided first thing this morning he was going to brown bag it. He'd learned to pinch his pennies from his mom's endless, but gentle, lectures. Replaying last evening's phone conversation in his mind, he contemplated his mother's ability to hide her disappointment. During other conversations she had not been so successful, calling it "ridiculous" of him to leave home for an unknown locality. *She's resigned herself to my absence. . . .*

When the shop door jingled open, Ben scooted his turkey sandwich beneath the lip of the counter as a matter of course. Looking up, he saw Zeke. "Welcome, neighbor," Ben said.

"How's business?" Zeke nodded curtly, then removed his wide black hat.

"Slow."

Zeke's golden brown hair was smashed down from his felt hat. He ran a big callused hand through his hair while glancing around the shop. "Anybody here but you?"

"Only the leather and me." Ben smiled, glad for the company. "Help you find something?"

"Well, s'pose I could go for a thick, juicy steak and some mashed potatoes and gravy 'bout now," Zeke said.

"Oh . . . you just missed the kitchen help. They're out for lunch." Ben laughed, and Zeke cracked a smile, unexpected for someone who seemed so hard-faced. But Ben had purposely set out to lighten things up between them.

"Thought I'd drop by, is all," Zeke said.

A man lost among his own people, Ben decided.

Appearing more at ease, Zeke went to sit near the long table where Ben laid out the harnesses for polishing. Zeke pulled out a small bag of pistachio nuts. "Care for any?" He held up the bag.

"I was just finishing my lunch here. But

thanks." He thought it rather generous of Zeke and not in keeping with his harsh reputation.

"Thirsty?" Ben asked, returning the gesture. "I've got a case of Pepsi out back."

Zeke's brown eyes lit up as if Ben had offered him a tractor, church approved. "That would be right good," he replied, getting up and going to lean on the counter where Ben's simple lunch was hidden, laid out on the back of a folded paper bag.

Returning with a can of cold soda, Ben offered it to Zeke, thinking now he ought to have brought along a large Thermos of hot black coffee instead.

Zeke continued to talk. "Our bishop— name's Andy Stoltzfus—and his great-grandson are neck and neck against two other fellas in a checker game to beat all games," he said. "You hear anything 'bout it?"

Ben wouldn't come right out and say Annie told him. "Yeah, someone mentioned it." He paused, observing this man who continued to exhibit all the signs of being a loner—or lonely. He didn't know which it was, though he knew full well that Zeke's wife and kids were still staying with Irvin and Julia.

"Well, there's not much goin' on this time of year, 'cept for mud sales . . . and a few checker games, like I said," Zeke said.

"Anyone play chess around here?"

"I do, but I shouldn't."

"Certain games aren't acceptable?"

Zeke's eyes grew suddenly darker. "In a manner of speaking, no. The fact that it's a war game . . . well, chess causes problems with some of the brethren. Same with playing cards in some of the more conservative circles. Most don't even know why it's forbidden. Just is." He walked across the shop to examine one of the larger harnesses.

"You mentioned mud sales. I'm curious about that."

Zeke turned and broke into a full grin. "Why, they're auctions—sometimes twenty or more auctioneers at once. Some on the back of hay wagons or flatbed trucks . . . some on a makeshift stage in a pole barn quilt room . . . and all to raise funds for our local volunteer fire companies. Last year's sale raised a whoppin' fifty thousand dollars." With a fleeting glimmer in his eye,

Zeke continued. "Lots of them take place outdoors, under a big tent. The ground can get mighty squishy with mud durin' the spring thaw."

"So . . . that's how mud figures in." Ben laughed.

"If you ever go, I'd recommend you get yourself some old work boots." Eyeing the ones Ben had on, Zeke said, "Some that are a mite worse off than them there."

Ben smiled. "I'll keep that in mind."

"First big one's comin' up here 'fore too long. 'Bout two weeks from now, over in Honey Brook on Firehouse Lane. Heard it starts at eight-thirty sharp."

Ben was interested. "What things are auctioned?"

"Oh, just everything. Livestock, farm supplies and tools, sometimes brand spanking new pine staircases, rings of Lebanon bologna, manure spreaders—I've seen as many as seventy handmade birdhouses. But if it's the chicken corn soup you're after, go early, 'cause the four hundred gallons the womenfolk bring is usually half sold out by nine o'clock of a morning."

Ben detected Zeke's almost jovial

change of attitude. "Next time you come, if you let me know when, I'll bring along some home-brewed coffee," he offered.

"All right." Zeke's mouth turned into another quick smile, then straightened again. "Do they have farm sales down where you hail from?"

"Thoroughbred auctions. I helped a lot at the county fairgrounds in Central City, every third Saturday. Quite a showing of tack, equipment, and fine horses . . . all to raise money to help locate stolen and missing horses."

"What kind of person steals a horse?"

Ben nodded. "I know . . . it's crazy."

Shaking his head and muttering under his breath, Zeke's otherwise ruddy face turned pale. "I daresay there are some wicked folk in this ol' world."

"Can't argue that," Ben said, looking up to see Preacher Zook pulling up to the side door with his horse and carriage. "We've got company."

Zeke spotted the preacher and immediately raised his hand to wave at Ben. "Best skedaddle," he said over his shoulder. "Be seein' ya!"

"Hatyee," Ben called.

Zeke turned suddenly, an odd smile on his face. "Ach, now, ya speak *Dietsch?*"

Ben was confused. "Why, what'd I say?"

" 'So long.' That's what."

Ben shrugged it off. "Must've picked it up . . . working around all these Amish farmers."

"Jah, s'pose."

Ben waved again, watching as Zeke stopped to greet Jesse Zook before heading outside.

Ben inhaled deeply and stood as tall as he could, glad for the boots he wore today. "Hello, Preacher! What can I do for you?"

Jesse Zook made his way toward the counter. "Oh, I've come for two black hames and the rosettes." He glanced over his shoulder at Zeke. "Do ya often see Zeke round here?"

Ben had a strong feeling the preacher was checking up on Zeke. It wasn't his place to squeal on the man who seemed in need of a friend. "Oh, Zeke was just saying he's counting the days till the first mud sale."

"Oh, jah. That one's a doozy. You should go, just for the experience if you've never been."

Ben was glad for the preacher's seemingly genuine ease. "I think I just might."

Jesse seemed to mentally agree, although he appeared to be somewhat distracted. "What was it I said I was here for?"

"Hames, sir." Ben led the older man to the wooden boxes filled with hundreds of harness accessories.

———

Esther was much too nervous to meet with her husband alone, even though she was residing in the safety of Irvin and Julia Ranck's home. She had confided her greatest fears to Julia, expressing what a frightening thing it was to be so displaced. Julia kindly agreed that she and Irvin should definitely accompany Zeke upstairs to meet his newest daughter.

Twenty-day-old Essie Ann lay sleeping soundly in her arms. Esther made an attempt to will her heart not to beat so hard, gazing at her beautiful baby girl. "Your dat's comin' up here to meet ya," she whispered in the pink little ear. "He loves ya so. . . ."

Well, she was ever so sure Zeke did love their wee babe Essie—or would. She just didn't know for certain how much Zeke loved her. Not after raising a hand to her. Not after she'd run off to Rancks' to have his baby. Run off and never told Zeke where she could be found . . . secretly hoping he wouldn't find her at all. Yet he'd tracked her down all the same. Came right out looking for her at Julia's, after the horse went trotting over to Irvin's tack shop instead of heading on home the way she thought for sure it would. Had it not been for Ben Martin, Zeke might not have figured out where she and the children were staying for quite some time.

But now she was about to present little Essie Ann to him. The sound of voices downstairs put Esther on edge all the more. *Ach, my life might've been easier if I'd never gone to that first singing seven years ago. . . .*

———

Mamma had been hesitant about having her go that September evening, the first Sunday following Esther's sixteenth birthday, pleading with Dat to think hard about having their daughter stay home for a few more months . . . "till she's older." Worries plagued Mamma for a full week before the barn singing. "Seems a body ought to know when her daughter's ready to be out alone with a boy nearly all night," Esther overheard her mother telling Dat. But Esther's father wouldn't hear of it. Sixteen was the "appropriate" age when such things were expected to take place. Tradition reigned.

Esther remembered fretting over what to wear and had ended up choosing her plum-colored cape dress, which her mother said made her blue eyes look even bluer, her "perty golden hair" fairer.

She met Ezekiel Hochstetler that night, a boy from Honey Brook, who some of the other youth whispered was "too far away from the Paradise church district to be included." Yet there he was, participating in the activities, along with the pairing up. Ezekiel took one long look at Esther and made it clear he had to have what he saw, and there was no turning back for either of them.

She let herself breathe deeply now, in and out slowly, so as not to awaken the little one who slept peacefully—*innocently*—on her lap.

I must be calm. Must smile convincingly when I see Zeke again. Oh, dear Lord, I must.

Chapter 7

Louisa, Annie, and Courtney stopped at the food court for cookies and a warm soft pretzel at Auntie Anne's Café in the Rockvale Square Outlet mall. Annie was still waiting in line for some hot cocoa, not the smooth espresso mochas Louisa and Courtney had chosen. "We'll grab a table," Louisa told Annie, motioning for Courtney to join her.

On the way to the table, Courtney said, "I wasn't going to say anything, but I think you probably suspect it already."

"What're you talking about?" Louisa sat down.

Courtney's eyes were blinking too fast. "Let's see . . . how do I put this?"

"Just say it."

"I think you're too comfortable here. I mean, what are you *really* doing? Did you have to come to Amish country to run away?" Courtney's face was red, as if holding back a torrent of words.

"I came to see Annie . . . I'd always wanted to visit. And I really do feel settled here."

"Oh, that's just great. You want to become Amish?"

Louisa wished Courtney might have the courtesy to lower her voice, but instead Courtney continued loudly, "You couldn't keep your eyes off that Amish guy last night. What was that about?" Courtney raised her eyebrows. "You're not *really* interested in dating men like that, are you?"

"Like what? Honest, gentle, caring? Men like *that*?"

Shaking her head, Courtney opened a bag of chocolate chip cookies, obviously disgusted.

Louisa forced a smile. "Boy, Court. Why is this such a big deal to you?"

"It's not a big deal just to me, Louisa."

"What's that supposed to mean?"

In place of an answer, Courtney offered a gooey cookie instead. "Here, this will make you think more clearly."

Louisa tapped her cup. "It'll take more than chocolate to change my mind. Trust me." She glanced over to see Annie at the cash register. "Look, this conversation is really pointless."

Courtney stirred her mocha, staring into the cup. "I don't know who you are anymore."

"Well, I guess I don't recognize myself sometimes either." Louisa sighed. "But, to tell you the truth, I actually think I like *this* me better."

Courtney's face registered complete shock.

"For the record, I've found something here. Is that so hard to believe?"

Courtney smirked. "I figured it was just a phase." She chewed carefully, slowly. "But this is nuts. I mean, it's like you need to be deprogrammed or something." Courtney was still for a moment, but when she spoke, her tone had changed to pleading. "C'mon, Louisa. Put all this nonsense aside and come home with me. Your parents would be thrilled."

"No, thanks. I'm learning things . . . I have a long way to go. And I know you'll be shocked, but I'm actually very happy here."

Courtney wrinkled up her nose.

Louisa leaned her elbows on the table, fixing Courtney with a serious gaze. "Why'd you come, Court? To visit or to get me to return home?"

"I came to see you, of course. We've been friends for a long time." Courtney paused, then she said, "Besides that, Michael wants you home."

Louisa leaned back, sighing, squeezing her eyes shut. "So that's it."

Courtney smiled too sweetly. "The guy's still crazy about you."

"He asked you to bring me back?"

"Well, hey, what's so wrong with that?"

"I'll bet he paid for your ticket here, too."

"What if he did?"

Louisa rose and huffed her disgust, heading across the food court, her shoulders squared. She was sick of defending herself to someone who should have understood her.

Annie headed to the table, wondering why Lou had rushed off . . . and where she was going. She sat down with her hot cocoa, glancing toward Courtney. "Louisa's upset?"

Courtney pushed her hair behind her ear. "She's a lot of things right now, I think. Probably offended, too."

Annie suspected Courtney had set Lou off somehow. But she refused to give way to her own anger over this worldly woman's glaring disapproval of Lou. The Good Book said: *The tongue of the wise useth knowledge aright: but the mouth of fools poureth out foolishness.* "It can be an awful frightening thing to lose yourself in the darkness," Annie said softly.

"What do you mean?" Courtney asked, her eyes hard on Annie.

Gathering her wits, Annie continued, "I recall a long-ago sermon my father gave . . . about letting yourself listen to the silence around you—getting in a place where you can actually hear yourself think, ya know? And, well, letting the Lord God make us— each one—into a servant."

"Please," muttered Courtney.

She's mocking me.

"No, now listen. Louisa was losing herself in the busy world. She came looking for peace, to make sense of her life." Annie paused. "Guess you might be needin' some of that, too?"

Courtney shrugged and pushed her chair out. "Later," she said, heading off to look for Lou, most likely.

"Something I said?" Annie whispered to herself. She gathered up the refuse on their table and carried it to the trash container.

Esther was aware of Zeke's dark eyes on her as he held their baby daughter. She trembled despite Irvin's and Julia's presence in the small attic room, transformed into a bedroom for her children—six-year-old Laura, three-year-old Zach, two-year-old John, baby Essie—and herself.

"Such a sweetie pie she is." Julia broke the silence, her light brown hair swept back beneath the cup-shaped prayer covering of white netting.

"Jah" was all Zeke said, still creating concern in Esther as he looked from the baby and back to her, meeting her eyes with disdain.

I've spurned him. . . .

"The Lord is so good to bless us with another healthy child," she managed to say, linking herself once again to her precious Savior.

Julia came and sat next to Esther, and Esther welcomed her nearness.

"Essie's a droopy one today," Esther whispered, scarcely able to think of anything except that her husband was terribly displeased with her. Not for birthing such a pretty baby, no . . . but for saying she was "saved" and a follower of the Lord Jesus, the reason for her recent temporary shunning. And for running off as she had three weeks ago, leaving him to fend for himself alone without even his children to comfort him with their laughter.

He must despise me for it.

Irvin glanced at Julia, an apprehensive look in his blue eyes. "When would be a good time for Zeke to visit again, Esther?" he asked, reaching for his wife's hand.

Esther made the mistake of looking at Zeke, who was already shaking his head in disgust and walking to the window with the baby. *He's ever so angry. But he's always that. . . .*

"I want my wife to return home," Zeke

said, his back to them, his feet planted firmly apart. He was breathing hard.

Irvin stood quickly. "We have an agreement on that, Ezekiel. You and I, together, will decide when that's a good idea. And we both know now's not the time."

Zeke turned to face them, still cradling Essie Ann in the crook of his big arm. "Esther's my wife. I say what she does . . . where she lives."

Now Julia rose to stand beside Irvin. "Zeke, please, not with the baby near."

It must have been Julia's gentle way, but Zeke relinquished Essie Ann, who was still sleeping in spite of her father's booming voice. Esther felt herself sigh, glad her husband would be seen out by Irvin—and right quick.

Without even taking time to say good-bye, Zeke followed Irvin to the door.

Esther heard the loud clumping of feet on the stairs, and she waited to speak to Julia, who went to her and held her near. "Oh, Julia . . ." she sobbed. "How can I ever go back to him?"

"You won't . . . not unless he proves himself to be kind and loving. Irvin will see to it."

Esther choked back her tears, for her

baby's sake, shaking her head. "There was a time when Zeke was good to me." She sniffled and rose to put the baby in the cradle across the room. "He loved me then."

"Dear Esther, you mustn't say that." Julia stayed seated. "He loves you now. Surely he does."

Love suffereth long, and is kind . . . love envieth not . . . doth not behave itself unseemly . . . is not easily provoked. . . .

"Well, doesn't seem so," Esther whispered. "Hasn't for ever so long."

"Trust the Lord that Irvin will minister compassion and help to Zeke, for now," said Julia.

"Jah, I need to trust more." But it was terribly hard when she knew what was in store for her should she succumb to her husband's demands and return to the farmhouse where Zeke now lived alone. A home where first-grader Laura, as well as Zach and little John, would be at the mercy of their father's quick and fierce temper. *And now poor infant Essie Ann, too. . . .*

She recalled the heart-wrenching times when Zeke had yanked their Laura into the pitch black belly of the cellar as punishment for not completing a chore quickly enough. Esther had heard the fearful sobs, knowing too well her little girl was sitting on the tip-top step, her body pressed against the door, no doubt leaning down toward the sliver of light beneath it.

Esther, too, had longed for a thread of hope, when first she'd married Zeke and dared to disobey him herself. Her heart had pounded so forcefully she'd scarcely been able to breathe. *Sent to the blackness*, she remembered with a shudder. *As black as Zeke himself.*

When Annie finally found Lou outside, Courtney was nowhere in sight. "She's off to do some more shopping," Lou explained. "Good riddance, I say. She only came to talk me into coming home. I should've known."

"I'm sure she means well," Annie said.

"But, get this—Michael paid for her to come here. She came at his request."

"Even so . . ." Annie wanted to help. "Wouldn't you want to patch things up with her?"

"What's to patch? She basically said I'm insane to stay here. She has no right to say that."

Annie pondered that. "Jah, maybe so."

Lou looked at her. "Maybe?"

"Well, I daresay all three of us need to separate for a bit." Annie didn't know what else to say. It appeared that Lou was terribly upset at everyone and everything.

"You're right. I think I need to cool off," Lou said. "How will you get home, though?"

"Oh, I'll just call one of our drivers at a pay phone. No problem at all." Annie waved to her. "I'll see you back at the house later on."

"All right." Lou's smile was a thin one.

She's hurt, Annie realized, wondering if Courtney really *had* come only to talk Lou into going home. She found it surprising that a modern woman would let a man pay her way, especially one she wasn't related to.

Annie hated leaving her friend there like that, alone and in a right fancy world looking ever so Plain. All the same, she set out walking across the vast parking lot and finally came to the edge of the sidewalk, shivering against the cold and waiting for the light to turn on the busy road.

Honestly, did Courtney think she could get Lou to return to Colorado by being rude? Annie couldn't help wondering how close Lou really was to her modern friend.

She pondered Lou's decision to go their separate ways just now as she stood waiting at the pedestrian light. Wondering why it was taking so long, she felt suddenly self-conscious, just as she often did while tending her family's market stand. So many staring faces. She not only felt terribly out of place, but she was freezing.

Suddenly she heard her name rising up over the din of the traffic—"Annie Zook!"

Am I hearing things?

Startled, she turned in the direction of the voice and saw Ben Martin waving to her from his car. "Stay right there, Annie," he called and motioned that he would park his car.

She couldn't believe it. How on earth had he found her?

"I mustn't let him persuade me to ride," she said beneath her breath. Yet she wanted to. All the good sense she'd inherited from her Mamm and Daed . . . where was it now? What was she to do in this crucial moment?

But she surprised herself and did as Ben requested, standing there as the light changed. *Er hot mich yuscht fer en Narr ghalde?* "Is he making a fool of me?" she whispered.

Well, I won't listen to him, she told herself, wishing she had already crossed when the light changed. But then, wasn't that downright rude?

Groaning inwardly, she grimaced, upset to no end.

"Annie! What are you doing all this way from home?" Ben asked, running toward her now.

She waited till he was closer so as not to raise her voice. "I've been out shopping," she said. "I came with Lou and her friend Courtney—mainly so Lou wouldn't be alone with her Amish dress, ya know."

His eyes searched her face, but she dared not look at him directly. She was much too drawn to this fine and fancy fellow.

"You're not going to walk home, I hope. It's a long way . . . and much too busy a highway, and . . ." He stopped short of saying she'd stick out the way she looked, but his kind intent was evident.

He's worried for me . . . wants to take care that I get home all right. And because of this and so many other wonderful things about him, she agreed to ride in his car. "As long as we go straight there," she told him.

She did something she'd promised herself she would never ever do. She let Ben walk her to his car, open the door, and wait till she got settled into the passenger seat. Then he hurried around the car to his own side.

With a contagious smile, he pressed the key into the ignition and the car roared to a start. Annie would not stare, but she was terribly aware that his hand was resting on the gearshift between them, ever so near. . . .

Chapter 8

Out running an errand after lunch, Ben's heart had nearly stopped when he saw Annie Zook alone, near the outlet mall.

Unbelievable, he thought. *I must be living right.*

Now here she sat in his car, gripping the armrest as they rode toward the countryside.

"I hope this won't cause a problem for you," he said.

"You drivin' me, ya mean?"

"It won't, will it?"

"Only if someone sees us."

He liked her quick comeback. She pulled no punches, this girl. "Okay . . . just let me know where you want to be dropped off, okay?"

She nodded, keeping her eyes forward, watching the road.

"Is this typical winter weather?" he asked, then cringed at how lame that must have sounded.

She responded politely to his inquiry. "Jah, I'd say so."

When that attempt at conversation fizzled, he was tempted to ask what she knew of the old covered bridge. Was it considered haunted, perhaps? Stranger things had happened. He *had* sensed something there. Maybe from his family's vacation years ago?

Here next to him was a beautiful, smart young woman with a lifetime of knowledge about the area.

Why not ask her?

He deliberated without bringing it or anything else up, which he viewed as an outrageous squandering of time, especially since he had been hoping for this very thing: a chance to be alone with Annie.

He turned his full attention to her. "Do you ever go to mud sales?"

She looked at him. "Most everyone does round here."

He mentioned his conversation with Zeke, that he hadn't known of such sales before coming here.

Then they lapsed into awkward silence, terribly aware of each other. Or, at least, he was of her.

Turning off Route 30, he knew the time remaining was relatively short. Inwardly he fidgeted, determined to make this serendipitous meeting count for something.

But before he could open his mouth and shove in another foot, Annie spoke up. "Julia says you've been spending time over there . . . several evenings a week."

Perfect, he thought, wondering what other things Julia had told Annie. "Yes, they invite me for supper sometimes. Julia is a fantastic cook, so how can I resist? And those kids of theirs are great fun, aren't they? So are Esther Hochstetler's children. That Laura's a real talkative little gal."

Annie brightened and seemed to relax at the mention of the little ones. "James keeps me laughin' nearly all the time when I clean house at the Rancks'. He says the funniest things, and dear Molly . . . well, she's just a darling two-year-old."

"Takes after her mother, I think."

Annie agreed. "Cousin Julia has the sweetest spirit 'bout her." She looked out the window. "Wonder if it has something to do with her . . . uh, faith," she added.

He found this fascinating. "Why would you say that?"

"Well, Julia—and Irvin, too—seem to think they have a corner on God."

"Maybe not just a corner . . . more like the whole deal," he said.

She looked at him suddenly, her heart-stopping azure eyes wide at his quick comment. "Jah, and just why is it some folk claim to have a full grasp of the Bible and the teachings of God's Son, while the rest of us seem so lost?"

"Lost? But your father's a preacher . . . isn't he?"

She blushed as if he'd caught her in a lie. "Jah, and of course I've learned plenty from Daed at Preaching. I'm hopin' to be taught the High German, too, so I can understand more of the Scripture readings. Still, Julia seems to know so much. . . ."

"Do you mean to say the Bible is read in a language only a few of the People comprehend?" He found this incredible.

"It's always been thataway. Our sacred tongue is German."

This was not the direction Ben wished their discussion to take, and he purposely slowed the car. There were other more intriguing subjects, at least for him, but their time together was running out. If he was going to make the link to a future meeting he *must* pay attention and talk about the things of interest to Annie.

He recalled Zeke mentioning High German during one of their initial conversations. "Say, Annie, how well do you know Zeke Hochstetler?"

"He's my best friend's husband. I've known him since Essie, I mean Esther, first met him," Annie said. "He's a hardworkin' farmer—raises pigs."

"He's a curious fellow, but I like him. A man of few words, though. He drops by the harness shop quite often."

"Nice of you to spend time with him."

As if no one else wants to? Ben considered.

Annie offered no more about Zeke. And Ben guessed he shouldn't ask why Esther and her children were staying at the Rancks', suspecting a good enough reason.

Glancing at Annie, he gripped the steering wheel. But Annie held his gaze now, too, and it was all he could do not to simply stare back at the most engaging girl he'd ever known. Pretty and innocent all rolled into one unique package.

The silence was thick.

At last, he said, "What do you know about the covered bridges in the area?" He knew he should've been more specific.

"Which ones?" she asked.

"The long red one, over on Belmont Road."

"Well, I know plenty. What do you want to know?"

Here they were already traveling the road leading to Annie's father's house. Should he pull over? If she protested, then he would continue on. But if she said nothing, he would buy himself extra minutes.

Tremendously aware of her presence, he raised his hand from the gearshift and let it come to rest at two o'clock on the steering wheel, turning off the road slowly. When the car rolled to a stop and she did not speak up, he believed he had not offended her.

"Did something, well, out of the ordinary occur there?" he asked.

"I didn't know for certain just what all the upheaval in the community was 'bout that bridge—not when I was little, I mean."

"Do you mean something bad happened?"

She nodded slowly.

Had he stumbled onto a painful topic? Had there been an accident here or . . . worse?

"Can you tell me more?" He turned to face her.

She sighed heavily, as if the telling were too difficult. "I best not say more."

"Sure, Annie. I understand," he said. But he didn't.

Then she surprised him and reached for the handle. There were tears on her face as she opened the door and stepped out.

What have I done?

Leaping out of the car, he hurried to catch up with her, stumbling through the remnants of snow and slush. "Annie . . . wait!"

She kept walking, fast. Not looking back, she slipped and nearly lost her balance several times.

"Annie . . . I didn't mean to—"

"*Nee*, no, it's not your fault." She stopped to look at him. "I never should've told you a thing. It was ever so wrong of me."

Exactly what did she say? He still was perplexed. Reaching out, he touched her black shawl. "I'm sorry, Annie. Whatever I asked about that bridge . . . I would never want to hurt you."

She looked at the ground, eyes downcast. "I don't know why it still pains me so."

What does? He refused to ask. His curiosity had done more than enough damage.

"Please, let me take you all the way home. It's too cold for you to walk. Too dangerous." Fact was, it was bitterly cold now and the sun was sinking fast.

He reached out to her yet again, hoping she might understand the gesture as merely an offer of apology.

But she surprised him when she accepted his help, her small mittened hand slipping into his own. "I really shouldn't, but . . ." She stopped midsentence, then began to walk with him toward the car, still clinging to his hand as they picked their way back through the frozen muck.

"Hold tight, Annie," he said. "I won't let you fall."

She gasped lightly, stopped walking, and stared at him. "What?"

Startled, he asked, "What's wrong?"

She looked confused but seemed to shake it off. "Oh, nothing, Ben. Just a trick of my imagination, prob'ly."

He smiled, hoping his fondness for her wasn't too obvious. "It's icy, that's all."

Her eyes were fixed on him again, as if she hadn't heard, as if she were suddenly deaf. A frown shimmered on her brow, and she blinked back tears.

What's with this girl?

"Come, let's get you home," he said.

Chapter 9

Once Ben had gotten her safely back into the car, he drove Annie closer to her house. She thanked him warmly for the ride and waved good-bye before heading up the road toward the turnoff to the driveway. She was glad Ben had agreed to let her out some distance from her house. *No sense worrying Mamm or anyone who might be observing.*

Confusing as it was, she would not erase her memory of having spent this forbidden time with Ben. She refused to berate herself and deliberately kept looking forward as she walked, even when she heard Ben calling to her.

He called again, and lest she be as rude as Lou's Denver friend, she turned around. Ben had gotten out of his car again and was motioning to her. "What is it?" she asked, her heart leaping.

"Annie . . . would it be possible for me to take you to dinner sometime . . . say, this Friday night?"

Oh, she wanted to accept, but first she must calm her breathing. "Well . . . I . . ."

"We could meet at a restaurant if that would suit you better," he offered quickly.

She shook her head, sighing, unable to control how she felt. *Oh, this is just so hard!*

He stood there looking at her, waiting for her answer. "Or I could meet you— anywhere you say."

No, I shouldn't . . . I can't.

He stepped toward her, eyes bright with hope.

I'll regret it if I agree, she thought, *I just know it*. But she surprised herself and said, "Well, I 'spose just once, maybe."

His handsome face lit up like a streetlight. "Where, Annie?" he asked.

"Up the road a ways, but wait till after dusk," she said. "Is that all right?"

He was nodding his head to beat the band. "That's perfect. I'll see you Friday!" Then, turning, he hurried back to his car.

Annie headed toward her father's house, willing herself to slow her pace. She mustn't slip and fall flat on her face here in the road with Ben watching, no doubt, as he drove past. And she would not second-guess this most peculiar situation to death. Still, it *was* a terribly dangerous place to put herself, seeing him again.

She sighed, wondering what would happen if ever someone were to see her with Ben. She'd had every intention of taking baptismal instruction next May. Now, though, nearly everything was topsy-turvy in her head. Not that she would go back on her word about her art, but Ben Martin certainly had not been a part of the handshake agreement with her father. She'd never considered him at all in the promises she'd made. And yet, how could she possibly prepare for becoming a member of the church now?

Ach, the wonderful-good feel of my hand in his!

Hurrying toward the house, she noticed the spot where the scarecrow had been but was no longer. *What the world happened to it?* She scanned the area, knowing for absolute certain it had been standing right there where she was looking . . . at the edge of the garden. Had the wind blown it down? But there had been no fierce gales recently. The thought that someone had come in the night and carried it off, the way some farm tools were known to disappear, bothered her terribly. She could not understand why she felt so traumatized when things seemingly walked off and were never returned. To assume certain things were permanent fixtures—such as the scarecrow she and her younger brothers had constructed last spring—was clearly a mistake. She thought of Zeke, poor man. He must surely be experiencing similar feelings, what with his wife and children gone from the covering of his house. And yet, far as she was concerned, Esther's leaving was his own terrible fault. *Puh!* Zeke was not the kind of man *she* would ever care to marry.

Her thoughts leaped swiftly back to Ben, and she decided then and there he was nothing at all like Zeke Hochstetler. Of course, she would never know that for certain, because she would never let herself fall in love with an Englischer.

Making the turn around the side of the house, she heard one of her brothers calling from the back door. "Hullo, Annie! 'Bout time you got yourself home."

She looked up and there was Yonie, sporting a worldly haircut. *What on earth?* Her favorite brother looked just like the fancy city boys over at the outlet shops. "What's that ya did to yourself?" she said, heading up the steps.

"Got me a haircut, is all." He was grinning.

"What's Daed gonna say?"

"Nothin'."

"You'll catch a tongue-lashing. You'll see." She pushed past him and waited for him to close the storm door on the porch.

"I already talked to Daed. He didn't seem to mind."

"Well, he must be blind, then."

"Not blind neither. And thanks to the grapevine, he knows plenty about the car I bought."

"You did what?" She stared at him. "Well, little brother, what's come over you?"

"I'm havin' me a fine, gut time, that's

what. I'll join church whenever I'm good and ready. Not before."

"And you're still seein' Dory Zimmerman," she said, flabbergasted. "Does our father know about *that*?"

"Not unless you broke your promise and told."

She shook her head. His ongoing relationship with the newspaper carrier's daughter wasn't for her to criticize. Still, she was miffed. "I did no such thing, Yonie. You know better than to accuse me thataway."

"Well, good."

She hung her shawl on the wall hook, then bent over to pull off her boots. "Seems to me there's a double standard round here," she muttered softly.

"What's that?"

"Just never you mind." Annie looked carefully at Yonie's hair cropped above his ears and parted on the side. She could not believe Daed had merely disregarded the deed. How could he not care one iota about Yonie looking as if he'd stepped out of a fancy barber shop like the one over in Strasburg, which was probably where he'd gone? And the even bigger issue—Yonie's having a car and brash enough to fess up to the preacher about it!

Who does Yonie think he is?

It wasn't what her brother had done that bothered her no end, it was Daed's reaction to it. That is, if Yonie was being straightforward.

She shook her head, truly perplexed.

How is it I have to give up my drawing and painting, and my brother can own a car and drive it to court his worldly girlfriend? Something's awful wrong with this.

She felt like blowing her stack and might have if Mamm hadn't called her to come and set the table for supper.

"You seen Yonie's hair?" she whispered to her mother after Yonie left the outer porch.

Mamm glanced at her. "Be careful not to judge, Annie."

"Judge? Well, look at him!"

"Oh, I've looked, believe me."

"And did you say anything to him? Did Daed?"

Her mother shook her head and raised her finger to her lips, intending to shush her. "Don't make a big stink out of this."

Well, I'll see about that.

"It's not one bit fair." She pushed the utensils onto the table.

"Sure, it ain't . . . but this is the way your father wants to handle it. So best be keepin' your nose out."

"So I'm guessin' being born a boy has more advantages," she muttered, hoping Mamm hadn't heard her once she'd let the careless words slip. Right this minute it was awful easy to ponder dear Esther's plight . . . her constantly being under the thumb of a hardhearted husband. *Jah, the difference between a man and a woman round here is altogether maddening!*

When she had finished helping in the kitchen, Annie rushed next door to the Dawdi Haus and upstairs to the bedroom she shared with Lou for the time being. She opened the door, cautious as always, since Lou's arrival had brought with it darling Muffin, the ever-smiling Russian Blue cat. "Kitty, kitty," she called, and he leaped off Lou's bed and came running to her.

She reached down to pick him up and carried him to the chair where she sat and petted him, talking softly the way she liked to do. "You sweet little thing. If all the barn kitties could see the special treatment you get just 'cause your fur is such a perty blue-gray, I'm sure they'd all be clawin' their way in here."

Muffin's elfin eyes alternated between half mast and squinted shut as he lay in her lap, his paws tucked under his plump little chest. His purring brought her a welcome sense of calm, even though she was not going to let the sun go down before talking things out with Daed. "Judgin' or not, I have to know what's what!"

Louisa found Courtney at the Gap outlet—one of Courtney's favorite stores—trying on a pair of jeans. Louisa recognized her black spiky-heeled boots visible beneath the dressing room door. "When you're finished, we need to talk," she said.

"Maybe you need to, but I'm done," Courtney answered through the door. "I'm leaving tomorrow night."

"Well, your mission wasn't accomplished, and you can tell Michael I said so."

"Actually," Courtney said, poking her face out, "to put it to you straight, I'm glad for Michael you didn't go through with the wedding."

"Well, that makes two of us," Louisa shot back. "Have a good trip home. And keep my name out of your conversations with your new boyfriend."

"What?"

"You heard me."

"No . . . that's where you're messed up, Louisa. He loves you. I promise you."

Promise all you want.

"I've gotta get going," said Louisa. "If I don't see you before you leave, have a smooth flight. I know how bumpy things can get near Denver."

"Hey, that's the nicest thing you've said to me the whole visit."

Yeah, maybe so. Louisa hesitated, realizing she was probably right. "Well, then, good-bye."

With that Louisa hurried through the store toward the exit. *Now, to call a cab and catch up with my real friend.*

But before Louisa reached the door, a chenille sweater caught her eye. Christmas red. *Do I dare try it on?* Still upset over Courtney, she pulled it off the rack, removed it from the hanger, and went to find a mirror.

Before coming to visit Annie, shopping often had a way of numbing life's disappointments for her. Maybe she needed a good dose of splurging right now.

Holding the sweater beneath her chin, she saw how perfect it was with her coloring. *Mother always said I looked splendid in red,* she thought, wondering why that memory had surfaced now.

Oh, why not. I'll try it on. But she wouldn't wear a red sweater here. Not after having dressed Plain for this long. She didn't want to offend Annie and her family.

Even so, she was mesmerized by the soft feel, the alluring color. *What would it be like to wear normal, modern clothing again?* she thought while heading to the dressing area. *Would I begin to crave more fancy attire? The finest clothes money can buy?* She sighed, feeling the old pull.

Returning to the back of the store, she saw Courtney standing in front of the three-way mirror, checking out her reflection in a pair of flared jeans and a plum leather jacket, price tags dangling. Courtney looked up and was obviously surprised to see her still there, let alone carrying the red sweater.

"Well, look at you," she scoffed. "Change your mind about being Amish?"

Louisa's cheeks suddenly felt warm.

"I thought you were heading out."

Louisa nodded. "I was."

"Hey, that would look chic over the cape part of your dress," Courtney taunted.

"Wouldn't it?" Louisa held it up for effect, feeling a bit catty herself.

A clerk appeared, looked her over—up and down—and frowned. "May I help you, miss?"

"Jah," Louisa said, then groaned.

Courtney rolled her eyes and wiggled her fingers in a mocking wave. "See you in the next life."

"Whatever that means."

Over her shoulder, Courtney called, "It means, plain Jane, that you're coming back as a full-fledged Englisher next time. I *hope.*"

Louisa felt lousy. *This visit was a bomb from the get-go.*

"Bye," she whispered, watching Courtney hurry back to her dressing booth.

Turning, Louisa spotted a mannequin with a lovely tan moleskin skirt and cream-colored blouse. "Nice," she said, hurrying to inspect it. *My suede boots would look so great with this!*

The same dumbfounded clerk asked if she needed assistance, and Louisa thought again of Courtney, still fuming. "I'll try on this outfit," she said. "Size two, please."

The clerk found the items and led Louisa back to the dressing rooms. Stopping outside the booth where Courtney's bare feet and hot pink toenails were now visible, Louisa paused, gathered her resolve, and said, "Hey, Court, I really want to apologize." She felt weird talking to the door.

The door opened and her friend grimaced.

"Look, I'm sorry," Louisa said. "Okay?"

"What for?" Courtney shrugged coolly. "You're following your heart, right?"

"But I hate this tension between us."

"So return to Denver with me. Make *everyone* happy."

"I can't do that."

Courtney scratched her head dramatically, then looked up. "Michael didn't want me to say anything . . . but since you're so stubborn, I guess I will anyway."

Louisa wasn't sure she wanted to hear about Michael.

Dressed now in her own clothing, Courtney led her to two waiting chairs in the common area and sat down. She patted the other for Louisa, who sat, too, her defenses rising again.

Courtney leaned close, pinning her with an intense gaze. "What if I told you Michael has decided not to partner at your father's law firm?"

Louisa swallowed. "He what?"

"He must love you a lot to give all that up. Don't you think?"

"No way he's walking from the firm."

"Don't be so sure. I think he wants to prove something to you in a big way."

"Then why didn't he want you to tell me?"

Courtney shook her head. "Maybe he wanted to say it himself. Remember, he wanted to fly out here? But you shut him down?"

"Courtney . . ." Louisa frowned. "Michael and I closed the door on our relationship . . . months ago."

Courtney stared at her. "He's a great guy, and putting it bluntly, you're nuts to ignore him."

"Sounds like you've gotten to know him pretty well since I've been here."

"All I'm saying is count your lucky stars

that Michael's willing to give the whole thing another chance . . . after you left him, basically, standing at the altar."

"Hey, you know that's not true."

"I don't see you throwing away that kind of love, Louisa."

"Honestly, I doubt Michael and I ever really had the devoted kind of love two people should marry for. The 'in sickness, in health' kind," Louisa said. The image of Sam's gentle eyes crossed her mind before she could blink it away.

"This is the real world, not some fairy-tale romance. No love is perfect, right? But Michael loves you and you love him. Or at least you used to."

"Yeah, I used to do a lot of things, Court."

Now it was Courtney's turn to sigh loudly.

"Listen, I don't want you to leave like this." Louisa reached over and squeezed Courtney's arm. "You have one day left here. Let's make the most of it—do something fun together, just the two of us. I'll take you to this art gallery I know, then out for lunch at a Dutch smorgasbord. Okay with you?"

Courtney's eyes were sad, even defeated, but she smiled gamely. "Sounds good, Ms. Stratford . . . but you're buying."

Chapter 10

Ben drove back to the harness shop where he found Irvin and another man negotiating a price on a new harness. Resuming his work, Ben checked the measurements for a custom miniature horse harness before cutting the leather.

He had never been awestruck by a girl before, and a Plain one at that. But Annie's personality was unlike any young woman he had dated. She was a peculiar yet appealing mix of beauty, naiveté, and spunk. She knew her mind and was rarely hesitant about speaking it, but only if she felt she was in a comfortable environment. Ben smiled to himself. *She's definitely become more at ease with me.*

Thinking ahead to the best choice of a restaurant for their first real date, he wondered how it would go . . . the two of them out together, and Annie vulnerable to the public eye. Inwardly he cringed at putting her at risk in any way and was contemplating rethinking where he might take her for supper when in walked Zeke Hochstetler.

"Ben, hullo again!"

Ben motioned him over to the large table where he worked. "What can I do for you?"

"Well, I came to ask Irvin if he could spare an hour or so," Zeke said, glancing over at Irvin and the farmer still haggling over cost. "Need some help mendin' a fence, and I mean that literally."

Ben smiled at his quip, though he found it curious that Zeke should drop by twice in one day. "I'd be happy to help with your fence," Ben volunteered. They both looked Irvin's way. "Looks like he might be tied up for a while, but I could get away once I'm done with this piece." Ben patted the dark leather.

"All right, then, I'll wait and take you over . . . then bring ya back."

Ben nodded in agreement.

Meanwhile, Zeke looked over at the wooden horses' heads of all different sizes along the shelf near the wall. He began to pace.

"Make yourself at home," said Ben.

"Don't mind if I do." Zeke wandered over to a chair and sat down. He pulled out a folded paper from inside his black work coat and began to read.

Nearly a half hour later, when Ben had completed his work, he went to speak to Zeke, who was dozing. Ben felt uncomfortable observing the man's chin and bushy beard leaning heavily on his chest. The tired-out farmer probably needed his forty winks more than Ben needed to wake him.

He thought of kind Esther . . . and how her husband was fending for himself these days, and he felt genuinely sorry for Zeke.

Ben and Zeke worked together to right the broken fence. The air was nippier than it had been earlier, even though the sun tried to peek through snow-laden clouds. Still, the exertion of sawing, toting lumber, and hammering kept Ben plenty warm.

When the job was complete and the fence was up and sturdy again, Zeke took him inside for some hot coffee. Dirty dishes were stacked in the kitchen sink, and Zeke apologized for the mess, saying he didn't know of any husband who kept a clean kitchen when the missus was away.

They sat and drank coffee, Zeke at the head of his table and Ben perched on the wooden bench. Zeke offered some sticky buns he'd gotten that morning from a "kindly neighbor," and Ben accepted, all the while thinking how terribly vacant this big old farmhouse seemed.

Later, on the way back to the harness shop, sitting under heavy lap robes, they rode near a cemetery, or as Zeke called it, "the People's burial ground." Ben was more interested in the interior of the fragile-looking coach, the Plexiglas windshield and the ultra-plain dashboard, than in an Amish graveyard.

Zeke held the reins as if it were second nature. He was clearly skilled in anticipating the signals, the slight nudges from man to beast and horse to driver that were their essential tool of connection. "Say now, what would ya think if we stopped off here for a minute?" Zeke asked, staring up at the fenced-in cemetery, set high on the hill.

"What's here?"

"I'd rather not be alone in doin' what I must." His voice had become a whisper, and the pink in his cheeks from the cold seemed to vanish.

Ben assented, though cemeteries made him feel on edge—always had.

Zeke turned toward him, the light slowly coming back into his brown eyes. "Been puttin' this off for too long, I daresay."

The horse slowed and the carriage came to a stop along the roadside. "I'm hard-headed, Ben, among other things," Zeke said. "I berated the brethren for the longest time . . . demanded to see where they buried my poor brother."

Ben wasn't sure he'd heard correctly. "Your *brother* died recently?"

"No . . . no. He was just a boy . . . his bones are buried back behind this here graveyard somewhere. Preacher Jesse and the bishop didn't even bother to give him a tomb-stone . . . nothin'."

Ben found this startling. "How did he die?"

"Not for certain on that."

"Wait now, you've lost me," Ben blurted. "Why are you only now going to see his grave?"

"You don't know the half . . . and it's too long a story, I fear." Zeke paused and said nothing for the longest time as they sat in the carriage. "I should never have uttered a word, and if you think twice 'bout telling anyone, well, I'll have your hide."

Ben bristled. "Who would I tell? And do you mean to say his death is a secret?"

"Jah, no one knows his remains were ever found. No one but two of the ministers, that is. And they intend to keep a lock on that." Zeke sighed loudly. "Up until last fall, I assumed he had been kidnapped. Then my memory of that night began to fade and nightmares began filling my sleep. I dreamed he fell into the hole I'd dug for his dead puppy dog . . . fell and hit his head. At least I think it was a dream. Then, lo and behold, if his bones weren't found buried in a farmer's field last year, not far from my own house."

Ben was speechless.

"None of this was ever reported . . . the kidnapping nor the death."

"Are you serious?"

"It's our way—*das Alt Gebrauch*—the old

way. Jesse Zook wants nothing to do with the outside world. Wants to follow the bishop's orders on that . . . ev'ry jot and tittle." Zeke gave a nervous chuckle, then composed himself. "Only the Good Lord knows why I'm tellin' you."

Quickly, Ben asked, "How long ago was this?"

"My brother was only four, and I had just turned eight." Zeke's hand shook briefly. "Sixteen endless years . . ."

"Sorry, I don't mean to pry."

"No . . . no. Don't apologize." Zeke was seemingly composed and was pointing out the narrow road that led to the hillside cemetery. "It's quite an elevated area, this here graveyard, so I'd suggest ya hold on but good." Zeke reined the horse to the right and onto the path hardly distinguishable due to drifted snow. "We've had some buggies actually tip over on this stretch."

Ben grabbed hold of the seat and held on.

———

Ben and Zeke stood at the back of the cemetery near the fence, looking down at the snowfields below—the vast white valley dappled with farmhouses, barns, and silos.

Like a picture on a calendar, Ben thought, although the sky was a gray-and-white mixture, the sun deeply cloaked.

"I've come here for many a burial," Zeke was saying. "But my brother never got a proper one." He stared at the rows of small grave markers. "'Twas Preacher Zook himself who unearthed the bones he and the bishop buried round here somewhere."

"I don't get it. Why weren't you and your family notified immediately?" Ben felt this was incomprehensible.

"I was told privately . . . then warned to keep mum. See, it's like this: Most of the People thought my brother had been abducted. No one wanted to think he was dead. But I thought it. Something in my gut knew it." He reached into his pocket and pulled out a paisley kerchief and wiped his face. "I want the killer found . . . punished. Whoever it is."

"What's the hold-up?"

Zeke looked around. "I need to find the grave first, but with all this snow . . ." He began muttering nearly incoherently now, and Ben felt sorry for him. "What was it again?" Zeke whispered to himself, shaking his head. "Eight long steps and . . ."

Ben didn't know what to think. The guy had a weird streak Ben hadn't noticed before.

Zeke trudged past a gravestone and headed toward the opening in the cemetery fence. Ben followed him up the slope and into the wooded area. And if he wasn't mistaken, Zeke was counting to himself as he walked.

Soon Zeke called to him from the thicket of trees. "I should've known the snow would be too deep."

Ben appraised the area. "Your brother's buried up *here*?" He glanced back at the actual cemetery.

Zeke nodded and struggled to speak. "S'pose it seemed fitting . . . since he disappeared . . . or died . . . in a grove much like this." His chin trembled. "I threatened Preacher Jesse with goin' to the police months ago. . . ."

Neither spoke for a moment; then Zeke brightened and turned to place a hand on Ben's shoulder. "But you could do it."

Ben frowned. "Do what?"

"Report his death." Zeke's eyes glistened. "I won't rest till I get to the bottom of this. But I'm forbidden, so I'm askin' you to do it for me."

Ben became instantly uneasy. "I agree, the police should be notified, but why would they believe an outsider? They'd want to know where I heard this, and then wouldn't the ministers trace it back to you?"

Zeke shook his head. "Maybe, but it wouldn't matter. The bishop can't control what outsiders do." He clenched his fists and turned his face to the bleak sky. His words were spoken just above a whisper, in a strange and chanting tone. "As the Lord God is my witness, I will see this through."

Ben experienced a strange stirring in his chest, as if Zeke were making a covenant with God himself. Then silently they headed out of the woods to the waiting horse and buggy.

On the ride back, as Ben continued to hedge about getting involved, Zeke's mood turned fiercely dark—alarmingly so. He slapped the reins down on the horse's back sharply and began muttering and cursing under his breath.

Ben could hardly wait for the buggy ride to end.

When they reached the thin road leading to the tack shop, Zeke turned to Ben again.

"Is that your answer, then? Or will you reconsider?"

Ben swallowed. "I need time to think."

Zeke nodded, averting his dark and brooding eyes. "Fair enough."

Annie found her father in the barn checking on the livestock, preparing to bed them down for the cold night ahead.

"Daed?" She walked toward him. "I best be gettin' something straight."

"What's that?"

"It's Yonie."

"Ah . . ." Daed frowned and straightened right quick. "You're upset 'bout his bobbed hair, I presume?"

"Well, aren't you?"

"Oh, he'll come around in time."

His response aggravated her.

"So, then, what's not at all good for the goose is just fine for the gander?"

"Aw, Annie . . . Annie."

"No, I'm serious, Daed. This is obvious favoritism, seems to me."

He leaned on his hay fork. "No one's favoring anyone. If ya think your sneaking round doing artwork is even close to what

Yonie's done with his haircut, well, you're wrong on that. And I'll be the first one to say it!"

She wouldn't let him wound her. Not the way he'd done in the past with issues of the Ordnung. She could see the bias too clearly. Why couldn't he?

"Listen, Annie. Truth be told, Yonie's bob has nothing to do with our agreement, yours and mine."

She thought of Ben Martin suddenly. His inviting her to dinner, her accepting. It wouldn't matter one bit now if she kept her word on the art and failed in the unspoken rule about courtship with an outsider. She was in no man's land, she knew.

She spoke again, willing away the tightness in her throat. "It doesn't seem fair what you're lettin' Yonie get by with. You even know 'bout his car." She wouldn't break her vow to her brother and tell what she knew of his romantic attachment to worldly Dory, also an Englischer.

"You've said enough, daughter. You best be goin' inside now. Awful cold out."

Cold or not, she refused to return to the house. "I'm headin' for a walk," she declared.

"Oh, Annie. Go inside and warm yourself."

She shook her head. "If Yonie can do whatever he wants, then why can't I go for a walk in the snow and not be reprimanded?"

"Listen here! Yonie's a man . . . that's different."

Annie was aghast and too stunned to talk. But only for a time. The pressure inside her was building and she managed to control her voice. "I'm a woman, ya say? Jah, Daed. Seems there *is* a mighty big difference between what's allowed for any man and what's permitted me."

The thin veil between her and the reality of the world she lived in had been torn, and there was no mistaking what flamed in her father's eyes.

———

Annie made slow progress over the hardened snow and ice on her treacherous walk. She was on her own, and it felt good, especially while struggling with her father's words, which still darted through her mind like so many hornets on a springtime morning.

"Daed's partial to Yonie . . . to men in general," she spoke into the frigid air. "All the People are." She felt her face tighten with the clenching of her jaw. It was too cold to be out here walking, just as Daed had warned.

I don't care . . . I need to vent my resentment so I don't burst out with something horrid! Except she'd already talked disrespectfully to Daed, so it was too late to spare herself from that embarrassment. Now she ought to go and ask forgiveness for questioning the man of God.

Yet how do I repent of something I'm not sorry for?

She kept on, careful where she stepped. The snow had melted down to fox-deep in some places where the sun had shone two days ago. Now the cloud-blanketed sun receded quickly, making dusk even grayer than the dreary day had been. Working up a bit of a sweat, she stopped to catch her breath. Not wanting to get overheated and then catch her death of a cold, she pulled her wool work coat tight against herself, looking out over the expanse of farmland across the road. She watched as a cluster of brown mules romped together—*trying to keep warm, just as I am,* she thought. Their winter coats were as dark as the moles that burrowed in the meadow.

She began to walk again, toward the

house this time. Thinking of the playful mules, she recalled the night their own mules had broken through a gate and taken off running down the road for a good long ways, gotten sidetracked from their flight, and disappeared into the woodlands high on the slope behind the People's cemetery. She, Yonie, Omar, and Luke had helped Daed by searching till the wee hours, taking two carriages and a pony cart and driving up and down the back roads, calling, looking . . . something akin to the night Isaac had gone missing, at least from what Mamm had told her. In the end, it was Yonie who had discovered the fresh mule dung near the turnoff to the cemetery road. She recalled the animals behaving as if untamed until rebridled, when they miraculously became Daed's own once again.

Like Yonie will become one day?

She had to laugh out loud. "Oh, jah. He'll run mighty wild. Maybe he won't ever allow himself to be haltered."

More sober now, Annie shivered in the cold.

I should talk. Will I?

Chapter 11

Snow had been falling all night, and the henhouse roof was beginning to sag. Jesse Zook Jr. and Annie's next oldest brother, Christian, arrived at first light to help their father remove the heavy ice. Sarah Mae, Jesse Jr.'s wife, came along, too, with their preschool-age boys, Little Jesse, Richard, and Davy, in time to help Mamm fry up a whole batch of corn fritters for breakfast.

As always, Annie was overjoyed to see her sister-in-law and wondered why Christian's wife, Martha, hadn't accompanied him, as well. When she asked, her brother said Martha was "under the weather," and

Annie suspected she might be expecting their third baby.

"Well, if Abner and Priscilla and their little ones were here, we'd have nearly the whole family," Annie said.

"We'll see everyone at Preachin'," Daed said.

Mamm agreed, waving at Dawdi and Mammi Zook as they made their way into the kitchen from the addition next door. Annie's grandparents sat at their appointed places at the long table, waiting for the hot meal to be served. Promptly, Mammi asked Louisa, "Where's that perty Courtney today?"

"She's getting ready to fly home this evening," Lou replied. "I think she's anxious to get back to Colorado."

"Jah, I s'pose," Annie said.

Sarah Mae carried a heavy platter to the table and set it down. That done, she got her stair-step boys washed up, with a little help from Annie, and then settled them onto the long bench on the window side of the table. "Some of the women are having a kitchen shower for Rudy and Susie Esh," Sarah Mae said softly, mainly to Annie.

It was their custom. After a couple married they spent each weekend at a different relative's home for the months following the wedding, in order to receive their wedding presents. And, in the case of a kitchen shower like the one being planned for Susie Esh, the womenfolk would bring enough canned goods and preserves to stock the young bride's cold cellar. Typically they would have thrown a large grocery shower by now, but with ongoing inclement weather and so many down with winter flu, they must have waited.

"That's real nice of you," Annie said, realizing again how happy she was for her former beau and his wife. "I'll be glad to come, if that's what you're askin'."

"Oh, would ya?" Sarah Mae's eyes lit up.

"Why, sure." Annie nodded. "I'll bring Lou along, too." Here she glanced at Louisa, who'd slipped in next to Annie's grandmother. "Would you want to?"

"Hmm . . . I don't have any canned goods to give," said Lou.

Sarah Mae smiled and tucked a napkin under her youngest boy's chin. "Ach, that's fine. Just come and have some hot cocoa and goodies . . . and wish the bride well."

Wish her well . . .

Annie pondered the before and after state

of marriage for young women. Some seemed to blossom under the covering of their husbands, while others lost their smiles nearly immediately. *Like Esther did.* . . .

"There'll be good fellowship," Mamm added, which meant she'd overheard the conversation. "Louisa should go along for that reason alone."

"When is it?" asked Annie.

"This Friday afternoon," Sarah Mae said, sitting across the table.

"Friday?" Annie wished she hadn't asked at all, because now Lou was giving her a peculiar look. *I haven't even told Lou about my plans with Ben that night,* she thought. Still, she knew she'd have to fill her in some-time. Yet how would she ever get to Susie Esh's kitchen shower, back home, eat sup-per, redd up the kitchen, and then out the door in time to meet Ben at dusk?

"Not sure I can make it," Annie blurted, not wanting anyone to see the frustration in her eyes. Because she must not let on she was seeing a fellow outside the Fold. Fur-thermore, she would not, under any circum-stances, let Ben down . . . at least not for someone else's kitchen shower!

Aware of her family's curious glances,

Annie could hardly wait to get going to Julia's. Ironing would be piled high, and she was itching to get to work. Since this was Lou's last day with Courtney, maybe today would be a good time to chat with Esther. *I really need to!* Annie thought.

Annie felt glad when Louisa told her after breakfast that she was going to "connect with Courtney once more." Omar had evidently offered to take Lou over to the B&B where Courtney was staying.

"You sure she'll be up yet?" Annie asked, glancing at the clock shelf on the kitchen wall. It was not quite seven-thirty.

"I can only hope." Lou seemed discouraged.

"Well, surely things will go better now that you've settled your conflict." Annie didn't mean any harm, and by the look on Lou's face, she understood.

Lou gave Annie a quick hug. "Thanks for hanging in there."

"That's why we're good friends. We never quit hangin'." Annie laughed softly.

Omar stood at the back door, smiling and waiting. Lou waved. "I plan to take Courtney over to the art gallery."

"Oh, good idea," said Annie. "To show her your work?"

"That and we need some time to relax together. So I might not make it over to Julia's at all today."

"Have fun, and don't worry none," Annie said. "I've got plenty to keep me busy." *And Esther wants to talk privately.*

Lou smiled and headed for the back porch and out the door. Annie strolled to the window and watched her get into the carriage with Omar.

Don't let Courtney talk you into going home, dear friend. . . .

Louisa realized, as she rode in the buggy with Annie's younger brother, she was no longer the same person who had first come to Amish country. *Three months has changed me big time,* she thought, judging from her reaction to Courtney's attitude. *Was I ever like that?*

She knew she must have been very similar. Why else would someone like Courtney have appealed to her as a close friend? Truly, she did not have the down-home sort of friendliness exhibited here in the Plain community. Come to think of it, Louisa didn't recall ever connecting with Courtney as a soul mate. Not the way she did with Annie. *A best friend who helped me find myself. . . .*

Suddenly Louisa shivered. She was freezing, even though she'd worn the "worldly" red sweater over her slip and beneath her dress and apron. Like expensive long underwear.

Perhaps Omar had noticed her shiver, because he spoke up for the first time during the ride. "Another cold one, jah?"

She nodded, smiling. All of Annie's younger brothers had kept to themselves somewhat since her arrival.

"Enjoy the Sunday singings, then?" asked Omar.

Taken off guard, she shrugged, not sure how to answer. She couldn't know if Omar had seen her and Sam Glick leaving together following the barn singing and dance. She felt strange being asked about it. "Umm . . . do *you*?"

"Well, to be honest, I've only been goin' for a short time." He slapped the reins and the horse picked up the pace. "Turnin' sixteen is the big thing round here, I guess ya know."

She was waiting for him to say something about the pretty girls lined up on one side of the haymow, or at the long table, when the singing began. But he volunteered nothing.

"I'm still figuring out how the Amish community works," she said.

He chuckled, tilting back his black hat. "Seems to me an outsider might never understand."

"Being born into it is the key," she said softly, more to herself than to Omar.

That really got a laugh from him. "Don't see how anyone could up and join the People without feelin' like they've given up everything important to 'em."

She gleaned that fancy Englishers like her were viewed as putting a higher value on modern conveniences than the tranquility and simplicity Amish life offered.

She pulled the heavy coat she'd borrowed from Annie more tightly around her, wanting to agree with Omar. She wanted to tell him how amazingly hard it would be if she or anyone from the "outside" decided to abandon electricity forever, or the warmth of a car on a horribly cold day like this—the modern world as a whole. But she figured her thoughts were of no consequence to

Omar Zook. They did get her thinking about the adoring gleam in Sam's eye, however.

I must be careful not to hurt him . . . or me.

The Maple Lane Farm B&B came into view as they made the turn. When she got out of the buggy, she looked up at Omar and said, "It was really nice of you to bring me. Thanks!"

He tipped his hat and beamed his appreciation. "See ya at supper, then?"

"Sure will." Waving, she wondered how it would feel to say her final good-byes to Annie, her family, and Sam . . . when the time came.

I don't have to contemplate that now, she told herself, heading up the walkway to the stately inn.

Later that morning at the Rancks', James and Molly helped Annie pick up the downstairs bedrooms. Four-year-old James kept talking about his "new chum, Ben Martin," and Annie wanted to ask the boy why he felt such a connection to the Englischer, but she merely listened.

When all the toys were stored and organized according to piece and color in the toy box made by their father, Annie dusted the furniture, shook out the braided rugs, dry mopped the hardwood floors, and made sure there were no cobwebs under the beds or dressers or dirt above the wide doorframes.

Julia was away from the house, assisting a young mother in childbirth, so Annie had not only her cleaning duties to attend to but babysitting besides. And since Esther's eldest, Laura, was off at the Amish schoolhouse not far from the Ranck home, Esther kept Zach and John busy cutting out snowflake designs at the kitchen table while the baby slept soundly in the borrowed cradle nearby.

Close to eleven o'clock, Annie stopped her cleaning and helped Esther make grilled cheese sandwiches and warmed up homemade beef barley soup from Julia's freezer.

It was after the meal, when the kitchen had been made spotless once again and the children were napping, that Annie sat at the table and talked with Esther as she nursed Essie Ann.

"Where's Louisa today?" Esther asked.

"With her friend Courtney."

Esther stroked her baby's cheek, looking down at the cute bundle. "Are you enjoyin' having Louisa here?"

"Sure. But some days I wonder if she's not awful homesick. Seein' Courtney again has made some things resurface, I'm thinkin'."

"I daresay it's been something of a culture shock for Louisa, jah?"

Annie smiled. "Oh, to say the least. But she's interested in experiencing our ways quite fully. I think she's done a right good job of blending in here."

"For now . . . jah."

"She's also quite curious about why we do what we do," Annie added.

"Well, sometimes I am, too." Esther smiled.

Annie assumed she meant the probationary shun placed on her for disregarding her responsibility to her husband. So far, there had been no indication that Esther could not fellowship with church members in good standing or others not yet baptized. "You doin' all right?" she asked. "What I mean is . . . do you know where you'll live next?"

"You're thinkin' I should go back to Zeke?"

Annie was hesitant to say one way or the other. "Might be wise to let the ministers have their say. . . ."

"Well, word has it I just need to pray more and be more submissive—then Zeke's temper will be quelled. But I know better, Annie." She stopped to lift her infant onto her shoulder.

"So Zeke's been gruff with you for a long time, then?"

"Ever so long."

"And it doesn't matter if you're completely obedient in every way?"

Esther shook her head, eyes tearing. "He has an affliction in his soul, is all I know."

"Isaac's kidnapping?"

" 'Tis one heavy burden." Esther patted Essie Ann's tiny hump of a back, then continued. "But the great burden-bearer is the Lord Jesus, and I pray Zeke might see Christ in me. Somehow . . ."

"Well, who can *not* see how sweetly long-suffering you are?" *But she's always been that way,* thought Annie.

"I want to be consistently loving, I do."

"Well, Esther, I know the difference

'tween you and a tetchy woman." Annie thought again of her conversations with both Yonie and Daed. It didn't seem fair that the men in the community could get by with mistreating their wives, as Esther had indicated. The favoritism annoyed her terribly, but she was determined not to bring it up with Esther just now. Maybe never.

Esther settled her baby to her other breast and covered herself with a light blanket. "I found the Lord just in time," she said softly.

"What's that mean?" Annie honestly didn't know.

"God's Word—the Good Book—has become my very food. I was tired, no, actually weary of constantly remembering the sins I committed on a daily basis. Now I am trusting in the Lord's grace to forgive me of all my transgressions. I can rest in His mercy and love."

"*You* feel you need to be forgiven?" Annie was bewildered. "You don't mean not fulfilling your family duties, do ya?"

"I mean just everything. The little fibs I might be tempted to tell now and then, the anger that comes up in my throat and flies out my mouth . . . the animosity I feel building up in me each and ev'ry day . . . toward my husband 'specially."

"Really?"

"Him and others."

Annie couldn't even begin to think who the *others* were, but at this moment she was eager to resume her work for Julia. Truly, she did not want to prolong this conversation.

But Esther needed to talk, apparently, so Annie sat still, feeling ever so awkward.

"Zeke was never treated right as a youngster, you must surely know."

Maybe that's the reason why he's so snippy with his own children, Annie wondered.

"He was constantly belittled by his father," Esther said.

"After Isaac disappeared?"

"Jah. Even Zeke's mamma joined in, instilling the notion that the full blame of the kidnapping rested on Zeke's shoulders."

"Why on earth?"

"Because Zeke disobeyed his father and left the house to bury Isaac's puppy that night. He had been told not to go at all. He was bullheaded and took Isaac to witness the dog's burial."

Annie had heard bits and pieces of this

account, but she had never observed such pity as was evident in Esther's face. "Do you believe it, too? That Zeke was punished by God for disobeying his father?"

"Oh, it's hard to say. And Zeke never speaks of that night—'cept in his sleep, that is. I know he's obsessed with his loss . . . and the fact that he believes Isaac is somehow watchin' over him, from on high."

"Well, it's not like Isaac's become an angel."

At Annie's mention of *angel,* Esther began to weep. "Zeke's had so many strikes against him, and here we are apart from each other. By my own doing."

"You felt you had a reason to leave—it was for your baby's sake. And now that Essie Ann's here, have you thought of goin' back?"

Esther sighed, brushing tears from her face. "Even if I were to return to Zeke, I wouldn't be allowed to share his bed. I'm a shunned woman, ya know."

"You mean you're going to keep on sayin' the prideful things—about salvation through grace 'n' all—that got all this started?"

"Are you askin' if I'm gonna hush up

'bout being saved in Jesus' name?" Esther stared into the milky blue eyes of her baby. "Well, no. I won't renounce my dear Savior. I wouldn't think of it, Annie."

She'll accept what she cannot see over what she can . . . over Zeke and the church?

"I best keep my opinion to myself," Annie whispered.

Esther reached out a hand. "You don't have to be put out."

"I guess I am in some ways . . . you're making a decision I doubt I could ever make. Or stick by."

"To open up your heart to the Lord?"

"If you must put it that way."

Esther did not attempt to persuade her otherwise. "It is a hard path . . . the one the church has set forth. We must come to our own fork in the road, and find God's Son waitin' there."

Annie squeezed her hand and released it. "I can tell you've been livin' here with Julia these days . . . hearing all her blood-of-Jesus talk."

"But I'm ever so happy, strange as that must sound, even with my future hangin' in the balance." Esther straightened and looked at her. "Maybe I'm speakin' out of turn, but I see a sad sort of look in your eyes when you hold Essie Ann near. And I can't help but wonder if you might not be longing to be a mother yourself . . . someday."

Annie quickly changed the subject . . . to the attic, where Irvin and Julia had made a special place for Esther and the children to sleep. She missed it terribly—*my former art studio.* Yet just entertaining the thought of working up there again was not acceptable. No matter, she asked Esther, "How do you like your little bedroom up yonder?"

"Well, it gets a bit chilly at times, but we sleep with lots of quilts and covers . . . and I even put Essie Ann in with me. It's not the best setup, but we're all together and that's what counts."

"Except for Zeke," Annie said.

"Still, I can't just rush back to his arms, Irvin has said. Julia says so, too."

Annie gave her friend a concerned look. "Cousin Irvin's not settin' out to convert your husband, too, I hope."

Esther's smile grew. "Oh, that would be just wonderful-good, I'm thinkin'."

"No . . . no. You'd both be shunned."

Esther nodded. "I'm not taking my heart back."

"Sounds mighty odd . . . like you're in love or something."

"Well, I surely am, Annie. I've fallen in love with my precious Lord Jesus."

No wonder the brethren slapped the Bann on her. . . .

Annie rose and excused herself. "I'll leave you be for now. Must complete things round here before Julia returns and finds me shirking, ya know."

"I'm glad we could talk frank like this, Annie."

Annie wasn't about to lie. In some ways she was sorry she'd ever sat down and listened to Esther go on so. It made little sense to her . . . and the last thing Annie wanted was to get caught up in Esther's zeal for a personal God and whatnot all.

After the cab dropped them off at the art gallery, Louisa introduced Courtney to Eileen Sauder, the owner, who had shown such interest in Louisa's work. Then, strolling about the corridor, Louisa pointed out her paintings to Courtney among the various framed oils and watercolors on display. Louisa made every effort to be cheerful and to solidify her apology. Courtney, too, seemed to be on her best behavior.

"Here's one of my first Lancaster paintings," she said, pausing in front of an autumnal landscape. "I'm mesmerized by the barns around here, the rolling countryside."

"Nice," Courtney acknowledged, and they moved to the next painting.

"Now, this is one of Annie's peacocks. Did I tell you I actually help feed these critters each morning? I think God was working overtime when He created this guy. I still don't think I did the colors justice, but isn't he gorgeous?"

Courtney shook her head. "Wow, I'll tell you what's gorgeous—it's your work. Seriously, Louisa, I don't think I've ever seen you paint so well, with such . . . peaceful beauty."

"Thanks. That means a lot."

After they had thanked Eileen, Louisa called a cab on her cell phone. Then they headed back outdoors, bundling their coats around them.

"Your students should see your recent

paintings, Louisa," Courtney said. "They're really something. What are you working on now?"

"Oh, I've kinda put my art on the back burner these last few weeks. Out of respect for my hosts—the Zooks. Besides, I've had other things on my mind."

Courtney's red lips parted in astonishment. "I can't believe it. You really *are* different. But I still wish I could talk you into coming home and giving Michael a second chance."

Louisa shook her head. "It's over. I know it; so does he."

"But what about the rest of us?" Courtney softened the question with a smile. "Giving up on us, too?"

Louisa smiled back. "No, Court. Never."

"So you'll stay in touch?"

"Sure, but I have no idea when I'm going home, so don't raise my mom's hopes, okay?"

Courtney nodded, then reached for her and gave her a hug. "If that's what you want."

"Jah, it is."

They both laughed as the summoned cab pulled into the parking lot. "Drive us to

Miller's Smorgasbord, please," Louisa said when they were settled in the backseat.

"Excellent choice for a buffet lunch," the cabbie said with a smile. "They have the creamiest cheesecake . . . and don't forget the shoofly pie!"

Louisa couldn't resist. "Wonderful-good cookin', jah?"

"Oh, brother," Courtney said, laughing.

———

When they parted ways, after a not-so-light meal, Louisa secretly felt glad about not having fallen for Michael's attempt at getting back together. She was rather impressed that he had given up the law partnership—an aspiration that had been the last straw between them.

But I won't let this news affect me, she thought, relieved the last day of Courtney's visit had gone so well. She was eager to tell Annie all about it . . . and surprisingly eager to start painting again, as well.

Chapter 12

Ben accepted payment for the newly oiled harness. He offered to help carry it through the snow to the waiting buggy, but the elderly Amish bishop and his great-grandson—introduced to Ben as a "wonderful-gut checkers player"—would not hear of it.

"*Denki*, Ben," Bishop Stoltzfus called over his shoulder.

Needing some fresh air, Ben walked to the back of the shop and pushed open the narrow door, standing where no one could see him. And where he could look out over the vast expanse of fields inundated with drifted snow. The skeletal figures of winter trees punctuated the horizon.

His gaze settled on a grouping of scrappy trees to the south. *What type of trees are they? I suppose Annie knows.*

How quickly his thoughts turned to her, as if she'd been his friend for years. His best buddy back home, Eric, had complained vociferously when he'd told him of his plan to move away. He hadn't been able to say then why he wanted to live in the middle of Pennsylvania Amish country, because he hadn't known himself. Truth was, he still didn't.

His eyes focused again on the distant grove, recalling someone from his childhood who had the uncanny ability to identify various trees. The astute person spoke of the Creator God—an all-powerful Being responsible for the majestic beauty of the woods and the meticulous design of the trees themselves. The tree expert, obscure in his memory, sometimes still appeared in his dreams.

Ben himself had readily recognized the glossy white bark of the wild river birches planted in various yards around Paradise. He had also spotted the tall-growing native cedars with their deep evergreen lacelike leaves. Yet his was a beginner's knowledge of trees.

Exhaling, Ben watched his breath float aloft in the frosty air. "Who was it?" he whispered, aware of the too-familiar sense of frustration he always felt when struggling to remember such things from childhood.

I'm not the only one.

He recalled his strained conversation with Zeke, dogged in his determination to discover the murderer of his brother. Yet as pivotal as that night seemed to him, Zeke was terribly confused about what actually happened.

Ben was incensed to think someone could sneak into this quiet community and steal away a small child. Yet wasn't it nearly equally unjust, in a different sort of way, for the People to keep a lid on things, evidently not wanting to make waves by reporting outsiders' offenses? Doing so left victims of such crimes unable to find solace in justice.

You could report this, Zeke had said when moved by Ben's pity, and later Ben had reluctantly agreed to consider it. But now he shook his head, for as much as he wanted to help raise Zeke's banner of justice, what would happen if it were known that *he* had caused the police to invade the People's sanctified privacy? It was bad enough for an Englisher to seek out an Amish girl. But this?

His hands were stiff from the subzero temperatures. "It's Annie who is most at risk by associating with me," he muttered, pushing his hands into his pockets. He remembered the spark of awareness in her expressive blue eyes . . . the way they held his gaze. At the same time an ever-present fear was etched on her face: She was afraid of being found with him.

I must make her feel comfortable . . . and trust me, he thought, then sighed. *If that's even possible.*

At once he smelled the familiar scent of pipe tobacco and wondered which of the regular Amish clientele had arrived, although he had not heard the clatter of carriage wheels nor the thud of horse hooves against the packed snow.

He wondered if Zeke had returned for yet another visit. Then again, Zeke was not one for tobacco. But Zeke *had* pulled a cigar out of his coat pocket—"from the preacher," he'd said—when Ben agreed to go tramp-

ing around in the woods, looking for an un-
marked grave, which they had never found.

Thinking back on yesterday's strange afternoon, Ben realized he could not assent to
Zeke's urgent request, not without further advice. And who better to advise him than another Amish person, namely Annie herself?
Being the preacher's daughter she would
surely know the issues at stake for Zeke—the
possible shunning aspect, especially.

Torn between frustration with Zeke's cir-
cumstance and anticipation of seeing Annie
again, Ben headed back inside to the
warmth and leathery tang of the shop to
tend to his unseen client.

Esther had never intended to overhear
Zeke's discussion with Irvin. She had
slipped downstairs, leaving her napping
children in the attic room to get a drink of
water in the kitchen. She heard Irvin talking
in the small sunroom off the kitchen, telling
Zeke he had proposed marriage to Julia on
the tan loveseat in their living room—"on
the same piece of furniture where my father
proposed to my mother." He chuckled. "Of
course, I reupholstered it since that time."

Zeke's response seemed to indicate he

was more interested in the process of up-
holstery than whatever point Irvin was trying
to make, which brought a sinking feeling to
Esther. *Is he that closed up to love?*

But she knew from being Zeke's wife
what sort of man he was. And she seriously
doubted if Irvin, or anyone, could change
his way of thinking.

As she sipped the cold water, Irvin began
to talk straight. "I'm not interested in wast-
ing your time, Zeke . . . nor mine. To put it
bluntly, I believe you have been treating Esther wrongly."

**Wrongly? Had anyone ever dared to be
this forthright?**

Esther doubted it. No one had ever suc-
cessfully dealt with Zeke's belligerent behavior toward her, nor toward the church
brethren. She knew from the grapevine that
her husband had been in jeopardy of the
Bann on several occasions. The fact that he
had escaped by the skin of his teeth made
her wonder what sort of things he had told
the brethren to quash their indignation. Perhaps the ministers had shown leniency out
of fear Zeke might eventually report his
brother's kidnapping, something he had
threatened to do off and on over the years.

"Here, let me read what the Scriptures say about the marriage relationship," Irvin's voice broke the quiet. "'Husbands, love your wives and do not be harsh with them.'"

"But that ain't all it says," Zeke snapped. "The woman's to come under the rule of the man . . . she's to submit in ev'ry way." Zeke paused. "And I wouldn't put a bit of weight on that Bible you're readin'."

There was a slight pause. Then Irvin answered thoughtfully, with slow words, "Well, we can read from the King James if you prefer."

Esther had to smile. Poor Irvin had his work cut out for him.

Irvin had evidently reached for a different Bible, and he began to read yet again. "'Husbands, love your wives, even as Christ also loved the church, and gave himself for it.' This means we are to cherish our wives, tend to them as we care for our own body. Give our love away sacrificially . . . surrender it to the good of our beloved."

Esther was stunned. She'd never heard such things coming from a man. *No wonder Julia wears a constant smile!*

But for Esther to trust that such a verse

might find its way into Zeke's stony heart, well, she would not get her hopes up. She had never known anyone to act like the devil, but she felt she'd seen his sneering face—when Zeke's rage overtook him. No, Irvin's attempt to convert Zeke was futile. She felt sure she knew what made her husband tick, and it had nothing at all to do with giving himself up for his bride.

After supper dishes were put away and Annie and Louisa were in their room, with Muffin purring in Lou's arms, Annie brought up her secret date with Ben Martin. "It's this Friday, after nightfall," she said, watching Louisa's expression.

A smile spread quickly across Lou's face. "I knew it. This is so great, Annie."

"Now, don't go jumpin' to conclusions. I'm not going to be his girl or anything."

"Well, are you sure?"

Annie let out a little giggle. "Now, listen. I agreed to go with him just this once."

"But you've spent time alone with him already . . . haven't you?"

Annie couldn't hide the truth. "Actually, we've run into each other quite a few times."

"Oh, so you're a couple now?"

"No."

"But that's what *he* wants," Lou said. Then she told her how Ben had asked about Annie some time back. "I said he should ask you himself."

"Ach, you did?" Annie held a strand of her golden waist-length hair in her hands.

"Sure, it beats wishing and hoping. Why should I try to set up a date with you for him when he can do it himself? It's better this way. You know exactly where he stands."

"I *do* like him, Lou. But he's English." Annie felt her heart do a strange dance at the thought of seeing him again. "What am I goin' to do?"

"Have a fine evening, that's what. Ben seems like a wonderful guy."

"But . . . he's off limits. My father will have my head if I'm found out. I shouldn't have agreed to see Ben again."

"Then why did you?"

"Because I have to know . . ."

"If he's the man for you?"

Annie turned abruptly and looked at her. "I'm not thinkin' of marriage. Honestly, I'm not."

"You wouldn't want to abandon your

Amish ways, of course. What's wrong with enjoying his company?"

"The way you enjoy Sam's?"

"Umm . . . we're not talking about *me*," Lou said.

Annie smiled at her friend. "Did Courtney get off all right?"

"You're changing the subject," Lou said.

Laughing softly, Annie nodded. "Jah, I guess I am at that."

Chapter 13

Annie sat in the barn on Friday morning, thinking ahead to her much-anticipated date with Ben that evening. She heard the sound of the milkers and stared at the far end of the barn. Squinting her eyes, she held up her fingers in midair—her thumb and pointer finger—measuring the distance as an artist might, appraising the shape and size of the milk-house beyond.

"Caught you!" Louisa said, sneaking up behind her. "What're you doing?"

Annie put her hand down quickly. "What's it look like?"

"Oh, I get it. You're missing something . . . big time."

Annie nodded. "The thought that I *must* draw and paint, well it never, ever leaves me. Not even for a minute." She pined for the feel of a paintbrush in her hand. "Some days I feel like I might just waste away."

"It's gotta be tough." Lou offered to help her lay out quilting squares again, like they had one other time when Annie's need to paint had hit ever so hard. "What about that?"

"Mamm was not so pleased with that crazy quilt pattern I created."

"She said that?"

"Oh jah. She was adamant it was much too worldly."

"I'm really, really sorry, Annie." Lou squatted near, smiling sympathetically. "What *can* you do to feed your artistic side now that it's winter?"

"Well, short of going back on my pledge to Daed, I just don't know."

Lou nodded and followed Annie when it was time to go to the milk house. "When's the next quilting bee? Maybe that might help."

"It's comin' up soon enough. I'll try 'n' think ahead to that," Annie replied, not wanting Lou's pity. Not on this day. "I know. I'll focus on Ben. Maybe that'll get my mind off my art."

"He *is* mighty *perty*!"

"Oh, you!" She chased Lou around the barn till the cows began mooing, which was not such a good thing. Not if Daed was going to have calm and contented cows for the rest of the milking hour.

"What would you do if the sounds of the country weren't humming in your ears every night?" Louisa said to Annie later as they swept the aisles. "I mean that hypothetically, of course. I know you're not going anywhere."

Annie wore a fleeting smile. "You're talking 'bout lying in bed and hearin' the owls hooting and the wind keening?"

"I guess, but sometimes it's more than that," Louisa admitted. "There are times when I think about the countryside being the least noisy place in the world. But how can that be true? I mean, the night sounds fill up my head and even sneak into my sleep, too."

"The restless peacocks?"

Louisa agreed. "And other sounds. Muffin

seems to hear them, too—she quivers in her sleep."

"Oh, I'm sure. There's something about animals. They not only hear, but they sense things like a brewing storm or, in the case of your cat, the agitation of the barn cats, especially when the moon is full. Ever notice that?"

"Not so much. I'm not into the phases of the moon. I do love the silvery look of the snow when there's a full moon, though." Louisa suddenly thought of Sam, wondering what sorts of sounds he heard each night as he fell asleep in his father's farmhouse. What smells did he love best?

Why should I care? she wondered.

Not allowing herself to linger on Sam, her thoughts flew to Courtney, who she knew would not understand nor care to embrace any connection with the Plain world here. Courtney was content with her flamboyant life.

So does a person have to be drawn to this? Or does life need to be messed up before you crave serenity?

At that moment, Louisa realized Annie was braver than she by far. Sam had asked to meet her later tonight, and she'd agreed. Yet she had said nothing at all to Annie. *How long can I keep this quiet?*

She daydreamed, feeling surprisingly mellow at the prospect of seeing Sam again, as she watched Yonie move in and out of the cow stalls, hitching up his work trousers as he went. His scuffed boots were ridged with caked mud, she noticed, with pieces of straw sticking out like a sort of barbed halo.

He, too, has secrets, she was willing to venture. One night, while Annie dreamed peacefully upstairs, sleepless Louisa had paced the main house's long front room, which was lined with shelves full of books with strange German titles. It was then she had spied the preacher's son outside, though Yonie had been too busy kissing his modern girlfriend to notice.

The next morning, Esther watched the sun come up, her body signaling it was past time to nurse Essie Ann. Propped up with pillows, she prayed silently in the stillness of dawn, her children sprawled in a row along the width of the bed.

I feel it in the marrow of my bones, dear Lord. I'll be forced to return home . . . and soon. I ask for the grace to do this thing which I dread.

She stroked John's head. *Touch my dear, frail child, I pray. Thank you for sparing his life on that most frightening night. Oh, I give you praise, Father.*

Essie Ann stirred in her cradle, making her usual soft sounds upon first awaking. Esther would not wait for her to wail. She slipped out of bed and went to her, longing to preserve the peace of this place, her retreat of safety, likening it to the shelter the Lord God had provided for the psalmist David.

How much longer will I find refuge here? She did not wish to be a burden to the Rancks, kind as they were, and would continue to help around the house wherever she could, especially with young James and Molly. But although she was inclined to, she would not allow herself to fret. *I will put my full trust in my Lord. I will not be afraid.*

Even so, she fought the looming sense of urgency that things were about to change for her and her dear, helpless children.

* * *

Annie was a bit surprised by Ben's somewhat Plain attire. She half expected he
might arrive wearing the shirt and tie asso-
ciated with church clothes or "dress up," as
the Englischers called it. But not Ben. His
solid blue shirt was open at the neck beneath his dark coat. In fact, he looked like
any one of Irvin's Mennonite friends.

Does he mean to impress me?

"How are you, Annie?" he asked, opening
the door for her. He'd parked out on the
road, about a quarter mile up from their
lane. The car was still running, and she marveled at how toasty warm it was inside.

"I'm doin' all right. How 'bout you?"

"Glad to see you again." He grinned irre-
sistibly and closed her door. She found herself smiling as he moved quickly around the
front of the car to the driver's side, got in, and
snapped his seat belt. That done, he turned
to her. "I hope you don't mind . . . I made
reservations for us at a restaurant quite a distance from here. I thought it might be best,
considering our circumstances," he said.

**He means: since you're not supposed
to be out with me!**

"Sure, I think that's nice," she said, surprised once more at how relaxed she felt

with him. She was glad, too, for a long ride before yet another meal—even though she was not so keen on riding in a car. Even so she'd waited with great anticipation for this night, and Ben seemed to be as careful as any of the drivers her father occasionally hired for the family.

"Am I going too fast?" Ben asked, seemingly mindful of her hesitancy.

She shook her head. "Usually, when I ride in the vans on the way out to Ohio or whatnot, I sit far in the back. But I'll get used to this, really."

"We'll be traveling more slowly tonight because of the weather."

Jah, good, she thought. "It's so cold the snow hardly has a chance to melt."

"And more is coming, according to the forecast." He went on to say he had made a habit of following the weather quite closely, via the Internet.

"Louisa has a portable computer," she volunteered. "Sometime she shows me the news and other things on the screen. That is, when we're at Cousin Julia's, of course. We don't have electric in the house, ya know."

He nodded. "I've wondered. Some of the

Amish who come into the tack shop have electricity and others frown on it. Can you explain that?"

Happy to clarify, she outlined the differences between several of the conservative groups in the area to the best of her ability. "And you may not know this, but there is a growing number of folk leaving the Old Order for a group called, not surprisingly, the New Order. They're more open to modern ideas. Over in the area of Gap there are Amish who drive cars and have lights in their houses, yet they dress similar to my family and me."

"Hard to understand why there are so many groups."

"Every Ordnung is different, if only a little, even from one regional district to another, my father says."

They talked about Irvin and Julia and Ben's fondness for them. And again about the blizzard that was supposed to blow in sometime during the weekend.

"In Kentucky we wished we had more snow," Ben said. "But here we complain if we get too much."

"Mer net zefridde," Annie said with a mischievous smile. *We're never satisfied.*

Watching the road carefully, Ben seemed distracted momentarily by a pedestrian, then turned to her, smiling. "You're right, we're not."

She looked at him, somewhat surprised. "You've picked up some Dutch, seems to me."

Ben shrugged casually, and she made herself stop staring. He was a curious man. She was careful to answer his questions— mostly about the "Plain society," as he referred to their community.

At one point she asked him if he'd ever read the book *The Riddle of the Amish Culture,* which was highly regarded as a good resource.

"I'll have to pick it up," he said. "You say your people approve of the book?"

"Well, sure, because it correctly represents the Anabaptist community as a whole. The author has lived and worked among us for a good many years now."

"He's English?"

"Jah, and well respected according to Daed. And my Dawdi Zook knows of him, too, which is sayin' a lot."

Ben continued to inquire about the author, obviously interested that someone who was not Amish could be so welcomed by those who were. Annie's mind flitted to the notion that, just maybe, Ben Martin was hoping to be well received, too.

When they arrived at the restaurant after a drive of some forty minutes, Annie could see from the exterior what a lovely place it was. It wasn't a regular sort of restaurant like some of those up and down Route 30, which catered to tourists with signs advertising home-style cooking.

Inside Ben stepped forward and quietly gave his last name to the hostess, who promptly led them to a table for two near a fireplace.

All during the candlelit meal, she found herself glancing toward the door, wondering if someone familiar might walk through and catch them. Several times, Ben asked if she was feeling ill, and each time she politely smiled and shook her head.

Despite being on edge, her conversation with Ben came rather effortlessly as they discussed their growing-up years. At one point something triggered a distant memory, one she had nearly forgotten. "Mamm and Mammi Zook—that's my grandmother who lives in the Dawdi Haus—were cookin' up popcorn in a skillet. My mother must've forgotten what was inside, so when she lifted the lid the kernels right then began popping out of the pan, flying every which way." She stopped, trying to suppress a nearly uncontrollable giggle but did not succeed.

When she had composed herself a bit, she continued. "I remember watching it pop wildly, some bouncing off the ceiling—that high, honest to goodness—other kernels soaring across the room. It was the funniest thing I think I've ever seen."

Ben grinned, glancing at her across the table. "I can see it, Annie. You describe it so well. How old were you?"

"I'm not sure, but this happened at a quilting bee, during the afternoon break, when the womenfolk stopped to stretch their legs and have their fill of . . . well, popcorn." She sighed. "I hadn't started school yet, so I was young."

"It surprises me you remember that far back."

"Lou says the same thing 'bout me."

He shook his head. "It's really remarkable." He reached for the salt and pepper shakers. "I have to confess I barely remember a thing before age five."

"It might be easier for girls," she said. "Maybe your parents could share a few memories to get you started."

He seemed uncomfortable all of a sudden, so she, too, ceased her talking.

She was thankful she'd taken only a very small portion of mashed potatoes, buttered succotash, and roast beef at home. And for good reason. Not wanting to call attention to herself by simply not eating with the family for supper, she'd sat down with them anyway. Now Annie hoped she would be able to eat enough at *this* meal to please Ben, though it was usually the man who would eat up to impress his girl. But she wouldn't allow herself to think that way— not about Ben.

Why on earth did I share my recollection of the exploding popcorn? One thing she had not mentioned about that day, and she didn't feel she ought to, was the fact that Isaac Hochstetler had been the only little boy at the quilting bee. Isaac's mamma had not been any too keen on his gravitating mostly toward Annie in play, although both Annie's mother and her grandmother had found it more humorous than cause for alarm.

"How's your meal?" Ben asked, jolting her back to the present.

Truth was, she had scarcely even touched her baked potato. "It's delicious, really 'tis."

"Are you a light eater?" he asked, surveying her plate.

"Ach, no." Then she realized he should know her little secret. "I best be tellin' ya . . . I couldn't just up and leave the house without eating. Mamm, 'specially, would've seen right through it." *She might have, anyway,* thought Annie.

Ben's eyes twinkled. "I wouldn't want to offend you or your parents." He glanced about him before continuing. "But I am hoping to see you another time."

Annie felt her face flush. *Courting?* "I . . . uh, Ben. I don't think . . . I mean . . . this can't go on."

Ben reached across the table and covered her hand with his. "Annie, please listen. I really want to get to know you."

She knew her face was blushing a beet red; she could feel it all the way down her neck, too. "Honestly, I'm not sure how we can get better acquainted." She wasn't going to explain how she'd promised her father she would be obedient for a change. Not since she was committing the sin of disobedience even now, sitting here with Ben in this pretty dining room with white linen-covered tables. Such a lovely, fancy setting for the Englischers present, which she was clearly not.

His eyes reached her heart. "I'm serious. I want to take you out again."

She lowered her gaze to stare at her plate. *It's not fair to ignore him,* she thought but couldn't help it. She slid her hand from beneath the warmth of his own and picked up her fork. She began to eat again, hoping he might do all the talking now. Forget that she had not responded. She was at a terrible loss, unable to comprehend what she felt when she looked into his handsome face with those ardent brown eyes.

"Annie, I don't mean to pressure you."

She nodded her head, because she didn't know what to say.

They passed the next few minutes in silence, except for the soft music she'd never heard the likes of before, which seemed to come from somewhere high in the ceiling.

In time, their conversation began again, returning to more casual matters, and the earlier tension was forgotten. For this Annie was ever so glad.

Chapter 14

Annie and Ben were making their way out of the restaurant, following a two-hour dinner, when Annie spied Louisa and Sam Glick walking toward them. Annie sucked in her breath.

Lou? Taken aback, Annie's stare met Louisa's, and she knew not what to say. Sam turned immediately red-faced, as though caught doing something terribly wrong.

"Well, funny meeting *you* here," Lou said, stopping to stand just feet from Annie as she rubbed her mittened hands together.

"Jah, 'tis." Annie realized her friend had

not wanted her to know her plans. "How'd you two get here?"

"Hired us a driver," Sam spoke up, pulling his black hat off in the night air.

"Hey, if we'd known . . ." Ben's voice trailed away.

"What's that saying about great minds?" Lou said, smiling directly at Annie.

"Well, enjoy your supper" was all Annie could say.

Sam and Lou waved and resumed walking to the entrance, and Ben and Annie proceeded to his car.

What's Lou doing? Then, realizing that she herself was in a similar jam, Annie squelched a laugh.

On the ride back, Ben talked of Lou and Sam, suggesting it might be fun to "double up," as he put it.

Double up? "I don't think we should be seen together—I mean you and me with Sam and Lou."

Ben chuckled. "Then you'll agree to see *me* again?"

"Did I say that?"

"Terrific. When can I come by for you?"

"Oh, Ben." Annie shook her head in frustration but couldn't conceal the small smile that tugged at the corner of her lips.

He's too fond of me. . . .

"We could drive even farther away," Ben persisted. "As far as Ephrata, if you'd feel better about it."

They were nearing her home now and Annie debated. It was a truly bad idea for Ben to creep up the road in his car so close to Daed's farmhouse. Awfully risky, especially with Omar, Luke, and Yonie coming and going. Her father's friends in the ministry also stopped by at odd hours for talks in the barn, where the bishop, preacher, and deacon made many private decisions.

She turned to face him. "Ach, I'd best be gettin' out right here."

He braked ever so slowly, till the tires ground to a halt against the crisp snow. "This far away, Annie? In the dark?"

She pulled on the handle before he could get out and come around to open her door. "I had a wonderful-good time. I truly did."

"Annie, wait . . ."

Quickly she slid from the passenger seat but made the mistake of glancing back, only to catch Ben's look of disappointment.

"When will I see you again?" he asked. "How can I contact you?"

She shook her head sadly. "We can't, Ben. We mustn't. This is good-bye."

Closing the car door firmly, she was determined not to break her father's heart on this matter, despite the strong tug of her own.

Louisa felt as oddly out of place wearing her Amish dress and head covering here in the lovely restaurant as she had at the outlet mall last Monday. Had it not been for Sam, who looked as Plain as she did, she might have considered wearing her pretty red sweater with her black suedelike pants. But she wasn't spending her time tonight with a suave guy like either Michael or Trey, and she really didn't miss wearing her own clothes enough to think twice about it. Only occasionally now did she still have passing twinges, missing some of her favorites back home or her normal hairstyle.

Besides, her fondness for Sam couldn't be linked to her feelings for either her former fiancé or her first boyfriend. For one thing, he had many more good character traits going for him. He also seemed interested in her as a person, and not just in what he could get out of her. *And he's cute, too.*

Despite all that, she was going to be cautious and not get too involved this time. She was too smart for that now; she'd learned some things from her past relationships. So, halfway through their shared dessert of New York cheesecake with chocolate sauce, she panicked inwardly when Sam lassoed her with his eyes and said, "I hope you'll stay on here for the time bein'."

"I have a studio of art students waiting for me." She picked up the wine list absent-mindedly, thinking a small amount might relax her. Then realizing what she was doing, pushed it aside. "They're anxious for me to return."

His face brightened. "You paint pictures?"

"Yes."

He leaned in closer. "Will you describe some of them for me?"

Immediately she was on her guard, so as not to implicate Annie. "Let's see. My most recent work focuses on country landscapes ... things found on Amish farms ... and other rural places."

"Windmills? Hand-held plows?"

"All that and more." She told him about her peacock painting, where every color had been matched to numerous photos she had taken of Annie's birds. "I followed those creatures around everywhere. Can't believe I did that—I actually started talking to them. But, I guess, according to Annie, she does, too, sometimes."

That brought a shared laugh.

"Ah, those peacocks," he said. "No doubt on that . . . a wonderful-good choice for a painting."

They discussed the birds' exquisite coloring and the fanned-out tails, and Louisa realized here was a person who apparently relished some of the same aspects of nature as she. *Is that to be expected from an Amish guy?* She had no other frame of reference, except for her friendship with Annie.

"I like it here in Paradise," she admitted, "but I'm only visiting."

"Well, word has it you're stayin' on awhile yet," he said, face full of hope.

She shook her head. "I haven't decided how long." She wouldn't lead him to think she was setting up a permanent residence at the Zooks', even though his smile faded rapidly with her words.

The light from the moon cast a shadow on the footboard of Annie's bed. Louisa stared at it for a moment, then rose and tiptoed over to Annie and placed the furry ball in her arms. "Here, you hold him awhile."

"Can't you sleep?" asked Annie.

"Can you?"

"Not yet, anyway." Annie let out a tiny laugh.

Louisa returned to her bed, sitting up. "Do you think we'll get slammed by that blizzard everyone's talking about?"

"The cattle seemed awful restless durin' afternoon milking."

Neither of them was willing to bring up the subject weighing on their minds. Instead, Louisa moved away from the topic of cows and snowstorms and mentioned something she had been thinking but had never voiced. "Have I ever told you this? When you wrote your first letter to me—when I wasn't expecting to get a letter from an Amish girl—I was absolutely ecstatic?"

"I'm sure you told me, jah. But it would be fun to sort through the letters sometime."

"Sure would," Louisa agreed. "What I

was getting to is I had felt so lonely, being an only child, up until the point your letter showed up in the mailbox. Of course, the one from your non-Amish neighbor, Jenna Danz, arrived around that same time, too . . . but I think yours actually beat hers."

Annie made soft kitty sounds to Muffin. "I know I was awful happy to hear back from you," Annie replied. "I wasn't sure if I would, ya know."

"I felt so disconnected from my family at that time, even though I knew I was loved. I don't know why I felt so emotionally starved, even as a small girl." She plumped her pillow. "Annie, you were the very friend I needed then . . . and now. The way you expressed yourself in your letters managed to break through my foggy, dysfunctional life."

"You must've been as forlorn as I was, floundering over my inclination toward art."

"Yeah, no kidding."

"Well, like Daed often says: Life isn't supposed to be happy all the time. You know—the rain falls on the just and the unjust."

"Speaking of which, what sort of trouble will Sam Glick be in if word gets out about his dating me?"

"I'd say he's fine for now. Who's gonna spill the beans?"

Louisa was relieved. "The last thing I want is trouble for him. He's just so nice." Louisa almost said "wonderful" but caught herself.

"I daresay you've already begun to fall for him."

Louisa tossed one of her pillows across the room. It landed on Annie's bed, and soon it was thrown back. "Okay, if it's an all-out pillow fight you want . . ."

"No, we best keep quiet. Dawdi and Mammi don't need to be awakened, ya know."

Stifling the temptation, Louisa hugged the pillow. "I need to get something off my chest while I'm thinking of it."

Annie giggled just a little. "Now what?"

"You talk in your sleep, did you know?"

"I don't!"

"Yep . . . and you answer questions when I ask them, too, while you're sleeping."

"Louisa Stratford . . . there oughta be a law against such things. Is there? I mean in the English world?"

Louisa couldn't stop grinning. "No laws

prohibiting the questioning of an unconscious person, nope."

Annie was trying to contain her laughter, trying her best not to awaken her elderly relatives. "Okay, one more thing before we call it a night," Louisa said.

"Jah, and we better, 'cause those cows will need milking at four-thirty, no matter."

"Here it is. You're a coffin sleeper, Annie."

"A what?"

"You look totally dead in bed."

"What on earth does *that* mean?" Annie asked, her voice higher pitched than usual.

"Legs straight out . . . your hands on your stomach." Louisa stopped to catch her breath, because she, too, was holding back a wave of hilarity. And not being too successful at it.

"So . . . you gawk at me when I'm unconscious?"

"No," Louisa said. "It's just if I wake up and look over at you, I see your coffin pose."

Annie shook her head, her hand over her mouth.

"If you think that's funny, listen to this," Louisa said. "One of my mother's cousins had an interesting situation happen when her husband died. I don't remember his name, but let's call him Jack, to keep it simple. Anyway, Jack's kids and stepkids were each jockeying for a portion of his ashes. So they were divided up in equal parts, and the undertaker advised them to 'puff out the remains with fireplace ashes,' so there was enough to go around."

"Well, for pity's sake!"

"Yeah, have you ever heard anything so weird?"

"I don't even know anyone who's been cremated. I think it's just awful, don't you?" Annie fell silent. Louisa wondered if she might be ready to go to sleep, but soon she heard Annie moving about in her bed. "I wonder if the Lord God will be able to find all of Jack's ashes on Resurrection Day," Annie said softly.

Louisa had never thought of that. "Do you honestly believe everything in the Bible?"

"Well, lots of folk must. I think my father does."

"Lots of it is suspect, if you really think about it."

"I'm tired," Annie said suddenly.

She doesn't want to discuss this.

"Send Muffin back to me," said Louisa.

"He's a coffin sleeper, too—look!" Annie said.

Bounding out of bed, Louisa went to see her cat in the glow of the moon. "Oh, you're right. Wow." Muffin was lying on his back, with his forepaws curled in the air and his hind legs stretched straight out.

"Do you think cats understand English?" asked Annie.

"Of course not." Louisa hopped back into bed. "Good night, Annie."

"Sleep well, Lou."

With that, they settled down, but Louisa couldn't stop thinking about Sam Glick, glad for the silly talk with Annie tonight, hoping to have toned down her own unexpected, even frightening, feelings for this really fantastic guy. *Amish, at that. So now do I have to consider joining church with Annie?*

She knew the answer was a resounding negative. She had actually begun to tire of wearing this long-sleeved cotton nightgown to bed. At first it had been a novelty to hang out with Annie in matching ultramodest floor-length nighties during their talks. But it was enough to mirror Annie's attire and hairstyle all day long. While sleeping, she much preferred to wear her satiny nightgown or her own pj's, but that was food for thought for another night . . . if at all.

I wonder what married Amishwomen wear to sleep.

———

Here we go again, thought Ben. *First thing in the morning—last thing at night.*

Annie was even starting to interrupt his nightly dreams. At least he was fairly certain the girl he often dreamed about was Annie, for she was every bit as pretty and as talkative.

The stuff of dreams was evasive, and he couldn't always remember the important details—a frustrating feeling. Yet he was fully persuaded something was lurking there, if not taunting him, on the edges of his consciousness, where he simply could not reach far enough to grasp.

He thought now of the delicate hands of the girl in his dreams, as well as real-life Annie's slight yet beautiful hands. The gentle, relaxed way she folded them in her lap as she rode next to him in the car . . . how her hand brushed her cheek while they were waiting to be served at the restaurant. Distracting things . . .

She doesn't want to see me again. . . .

"Annie, Annie," he said, heading to the kitchen for breakfast. "What have you done to me?"

Chapter 15

The predicted blizzard swept into Paradise with such force even Preacher Zook was taken off guard by it. Prior to this storm, a good number of farmer friends had shared complaints about the inaccuracy of weather reports from Englischers, despite their access to radio and television forecasts based on the latest technology. Jesse much preferred the People's shrewd predictions, which were rooted in their knowledge of the land. A man could tell a lot from his mules, who might lie on exposed terrain in full sun one day and stand the next day with their rumps against the wind, signaling a coming storm.

It had taken Jesse and the boys nearly an hour, well before daybreak, to create a tunnel-like path from the back stoop to the barn door. Now Jesse watched Annie, minus her sidekick, emerge from the kitchen door bundled up like nobody's business. *Barbara's doing,* he thought, knowing his wife's determination to still mother Annie whenever possible. Annie paused as if to investigate the size of the yard drifts, running her gloved hands along the tops of the waist-high piles.

Bands of blustery wind came each time Annie lifted her head while picking her way across the yard. The animals' water tanks needed to be filled no matter the weather, and watching her come plodding out to help with chores amidst the gale of wind and white, Jesse had a sudden warm feeling for her.

My one and only daughter . . .

He had never forgotten the day her newborn cries pierced the stillness of the bedroom, the day this sweet infant joined his household. To think now there would be only one set of braids in his house, one small girl with her faceless dolls lined up beneath the bedroom window. That girl had grown into a young woman who possessed something of an artistic gift, as Barbara had pointed out on more than one occasion. Their Annie—with the determination of a man and the openness of the sky.

Quickly, so as not to be caught staring, he darted back into the milk house.

Why had she made such a fuss over who—sons or daughters—was most favored? Women were fine for marrying and birthing babies, but men were elected by the Lord God to lead the community of mortal saints. For Annie to have questioned him at all on this point irked him some, yet he would not allow her to know it.

Truth was, he had managed to shield her from outpourings of disapproval by the hiding the magazine featuring her art. Just what would she say to that if she knew?

Regrettably, it would not be long before the People would hear of the contest award. He couldn't keep the magazine from finding its way into the hands of a few good farmers who'd insisted on subscribing to an English periodical. And he couldn't fault them. The *Farm and Home Journal* was a fine one, as he knew from reading its pages any chance he could. It was not his place to order those farmers to cease getting the magazine based on a mere art contest. *Exposing my daughter* . . .

There had been plenty of other times when he'd attempted to protect someone from the potential of pain at their own hand, he recalled. Daniel Hochstetler for one. Zeke's father kept coming to mind, even though Jesse wanted to put the unresolved issues to rest. In all truth, he did not believe the burden of blame for the loss of Isaac lay only on disobedient young Zeke, nor did Jesse view Daniel's carelessness at having caused the puppy's demise as the sole reason for the kidnapping. Daniel had been so distracted during his heated debate with Jesse, he'd accidentally rammed a hayfork into the quivering pet's body. Young Isaac had sobbed his way through supper that crucial night.

No, there had never been any doubt that Daniel's defiance of the Holy One had resulted in the disappearance and eventual death of the man's second son. Why the thing ate away at his thinking Jesse didn't rightly know, but it did, and his pondering was an endless stream of irritation. He'd believed he'd known Daniel through and through, only to realize the man he had embraced as a true friend had been a fraud. Why else would a man of devout upbringing turn his back on the divine appointment?

Sighing loudly, Jesse closed the lid on the cooler where milk was continually stirred by power from their bishop-approved air compressor. Now he could hear Annie's voice, hers and Yonie's, across the way, in the milking area. Their terse greeting reminded him that, of all his sons, Yonie had always been most tender to his sister. Until now.

"Aren't you and Mammi goin' to the work frolic this Thursday?" Annie asked her mother some hours later.

"Mammi's under the weather," Mamm replied. "So not this time."

"Well, she didn't look sick to me," Annie replied, wondering if the blizzard had caused some depression. "What's ailin' her?"

"Lower back pains. She could scarcely get out of bed this morning."

"Will she see the doctor?" Annie asked.

"Oh, you know her. She puts it off as long as she can. Needs to have one foot in the grave, nearly, 'fore she'll go."

What's really troubling Mammi? It wasn't like her grandmother to complain one speck. Never, in fact, that Annie recalled.

"Well, tell her I'll take her to the doctor when she's ready . . . once the roads clear some," Annie offered, heading to the Dawdi Haus to read, as she often did on their off Sundays—"no church" days. Sometimes, though, they attended church in neighboring districts, since Daed was a preacher.

"Right nice of you, Annie," Mamm said, eyeing her more closely. "She's growin' older, just as we all are."

Annie couldn't help but think her mother was attempting to send a not-so-subtle message that she wished a replacement beau for Annie might hurry and show up.

———

To Annie, the best sounds of winter were the stomping of boots in crusty snow and the scrunching of skate blades against hard silvery ice. Once the snowstorm blew itself out, Annie had taken Lou off to tromp through drifted pastureland and then skating on neighbor Lapp's pond during the week.

But today Annie was ready to help lay out an intricate "album patch" quilt with the womenfolk at her brother Abner's house. Her sister-in-law Priscilla, who was fond of researching old quilt patterns, had discovered an old Zook family quilt stuck away in an attic. She declared up and down it had been made in the early 1920s, complete with hundreds, if not a thousand pieces.

Louisa had been talking of Annie pouring her artistic inclination into quilt making, so despite oodles of snow, Annie was excited to take the sleigh out for the first time since the blizzard. "I hope the colors haven't been decided on," Annie told Lou as they strung the reins through the horse's bridle.

Lou laughed. "You think you'll have much say in that, Miss Annie?"

"I can hope. After all, this one's for my cousin Fran, who's gettin' close to marrying age."

"Has anyone decided to make a quilt for *you*?" Lou looked at her with a sly grin.

"Oh, you . . . don't you know better than that?" No one knew of her having seen Ben but Lou, who had been sworn to secrecy, especially because Annie had vowed to herself she would never go down that path again. *Going with the likes of Ben Martin. What was I thinking?*

Yet she felt terribly susceptible to him, wishing to know him better, longing for the things she saw in his face. His eyes seemed to open up vast woodlands to her. No, it was the sky . . . or the sea, or something she knew he possessed. Was it merely his Englishness? She didn't believe so, yet, irrational as it was, she longed to be with him.

Years back, she had also felt stirrings of affection for Rudy Esh, but this was not akin to that. Something far different was drawing her.

Annie knew with conviction where her thinking should be in regard to Ben. As wonderful as she believed him to be, she dared not let her heart beat only for him.

She rehearsed their good-byes that lovely night once again, pushing down the keyed-up feelings she had experienced then. *He wanted the promise of another meeting.*

"I hope this get-together with the women puts some zip back into you," Lou said, changing the topic back to where they'd begun.

"Well, look at you talk. I haven't seen you drawing much anymore, Lou. Why's that?"

"I've put my art on hold for you."

Annie couldn't help but frown. "You mean it?"

"Why not, silly?"

"I can't let you do that."

"Hey, my coming has caused you enough nuisance. So postponing my work is all right with me."

"It's awful nice of you, Lou, but—"

"No 'buts.' That passion can wait."

Annie climbed into the sleigh, amazed. "I don't know what to say."

"Say: 'Sure, that's cool, Lou.' "

Annie laughed. "You're such a *Schpundi*— a nut!"

"Look in the mirror . . . er, I mean . . . oh, you know."

Annie picked up the reins, looking fondly at her friend. "All righty. Let's go and use our artists' eyes to lay out a perty quilt for Fran."

Lou tucked the lap robes around her. "Are purples and yellows allowed in the same quilt?"

"Well, if reds and purples are, why not?"

"I haven't seen yellow or white used in any of the quilts here, though."

"Mammi Zook says those aren't such good choices . . . the other deeper colors run into them when washed.

"Makes sense," Lou said.

They were off to Annie's sister-in-law's place on another gray sort of day. Not a soul could possibly see a shadow on the snow that spread itself out in all directions. She wondered if there would be a moon tonight. Even a hazy one, as she often saw during winter nights, would be nice.

Will Ben look up at its muted radiance over knoll and woods? And will he think of me?

When they arrived, Annie noticed a few buggies parked in the side yard. *Highly unusual to cut out and piece a quilt as a group,* she thought, assuming Fran and her mother were simply wanting fellowship at this bleak time of year. *How nice of Priscilla to open her house for this.*

Once inside, Annie took a deep breath and peered down at the choice of colors Fran had already picked for the wedding quilt. Nothing out of the ordinary—plum, reds, blues, and touches of orange. *In keep-ing with her color scheme, no doubt.*

"What 'bout different combinations?" An-nie suggested.

"Fran's favorites are these here," Priscilla replied, her black apron tied loosely to cover her round middle. "Besides, how many colors do ya want?"

A rainbow full, she thought. No need to speak her mind, though. Priscilla and the others had no idea Annie longed for things she ought not to.

A little more than a handful of women worked to piece together the blocks, creat-ing the small nine-patch squares—twenty-five larger squares in all—set against an even larger gray background, and a plum-colored border, hemmed in the same dreary hue as the middle block.

She didn't quite know why it plagued her, this urgency to recreate the pattern. Per-haps if Lou hadn't brought up the possibility earlier. That, and if she weren't so head-strong herself. At any rate, Annie resigned herself to Fran and her mother's plan of ac-tion. Rightly so.

Her mind wandered back to Mamm's in-sistence that she and Lou attend without her. "Mammi and I, we'll fill the gas lamps and lanterns while you're gone," her mother had replied, which seemed odd. Mamm wasn't one to miss out on some good fellowship. Annie suspected Mamm of being overly worried, truth be known. Mamm was a brooder . . . and this was another case in point.

At the moment there was abundant chatter around the worktable. One of Fran's aunts mentioned having heard a cousin of hers clear out in Wisconsin had cut her knuckle badly while drying a glass. "It broke apart right in her hands. Ever have that happen?"

Across the table, Fran's mother nodded and made a little grunt.

"Well, anyways, both a nerve and muscle were cut and six stitches were needed," the woman continued.

Several low *oohs* were heard, and the woman next to the first began talking. "An Englischer friend of mine from Shipshewana, some of yous may remember, well, she and her husband stopped in at Wannacup for some hot cocoa last week sometime, and here came—least she said this was true—a Plain fella with two perty girls, one on each arm. And neither one was his sister."

This brought a round of *ahs* and a few curious smiles.

Annie liked the table talk. It was one of the reasons she enjoyed work frolics, although typically they were canning or quilting bees. So many stories to hear. Sometimes, between the work and the talk, she imagined drawing a collage, a wall hanging of sorts portraying all the images of things women shared round the worktable.

"And listen to this," another woman close to Annie said. "One of Zeke's cousins over in Honey Brook heard from Daniel Hochstetlers, who've been living on a farm up near Wingham, Ontario, of all things."

"Oh?" said Fran. "Wonder what took them so far away?"

The woman could only shake her head. "Don't know, really. Only heard that Mary died in her sleep sometime recently."

"Zeke's mother?" said one.

"Ain't it just awful?" said another.

Annie's heart sank. Zeke's—and Isaac's—long-lost parents . . . chastised yet again by the Almighty? "Wonder if Hochstetlers have gone fancy," Annie said.

"Well, seems so."

A weighty pause followed. Then Annie

filled the silence with her words. "Could it be the nickname caught up with them?"

"Ichabod," someone whispered.

Lou looked at Annie, frowned, and went back to her slow stitching, making Annie feel awful for speaking her mind yet again.

"Daniel oughta be a lesson to us all," said Fran's mother suddenly. "First Isaac's kidnapping . . . now the man's own wife, dead too soon. What a shame."

"A word to the wise is sufficient," said another.

Annie forced her eyes back on her work. So Zeke's family had been located after all this time . . . if the Amish grapevine was accurate. And his poor mother dead.

She felt she must talk to Esther about this. Wouldn't Zeke be comforted to hear something—*anything*—but also terribly grieved at his mother's passing? Annie wondered what Zeke's reaction would be to such news. To put it mildly, Esther's husband was truly a conundrum, not only to her, but to all the People.

Chapter 16

Annie had not come to Julia's attic to discuss bygone days, but the past certainly seemed to weigh on Esther's mind today. During the course of their conversation, Annie was surprised to discover she and Zeke had talked only minimally through the years about Isaac's kidnapping.

"Zeke's kept it to himself," Esther had said out of the blue. "Sometimes I wonder just how much he remembers, really."

"I s'pose things would become hazy over time," Annie replied, watching Esther stroke her baby. Essie Ann squeezed her tiny lips into a pucker, then relaxed them again into a faint smile.

"He's had nightmares . . . well, I don't know so much now, since I'm not home with him." Esther avoided Annie's eyes.

Annie had hoped Esther and Zeke might have heard of Mary Hochstetler's death directly from Zeke's father, but since it seemed Esther was in the dark, Annie forged ahead. "I don't like to be a bearer of bad news, but I heard something awful sad at Priscilla's frolic. Mammi Rosa said word came from one of Zeke's cousins . . .'bout Daniel Hochstetlers."

"Oh? That's odd . . . no one's heard from them for years—not even Zeke's uncle, Preacher Moses. Not since after Zeke and I married, anyway. His folks have never even seen our children." Esther's voice quivered.

"I hate to tell you this, truly I do, Essie."

"Well, what the world." Esther frowned, her eyes searching Annie's. "Did Daniel pass away?"

"Not Zeke's father . . . his mother."

Esther's eyes clouded from blue to somber gray. "Ach, such terrible news." She lifted Essie Ann up close to her heart, hold-

ing the wee babe there, whispering something against the infant's peachy head.

"Awful sorry," Annie murmured.

The small room felt dismally devoid of
light, as though an invisible hand had
blocked off the sun from the dormer win-
dows.

Annie felt she ought not say another
word. She held her breath, sad for the an-
guish on Esther's face.

At last, when Annie felt sure her friend
might not speak again . . . that Annie might
simply have to say her whispered good-
byes and slip out of the makeshift bedroom,
right then, Esther raised her head. "This will
bring such sorrow to Zeke," she said.

"I'm sure" was all Annie could eke out.

"You see, he was always convinced his
mother loved him . . . even though she was
forced to take her husband's side all durin'
Zeke's growing-up years."

"Take sides on what?"

Esther looked away again. When she
spoke, her words were faltering. "Mary
Hochstetler . . . believed she must follow
her husband's approach to Zeke by not in-
terfering. So, in a way, they both belittled

him. Zeke once told me the ridicule was near endless." She sighed. "It's one of the reasons I think I must've married him. I felt sad for the way he was raised . . . with no real sense of parental acceptance. His father clearly hated him."

"Hate's a strong word."

"Even so, Daniel *did* put the blame firmly on Zeke's head."

"For Isaac?"

Esther nodded forlornly. "And hearin' of Mary's death, well, I just don't know what it'll do. . . ."

Annie wished the news might soften Zeke's heart toward his wife, but she wouldn't hold out much hope of that.

"Does your Laura know about her uncle Isaac?" Annie asked.

"She's never to know—Zeke is adamant on that."

"I understand." Annie felt herself frowning hard.

"Well, lookin' at you, I'm not so sure you do."

"No . . . no, I don't mean to complicate things." Annie shook her head, pushing away her own happy memories of the boy.

"What Zeke says goes."

"Jah . . ." Annie wanted to cry. "I want you happy again. Honest."

Neither of them spoke for a time. Then Esther looked right at her, her eyes pained. "Happiness is hard to pin down. My joy comes from the Lord Jesus now. He's my everything. . . ."

Annie nodded sympathetically, feeling awkward at Esther's too-familiar remarks about God. "Would you want me to say something to Daed? Have him break the news of his mother's death to Zeke?"

"Jah, in fact, Julia says your father's takin' Zeke to the mud sale tomorrow. Maybe Preacher Jesse's the best one to tell Zeke. But it's in the dear Lord's hands, that's for sure."

Annie rose and kissed the sleeping baby's forehead, then touched Esther's back lightly. "Take good care, Essie."

"You do the same."

Moving slowly toward the door of her old sanctuary, Annie turned and looked back at her friend with her darling baby. She stood in the doorway a moment longer, her old yearnings building with each breath as she allowed her eyes to take in every inch of her former art studio.

I miss this place!

She let her gaze linger in the far corner, and something welled up in her as she spotted her framed painting all wrapped in brown paper, part of her secret still secure.

" 'Bye, for now," she said, turning to leave.

Louisa made good use of her time while Annie did her regular Friday work routine at Julia's. Making herself scarce in a private corner of the sunroom area, adjoining the kitchen, she plugged in her laptop and began catching up on email. First her art students with more than a few questions, then other friends who continually bugged her about "coming back to civilization," and one lone message from her mother, who urged her to "come home for Easter, won't you, dear?"

Cringing, she felt as if she could actually hear her mother's voice.

I still haven't been gone long enough.

Caught up on her email, she sat and stared out the window at the snow-covered yard and trees, wondering if she dare contact Trey. Her response to his repeated overtures was definitely overdue, so when she checked to see if he was online, she was relieved that he was. "Better this way than by phone," she whispered.

Louisa knew now that continuing their relationship was pointless. Not only had she begun to feel differently about Trey and his interest in her, she was in the process of reformatting her view of the world, her life in particular.

Clicking on his screen name in her IM buddy address book, she got the conversation going.

Hey!
Hey back!
I've been thinking. . . .
Yikes! That's scary, Louisa.
I'm serious. I can't meet you either here or in London.

She waited a full minute before she saw the indication that he was writing a response. She leaned forward to read it:

Come on, girl, you know you want to.
I thought I made that clear on the phone last time.
Well, reconsider.

**Don't be mad. Just please under-
stand.**

She felt stronger than ever. This was the
right thing . . . letting him know once and
for all.
Trey again:

You're kidding, right?
No.
**I want to see you again. I can change
your mind. . . .**
No. Gotta go.
Wait . . . got power where you are?
I'll call your cell.

She had power all right. She'd recharged
again here at Julia's and was using her Palm
to connect her laptop to the Internet. But
she didn't want to hear Trey's voice. Was
this Sam's influence? Had she fallen for him
like Annie said? No, she merely looked up
to Sam . . . and looked down on her past.
There was no questioning her resolve where
Trey was concerned. He was not in the
landscape of her future.
Don't call me. Bye! She typed it quickly
and signed off.

All guys aren't like this. She thought of Sam again, hoping she was right. Yet how could she possibly know? She knew one thing: she was weary of the modern dating scene. The Plain culture had it right. You courted. You married, settled down . . . had a bunch of kids.

Whoa, Mamma, am I losing it or what?

The realization that she had just slammed the door on her first romantic interest over-whelmed her. And, of course, there was no going back to Michael. She was guy-less for the first time in years. *At least, not a man out in the real world. . . .*

Suddenly sad, she heard Julia's voice. "Louisa, are you in there?"

"Uh-huh," she managed to say, through her sudden tears.

Julia appeared, looking prim as always, her long-sleeved white blouse open slightly at the neck, and her navy blue corduroy jumper brushing her legs at midcalf. "Aw, Louisa . . . what's-a-matter?"

She couldn't speak now. That always happened if someone paid too much atten-tion when she was losing it.

"Well, bless your heart." Julia tiptoed over and pulled up a chair.

"It's not my heart . . . just my dumb head." Louisa wiped her eyes, glad for zero mascara. She sputtered, "I admit to being foolish—I've made some stupid mistakes. That ever happen to you?" She doubted she was making sense.

"Oh my, yes." Julia seemed to understand.

Louisa looked at her and saw the depth of compassion in her eyes. She felt as if she'd come to a fork in the road, made the turn, and refused to look back.

Julia's only a year older than me, but much wiser. . . .

"I wish I'd come to Paradise earlier . . . when I was, oh, sixteen. I might've spared myself many things."

Julia nodded. "Plenty of folk have said the same. There *is* a kind of peace here. Some want to soak it up but return home unchanged. Others attempt to box it up, only to lose it along the way. Others embrace it—not only the peace, but the Peacemaker himself."

"Who?" She knew all too well whom Julia was referring to. She had heard similar statements from her deceased aunt Margaret, who talked about Christ as her "dearest friend."

Julia tilted her head, a glow of a smile on her face. "Well, some call Him the Light of the World, others call Him Redeemer and Friend."

"No more *male* friends would be great," Louisa said. She didn't consider Sam just any male, of course. He was the clichéd special person. One of the most important to her at the present time, aside from Annie.

"You've been hurt," Julia said, extending a hand.

"More than once. . . ." She sighed. "I've been wanting to talk to you about God and . . . just stuff."

"Well, I'm here . . . whenever."

The house seemed unusually quiet for as many young children as were present, though Annie and Esther were no doubt keeping them occupied.

"What about right now?" asked Louisa.

Julia folded her hands. "Sure," she said softly.

"So . . . let's see. How do I start?"

The room was still. "Just speak your heart" came the gentle words.

Even though Louisa had been waiting for this moment, she felt nearly tongue-tied, so many thoughts swirled through her head.

"To begin with, what's your take on faith exactly? How does it start . . . and where does it lead?"

Julia straightened in her chair. "I can tell you what I've learned . . . what I know in the deep of my heart. Faith is trusting in a person." Julia stopped a moment. "Take, for instance, when my little girl wants to jump off the back step and into Irvin's arms. She knows instinctively that he will catch her. There is no hesitation in her mind. But she has to make the jump . . . take the first step in making that happen, I suppose you might say."

"So faith depends partly on you . . . not just God?"

"Yes, Louisa. Faith is a divine gift, but it is also based on evidence."

"Found in books like the Bible, right?" Louisa recalled Aunt Margaret's comments on this.

"I'd say the Bible is the best source."

She wished she might have been more exposed to religion while growing up. Margaret's belief system and life was such a shadowy memory. "Do you think there is any correlation between faith and love?"

Julia turned at the sound of her children

coming into the room. "Why, sure," she said, pausing to give her attention to Molly, who was pointing to an "owie" on her thumb. She scooped the two-year-old into her arms and carried her back to where she had been sitting. "Simply put, faith is trust in a person, and love is a plan of action. It may be described as a feeling, a commitment . . . a decision. But in the end, it's a person you belong to . . . a person you are devoted to, through thick and thin."

"So love and faith are similar?"

Julia kissed Molly's hand. "The power behind creation is really very personal. You are aware of this, Louisa, being an artist. God's power and His infinite love go hand in hand. We matter to Him. Our lives have meaning. I've chosen to live in recognition of this amazing power . . . this love."

"You make it seem so clear," Louisa said. Just then Esther's two boys burst into the sunroom accompanied by Annie.

Louisa was careful not to signal to Annie that she'd bared a corner of her soul to Julia. But it was past time to open up about Sam Glick with Annie. They'd lost some closeness lately, and Louisa missed it.

"Time to wash hands for lunch," Julia told

the children. She turned to Louisa momentarily, offering an encouraging smile as if to say, *we'll continue another time.*

Louisa nodded back, to let Julia know she understood. She watched her carry Molly to the kitchen. Julia's confidence was more than appealing.

What would it take to live like that?

———

It was not easy for Annie to approach her father with the news of Mary Hochstetler's death, not since her derogatory remarks about his treatment of Yonie. But Daed surprised her by verifying that Mary Hochstetler had died of a brain aneurysm, slipping into unconsciousness instantly. "We can be glad she suffered very little, if at all."

"How'd you hear?"

"Your grandmother received word from a grandniece in Canada, is what she said."

No wonder Mammi wasn't well enough to attend the quilting. She loved Mary Hochstetler so. . . .

"Mary was on the young side, ain't?"

"Early forties, if I recall. Too young to be dyin', I'd say."

Annie sighed. "I saw Essie—Esther, I mean. She hadn't heard and doubted Zeke had, either."

"Well, I'm sure he knows by now," Daed said.

"One would think so . . . but if he doesn't, will ya break it to him?" She wondered how she would feel if Mamm were to pass on at her present age. She would sorrow for her, no question on that, and she'd feel cheated out of the years ahead. *Just as Zeke will . . . and has.*

Daed's jaw was rigid. "Zeke'll be beside himself. Could push him over the edge."

"I think Esther fears as much."

Daed rubbed his pointer finger under his nose. When he did speak, his words were sharp. "Why on earth can't Esther break this news to Zeke herself?"

Annie wouldn't say. It was perfectly clear why not. Fact was, Esther and the children were out of harm's way at Irvin Ranck's— best not to have Esther interacting with Zeke just yet. The bigger question loomed: Would Mary's death soften or further harden Zeke?

Annie made a stronger determination to protect her dear friend. *If need be . . .*

Chapter 17

All Zeke seemed interested in talking about on the way to the mud sale was his growing-up years in Honey Brook. He pointed out the street where he'd once walked to a corner store to run errands for his mother, even asking their driver to take them past the small brick house where he'd lived with his parents till he was courting age. "Till Esther came into the picture."

Zeke said this so halfheartedly, Jesse turned to look at him. *He's not too fond of his wife.*

"I've often wondered why your parents just up and left," Jesse said much later, as they made their way across the grounds at the firehouse.

"Honestly, I think they were opposed to Esther. And Dat wasn't happy I'd taken up with the Paradise church district." Zeke twitched his nose. "I never knew why, not for certain."

Jesse figured as much, although he'd never breathed it to a soul. He wondered how long before Zeke might say something about his mother's death—if he knew at all, which seemed unlikely. He didn't want to spoil the day by telling Zeke too early. *Then again, if I tell him late, the poor man might not sleep tonight.*

So Jesse was torn, not knowing when or how to address the miserable news he held warily in his grasp.

———

It was after they'd enjoyed some chicken corn soup that Zeke asked Jesse if he thought his father's "rebuff of the lot" had, in some way, caused his brother's death.

He should know it did, Jesse thought.

Zeke didn't wait for an answer. "This is selfish, on my part . . . I know. But why did I have to suffer for Dat's choice on the matter?"

"God made the choice, Zeke. You know as much."

Zeke fell silent.

"Isaac's kidnapping and death were never about you goin' against your father's wishes . . . buryin' Isaac's puppy." There. He'd said what he'd been fixing to for the longest time. "Your father was wrong to put the blame on you. *He* caused a tragedy, when all's said and done."

Zeke made a muffled sound, eyes raised to meet Jesse's own. "I believed my father . . . all my life I did."

"Well, quit."

"Hard to do when I hear his shouts in my ears, Preacher."

Jesse had never seen Zeke so open and responsive. He would wait for a better moment to tell of Mary's death.

"Dat never forgave me, ya know."

Jesse nodded. "Would seem that way."

"He took Mamm and moved far away from me . . . from you . . . all the brethren here. As a punishment of sorts." Zeke pushed off his hat and scratched the back

of his head. "Uncle Moses always thought
Dat and Mamma went to another state.
Moses has strange feelings 'bout things
sometimes. He never got over Isaac's disappearance, either, seems to me."

"Oh jah." Jesse inhaled, feeling the cold
air fill up his lungs. *I can't let him keep ram-
bling on.* . . . "Word has it your father lives in
Canada somewhere."

"Dat does?" Zeke turned quickly to look
at him. "He's not with Mamma?"

"No. What I mean to say is: There was
word about your mother. They were livin' in
Ontario when your mother fell ill."

Zeke's eyes were sudden darts of fire. He
shook his head, turning red in the face.
"She died, didn't she? That's what you're
tryin' to tell me."

Jesse placed a firm hand on his shoulder,
just as he had on other occasions when the
younger man was out of order. But now he
offered his sincerest concern. "I wish it were
better news, Zeke. Truly, I do." He removed
his hand. "Your mother passed away in her
sleep, here recently."

Zeke put his head down, nearly between
his knees as they sat. What little warmth the
winter sun had to offer seemed to disap-

pear, and Jesse was aware of the growing knot in the pit of his own stomach.

Suddenly Zeke rose and faced Jesse, his tall body blocking the sun. "It's not okay what I did that night. Isaac went missin' because of me. You know it, and I know it. Just 'cause you say so, Jesse Zook, doesn't mean anything's different!"

With that Zeke strode stalwartly away.

What have I done? Jesse wondered, hands clenched.

Ben had driven himself to the mud sale in Honey Brook, assuming Zeke was put out with him. Zeke hadn't shown up at the tack shop since asking Ben to contact the police, or Ben might have suggested the two of them go together.

He's still waiting for my answer, most likely.

Ben recalled Zeke's comment about the chicken corn soup and made a beeline to the concession stand. He shivered, even though he'd earlier donned his long johns and the black scarf his mother had knitted for him last Christmas.

He was rounding the bend of one tent when he spied Zeke walking briskly, his arms stiff as a robot as he rushed past him. "Hey, there, Zeke," he called.

Zeke stopped in his tracks, turned, and scowled. "You do what I asked yet?"

Taken aback, Ben shook his head. "Look, I can't just jump like that."

"Why not? You do what your boss tells ya, don't you? You do what your father says to. . . . You need to do what's right 'bout this. Do it for an innocent boy's sake."

Ben wanted to wait and discuss it with Annie, but Zeke was the one in his face at the moment, and in a big way.

Zeke stepped forward; his breath was foul. "Don't dally, Ben."

"Then don't push me," he muttered, saying it more for his own sake than for Zeke's.

"I didn't take you for a bullheaded sort."

Ben stepped forward. "I said I'll think on it and I will."

"Well, fine. But would ya hurry it up?"

Next time I see Annie . . . if I do, I'll get some levelheaded advice, he decided. But he wouldn't tell Zeke yes or no now. He wouldn't let him force him into a decision, dead brother or not.

"I'll be seein' ya," said Zeke with a brusque wave.

Not anytime soon, I hope, thought Ben.

For the first time since meeting Zeke, Ben had glimpsed his controlling nature. And he was worried for Esther and the children.

Annie was glad for Louisa's eagerness to chat. They were heading out with the enclosed family carriage to deliver a turkey-and-noodle casserole to a sick neighbor. Lou had jumped at the chance to go along, which made Annie wonder what was on her mind.

The air was biting and snow was flying again. Coarse, short hair from the horse blew in on their lap robes. "I'm glad you're comin' along." Annie glanced at her friend.

"Well, hey, I thought it might be fun to get some fresh and frigid air." Lou looked at her. "Actually, I wanted a chance to level with you."

Annie's face grew serious. "About Sam?"

"How'd you know?"

"Seeing you out together, well, I assume you must like him."

Lou looked out at the snowy landscape. "I think I might be falling for him."

"Well, he's awful nice." Annie didn't know what to say, really. "And not one to court many girls."

"That's scary."

"Well, why?"

"If he hasn't dated much, then he's more prone to being hurt."

Annie let the reins fall across her lap. "Well, you're not plannin' on hurting him, are you?"

"He'll be way too vulnerable."

"What 'bout you?" Annie wanted to be careful what she said next. "You might be heading in the same direction."

Lou nodded. "I'm afraid of that. I mean . . . when he walks toward me, at barn singings, or outside after the common meal . . ." She stopped.

"What?"

"I don't know how to describe it. It's just the most incredible feeling. You surely know what it's like to be in love."

"In love or real *love*? There's a difference."

"Yeah." Lou pulled on the lap robe, bringing it up higher, covering her gloved hands. "I know all about infatuation."

Annie looked at her. Lou's cheeks and nose were red from the cold. Or was it something more? "Well, which is it with Sam? Do you even know?"

"That's what I'm sorting out. Trying to make sense of things."

"You'll know in time, Lou. You will."

"But time's my enemy, don't you see?"

"How so?"

"The longer I stay . . . and the longer I agree to see him, the more hurt he—*we*—could be. Oh, Annie, it's a total dead end."

Annie leaned her shoulder against Lou's. "What was it you said to me, not so long ago?"

"Just enjoy the friendship?" said Lou. "See where it goes?"

"Jah, that's right." No matter how much she wished it were otherwise, Annie's heart could not be swayed from thinking about Ben. But she hadn't come clean with Lou on that. No, she'd kept it tucked away where only she could ponder it, protect it. Especially because she'd sent Ben on his way for good, and the memory of it tortured her.

"Where does friendship that's bound up with genuine love end and romantic love begin?" Lou asked.

"I'd guess it's a fine thread of a line. But you'll know when you cross it, for sure."

"Meaning what?"

"Well, doesn't deep sharing—talking and whatnot—include physical longing, too? A desire to touch hands, face . . . lip kissing." Suddenly, she felt sorry she'd said anything. Many Amish young people, she knew, saved their kisses for after marriage. There were some groups in Ohio who never even held hands until after the wedding.

"Lip kissing?" Lou laughed softly. "As opposed to what other kind?"

Annie picked up the reins. "Oh, go on. You know."

"Pecks on the cheek?" Lou laughed again.

"Well, Rudy wasn't one to let things get too much out of control. I'm awful glad of that now, 'specially since he and I didn't end up married."

Lou leaned back in the seat. "You're long past Rudy, I think."

"You can say that again, even though we courted ever so long." Truth was, Annie sometimes wondered if Rudy and she would have *ever* married ultimately, even apart from the art issue. "I wasn't meant for him," she admitted.

"Julia says things about love I've never realized," Lou said.

"She's a sensible person, no question on that."

Lou nodded her head, shivering in earnest. "I can see why Esther ran to her for safe haven."

"She's got a way about her . . . draws people," Annie replied. "Makes you feel so comfortable." *The way I felt with Ben. . . .*

Their destination could be seen now, and Annie craned her neck to see the gray curl of smoke from the brick chimney. "Well, here we are. Want to come inside and warm up some?"

"Sure."

"You tether Betsy and I'll get Mamm's basket from the rear of the buggy." She climbed out as Lou hurried to tie up the horse. Annie moved back around the carriage and opened the tied flap to remove the sturdy wicker basket, filled with the hot dish and other goodies.

Did Ben go to the mud sale today? she wondered as she made her way toward the house. *Will I ever see him again?*

Zeke wasted no time in hunting down Preacher Jesse for the second time during the mud sale. Running into Ben Martin had stirred him up even more. He didn't know why he was so upset just now. Perhaps it was the news of his mother's death. Missing Esther made him scattered in his thinking lately, too. *Murky-headed.* He wanted her back, no matter what Irvin's plans for discussion were. He was tired of cooking, of washing his own clothes. Tired of the wrinkles in his for-good shirts and trousers. *Tired of sleeping alone, too. . . .*

There was a problem with that, though. Even if he got his way and Esther and the children returned, he would have to leave her be. The probationary shunning meant life without the things he missed most. But no, once he got Esther home again, he'd get her to see the light . . . the recklessness of her ways. You couldn't claim to have salvation and still be saved in the long run. He would make her see what nonsense all that talk was if he had to shake it clean out of her.

He found Jesse standing in a long line, waiting for a cup of coffee or cocoa. Knowing the preacher as Zeke did, it would be coffee. Zeke inched forward when Jesse had his back turned, then stood right by him, to the dismay of several customers behind them. "You won't mind if I butt in right here, will ya, Preacher?"

Jesse grimaced. "S'pose not."

" 'Tis a cold one," Zeke ventured.

"Jah," Jesse agreed.

"Good for the soup and coffee business."

Zeke decided he'd best be keeping his tongue still till there was opportunity to talk in private. Jesse was the type to speak little, but folks paid attention when he did.

Like Mamma . . .

The thought of his mother lying in a wintry grave put a tense feeling in his chest, and a barricade in his brain. He had purposely refused to acknowledge Jesse's news. Fact was, Mamm was the one good thing in his life, like salve on a wound. But the ability to soothe was not always granted her, thanks to his father. *A tyrant of a man,* Zeke thought. *Like I've become. . . .*

When they had their cups of black coffee in hand and had wandered over to an out-of-the-way place, Zeke said simply, "Esther's been gone long enough. I want her home."

Jesse nodded, as if recalling his comment about speaking to Irvin about this. "I'll go 'n' see what can be done," he offered.

"Time Esther gets away from them Rancks."

"I'm with you on that."

"Well, then, I'll expect my woman back tomorrow."

Jesse shook his head. "Did I say that, Zeke?"

"No, now you listen to me. I'll have Esther home if I have to carry her out of Irvin's house. You hear?"

The preacher lowered his eyes. "If you lay a hand on her, she'll leave you all over again."

"I'll bite my tongue more . . . if need be. But I'm not lettin' her have her say!" And he wouldn't. She had a good many lessons to learn yet, and he was just the one to teach them to her.

"Esther's young yet. She'll come under, in time," Jesse said.

Zeke could only hope. A difficult wife was a detriment to her husband. He'd seen this firsthand as a child, because occasionally his mother had the gall to voice her opinion and was squelched for it. Even punished. Like the time the house was so cold she threw extra logs on the fire to warm the kitchen, and from then on the wood was severely rationed.

Often he wished she might have spoken

up even more, attempting to spare him numerous thrashings. *Just as Esther does with our children.*

He was startled by this sudden realization. Yet he felt blinded, unable to escape the towering walls of his anger and condemnation, unable to fathom the freedom he longed for.

I'll be fine when Esther's home.

More and more he did not trust himself alone in the house. Visions of the past came to him continually, small pieces of a haunting riddle. A clearer recollection forming with each new day: a deep hole, the shovel, Isaac leaning into the puppy's grave, grieving mighty hard. . . .

There had been a deep black sky the night Zeke defied his father. The night when all of the years to come were forever altered. Only a distant yard light had broken the darkness, he recalled. Not a single streetlight shone the way to either the banks of Pequea Creek nor to farmer Fisher's field. Zeke had used his flashlight, a gift from Uncle Moses on Zeke's eighth birthday, to help him see to dig the hole. Or was it *two* holes? Jah, it was all becoming chillingly plain now.

Ichabod, he thought and shuddered.

Chapter 18

Annie tromped quickly all the way out to the barn, scarcely able to wait till she could return to the cozy kitchen and help Mamm with Sunday breakfast.

Too cold for people, she thought.

But it was Ben who was the person most on her mind today. More time than she cared to ponder had passed since her impulsive, though needful, good-bye. She couldn't believe she'd left him sitting there, abruptly getting out of the car as she had. But what other choice had she?

Aside from her friendship with Louisa, she felt as if she were going through the motions of her life—no art and no Ben—whereas before she could skip through even the coldest day.

Nothing's right with me now.

While helping to put the milking machines on the cows, she overheard Daed talking to Yonie. "I picked up the wrong bridle rosettes by accident over at the tack shop."

Her pulse sped up. Lest she react too enthusiastically, she held back, ever so glad for Yonie's apparent reluctance to make the exchange for their father.

She muffled her smile with her hand. Then, creeping out from between two cows, she stepped forward. "I have to go that way tomorrow, Daed," she said. "I could return the rosettes if you want."

Her father brightened, shooing Yonie off. "That'd be right fine."

One for me, she thought, not sure she ought to be keeping score, so to speak.

———

Right after the common meal, following Sunday Preaching, Jesse motioned to Barbara, and she hurried to get into the carriage for the ride over to Cousin Irvin's place. The day had brought more snow, but it was tapering off now, and he could see the sky was clearing in the north. "We're due for some sunshine," he said to his wife, who sat to his left in the front seat.

"I should say." She leaned against him briefly.

"Is there enough room in here to transport Esther and the children to Zeke's?"

Barbara nodded. "We'll make do."

She wouldn't question him on this, he knew. Barbara was nothing at all like Esther Hochstetler, who had a mind of her own. *Just as Annie does,* he thought.

Jesse was unwavering in his plan. He would not rehearse it again in his mind, as he had lost a good amount of sleep last night, deliberating over today's visit to the Rancks on behalf of Zeke.

When they pulled into the drive, Barbara asked, "How is it Esther fled here?"

"I daresay Julia's responsible for Esther's temporary shunning . . . if you get my meaning. Too much worldly influence. Besides, Esther might've thought she had nowhere else to go."

"But it's not true." Barbara pushed a stray

hair back from her forehead. "I s'pose it's time she got back under the covering of our brethren, jah?"

"Which is precisely why we're here," Jesse said as he tied up the horse.

They made their way toward the side of the house, Jesse steadying Barbara as they stepped carefully on the encrusted snow, icy in places.

"Come in, come in," said Irvin when he saw them at the door.

Soon, Julia was present, and she and Barbara went off together, arm in arm, into the front room.

Irvin and Jesse made the turn from the kitchen into the sunroom. "What brings you here?" asked Irvin. He was never one to mince words, Jesse recalled. If Irvin suspected an agenda, he wasted no time discussing the weather or anything else.

Jesse took the seat his cousin motioned to. "It's time Esther goes home."

Irvin reached up and scratched his blond head. "I wouldn't advise it, and I'll tell you why."

Jesse had no interest in listening to his Mennonite relative expound on matters that pertained to the Amish fold. Still, he sat patiently.

"Zeke's in no way ready to resume his role as the head of his house" came Irvin's definitive words.

"Well, ready or not, I'm taking Esther and the children back today." Jesse rose. "It's out of your hands." He might've added: *You had your opportunity and failed,* but he thought better of it.

Irvin got up quickly. "I say she stays here."

"Say all ya want, Cousin. Truth is, Esther's been gone long enough."

Irvin shook his head. "It's a shame for a man to treat his wife as Zeke has . . . and will again, no doubt."

Jesse wasn't interested in Irvin's opinion. "Esther's goin' home. That's all there is to it."

"Well, why not leave it up to her? See how she feels about returning?"

Jesse was irritated at the suggestion. "She's exerted her will enough already. Esther has no say now. Go and have Julia get her ready."

Irvin pushed his hands into his pockets.

"The children are all napping, so there must not be any loud talk."

"So be it," said Jesse, glad for no significant ruffle of wills thus far. Despite Irvin's strong character and opinions, he was not a fighter. Not like Jesse, who still recalled the fuss between himself and Annie . . . over Yonie, of all things.

He assumed with his son well into courting age, Yonie would be settling down with a girl soon enough. He wouldn't want to embarrass himself much longer at singings and whatnot. He'd be letting his hair grow out again like his counterparts—the ones headed for the kneeling vow, that is.

Irvin left the room, heading back to the kitchen to talk quietly with Julia.

Irvin's young enough to be my son, thought Jesse, hoping the rest of the afternoon would go off without a hitch. He heard multiple footsteps now, Barbara and Julia both going upstairs to get Esther.

Wandering into the kitchen, he was conscious of the peace of this house. He pulled down a small paper cup from a wall dispenser and drew water from the faucet, contemplating his earlier words. *It's past time for Esther and Zeke to reunite,* he reassured himself.

He went to the front room, and in a few minutes, here came Esther accompanied by Barbara and Julia. "Hullo, Preacher Zook," said Esther, looking as though she'd just awakened. She held in her arms her infant, wrapped in a pink knitted blanket.

"Barbara and I will help get you and the children home," he said.

Esther glanced at Barbara and Julia, a worried look in her eyes. "Laura, Zach, and little John are sound asleep," she replied.

It was Irvin who stepped in. "Why not wait awhile, Jesse?" Then, turning to Julia, he suggested, "How about some coffee, hon?"

Julia nodded and quickly headed to the kitchen, followed by Barbara. Jesse wondered if Esther might go along with the women, too, and for a flicker of a second he saw by the angle of her head and the look in her eyes that she truly preferred to.

Sitting in the rocking chair instead, Esther held her baby close. "I'm not sure Zeke's ready for us, Preacher," she said, looking right at him.

"Oh jah, he is." He wouldn't reveal that Zeke had come and demanded her return yesterday.

"Well, what 'bout you, Irvin?" She turned her head and looked pleadingly. "What do you say?"

Irvin glanced at Jesse and back at Esther. "From my discussions with Zeke, I'd say hold off. He's not made much progress . . . and now, from what you've told us about his mother's death, I just think it's too soon. He's irate and distressed. Unreasonable, too, in some of his remarks."

Esther's eyes registered panic. "I have young children, Preacher. A nursing babe . . . two small boys. And . . . Laura is tenderhearted. It troubles her greatly when there is a noisy dispute in the house, or . . . worse."

There should be no disputing at all, he thought. Truth be told, Esther seemed to have had too much say already. And looking at Irvin, Jesse wasn't sure how to proceed without causing a squabble here and now.

"Can't I stay put?" Esther pleaded. "We— all of us—are safe . . . looked after here."

Jesse's heart momentarily went out to her. Was he doing the right thing, passing her off from the Rancks to Zeke's volatility? He looked at the sleeping babe; one small fist had managed to escape the blanket. *Lord God in heaven, am I doing right by this family?*

He felt strongly that Esther needed to be the submissive wife she was meant to be. But he also had a nagging feeling in his gut about sending her back prematurely. It was true; Zeke had seemed truly unstable at the news of his mother's passing, angry at his father and at the world in general.

"Just a few days more?" Esther entreated.

He spied the Holy Bible lying on the lamp table nearby and assumed Julia and Irvin had been filling Esther's head with alien beliefs. Something clicked in him just then. "No, I daresay your time here has come and gone. Have Julia help you gather your things . . . and the children."

He did not want to be on hand to witness the removal of Zeke's little ones from this house, their faces pink and their eyes glazed from a Sunday afternoon's rest disturbed.

Excusing himself, he went outside to wait in the cold, breathing deeply, thinking about the cows waiting to be milked . . . and contemplating Zeke, too. But it was a waste of time to think too hard about Zeke Hochstetler. This would not be much of a reunion for the couple, not with Esther still under the probationary shun.

It remains to be seen how this will go, he thought woefully.

He must not back down. Taking Esther home to the People was the right thing to do. If nothing else, it was high time for her to come back to the fold.

Fearful, Esther headed back to the attic room. *This is a horrid thing.*

Even so, she began to awaken Laura, then Zach. Little John was always the hardest to rouse from slumber.

Turning, she saw Julia standing near. Barbara Zook had stayed downstairs, for which Esther was relieved. This way, she and Julia could have their parting words in private.

Julia offered to hold Essie Ann, and Esther continued patting her children to wakefulness.

"You must remember what I'm going to say, Esther," Julia said ever so softly, bending to kiss Essie Ann's tiny forehead.

"I must not hesitate to leave Zeke again . . . if need be. Ain't so?" Esther said.

"Why, yes. No question on that. There is a shelter for women—and children—at the Water Street Mission, but it's all the way in town . . . Lancaster." Julia paused a moment, standing and swaying with the infant as she looked first at Essie Ann, then back to Esther. "That is, if you should feel uncomfortable, for whatever reason, returning here to Irvin and me."

Esther could read between the lines, and she was touched deeply by Julia's thoughtfulness and compassion. "Jah . . . you're most kind."

"And . . . we mustn't forget about the newly opened Green Pastures facility, run by Amish. I'm sure you've heard of it. I doubt, though, they have room for more than a few beds, but I can find out for you . . . just in case."

Esther recalled that following communion last fall, there had been a call for Amish house parents, after the main facility in Mt. Gretna first opened. Members of the Lancaster County Amish community had built the place, and it reflected their simple ways and cultural differences—no TVs or other modern amenities.

A helpful place for someone troubled like

Zeke? Or is Julia afraid I might be the one to crack up? Esther wondered, feeling the tension in her jaw. *Why don't I just stand up to Preacher Jesse . . . tell him I'm staying on here?*

She wanted to speak up more than anything, but sometimes she felt as if she were losing her ability to think clearly . . . to sort things out. In the past she *had* worried she might not be able to manage her domestic responsibilities alone. Yet while living with the Rancks she had sensed none of that hesitancy, not since opening her heart to the Lord.

So here I am heading back to a hornets' nest. Is this the Lord's will for me? She cringed at the thought of Zeke tormenting her with the stipulations of her shunning . . . how it would keep her from the family table and the marital bed unless she renounced her salvation.

Never, she thought.

"The Lord Jesus go with you, Esther." Julia watched as Esther lifted John out of the bed and stood him on his feet, the two-year-old whimpering softly, rubbing his sleepy eyes.

"And with you, Julia."

"You know you're always welcome at our church . . . let us know if you would like a ride there, or whatever you need."

"I doubt I'd ever be allowed to go, considering the children."

"Well, if so, Irvin and I are here for you. Please keep in touch."

"Jah, I will." Tears blinded her vision. Then, suddenly, she was leaning on Julia's shoulder.

"Prayer is powerful . . . always remember," Julia whispered. " 'For the eyes of the Lord are over the righteous, and His ears are open unto their prayers.' " Julia kissed her cheek, and then those of the children.

"I best be hurryin'," Esther said, reaching down to lift John before asking Laura to take Zach's hand down the steps.

"Jesse and Barbara will look after you." Julia stopped short of saying more.

For the time being, Esther felt protected. After her arrival home, she could only imagine what she would face.

Chapter 19

She had not been a spiteful child. Esther knew she had been a joy to her parents' hearts. But now . . . *now* she felt just horrid, wishing Irvin and Julia had spared her from returning to Zeke.

Slowly she made her way inside the house, carrying the baby and holding little John's hand. Laura and Zach followed behind, dawdling, and she knew why. Preacher Jesse and Barbara helped carry the few things they'd taken with them to the Rancks' place and set the overnight bag on the kitchen floor. There was also a suitcase, borrowed from Julia, with the items of clothing Esther had sewn for her children and herself while there. A pillowcase full of toys and books Julia had purchased had been left behind in the Rancks' attic, as well as several crocheted items.

"Hullo, Preacher," she heard Zeke call out to Jesse when he saw him. The two men shook hands good-naturedly, though Zeke's eyes were on her as she sat near the table with Essie Ann in her arms.

The kitchen looked remarkably clean for her having been gone so long. She wondered if perhaps Zeke had asked her mother to come over and scrub things up some.

Barbara pulled out a chair nearby, calling to Zach to come sit on her knee. But Zach and John hurried away, with Laura following them into the next room, and Esther heard the lid on the toy box creak open.

"They seem content to be home," Barbara offered.

For a time maybe, thought Esther. *Till their father shouts at their mother or pulls their hair and drags them across the room.* But she dismissed thoughts of their wretched past, trusting for a new beginning. Now that she was a child of the living God, her hope for a more suitable life with Zeke was becoming stronger. Still, she felt weary just entering this house, sitting here, looking around at all she'd left behind to escape Zeke's wrath, if only for a season.

When Preacher and Barbara said their good-byes, Esther tried to be as pleasant as always, but she could feel the tension in her face and neck. Her entire body strained under the awareness of her old surroundings, despite Zeke's grinning his welcome.

"You're home," he said, looking her over but good.

"Jah . . . home" was all she could say.

———

On Monday, Annie was careful not to jingle-jangle the bell on the door of the tack shop more than necessary, thinking it best not to draw attention to herself, since several men were standing around. But after a quick scan of the shop, she saw that Ben was nowhere in sight.

Quickly she headed for the window, facing out toward snow-covered fields, keenly aware of the smell of leather mixed with oil and a hint of tobacco rising off the farmers' woolen work coats.

Oh, I must at least catch a glimpse of him.

She straightened, wondering now if her trip here was to be a waste of time. But, no, she wouldn't think selfishly—she still had an exchange to make for her father.

Slowly she wandered through the shop, stopping to look at the assortment of bins filled with bridle accessories. A variety of horse collar paddings in different colors— she couldn't help noticing the brightness of reds and blues.

Is Ben at work today?

She pushed a smile onto her face, staying aloof from the other customers, a large group of them now heading for the door. Was it safe to search the shop for him?

She felt suddenly shy. But Ben Martin was her friend, or had been.

Just when she was about to approach the counter and return the bridle rosettes to someone other than Ben, she heard his voice.

"Annie . . . it's great to see you!"

She turned and there he was, smiling. "I've come to return this." She pushed the paper bag toward him. "Daed picked up someone else's bridle rosettes—he wants the ones with the little peacocks." She couldn't help but smile. "I wonder why."

His eyes shone as he took the bag from her. "I'm glad you're here," he said with a lowered voice. "I've wanted to talk with you about something . . . important. I have a few questions about your Plain customs."

She breathed in the dense aroma of the harness shop. "Ask me now."

"Well, it's rather complicated. It could take more than a few minutes."

His eyes were earnest. He must have legitimate questions.

She frowned, because at second glance he seemed almost tormented.

He leaned near. "It's regarding Zeke Hochstetler."

She had told herself she would never see him again, but Ben's request seemed urgent, and she worried there was possibly more trouble for Esther.

All right, she told herself. *This doesn't count.*

"I'll talk with ya, Ben. When?"

"Tonight?"

She nodded. "After supper?"

"What time would that be . . . for you, I mean?"

She stopped to think when she'd be finished eating and with kitchen chores. "About six-thirty or so."

"Sounds fine." He couldn't seem to keep his eyes off her. "Where should we meet?"

"Same place . . . just farther up. Near the big white pine tree on the north side of the road."

He nodded as if he knew which one.

"It's the largest tree round these parts. Some say it's nearly four hundred years old."

"You seem to know trees, Annie."

She shrugged. "A little, maybe. But you should talk to Zeke 'bout foliage and whatnot." She waved to him then and headed toward the door, feeling suddenly tongue-tied.

"Annie . . . didn't you forget something?" He held up the small sack with the wrong bridle rosettes inside.

She felt ever so foolish. *He must surely know how he affects me.*

"Oh, puh! I forgot what I came for."

She walked back to the counter, unable to prevent her smile. *I'll see him tonight!* her heart sang.

Lou and I are two peas in a pod . . . both attracted to fellas we can't have. Her throat suddenly felt terribly dry. *Am I a* Dummkopp *to meet Ben?*

He was pleased Annie had agreed to see him, and marveled at the landmark tree she had chosen for their meeting spot. The towering white pine must have been seventy feet high, its blue-tinted evergreen boughs spreading a good thirty feet. He parked his car beneath it, opening the door and getting out to wait for Annie.

He would have preferred it if she didn't have to walk all this way to the car, and on such a cold day, even though the afternoon had been fairly sunny.

She was right on time, and he could not suppress his excitement at first sight of her as she rounded the bend, wearing snow boots, a long black coat, gray gloves, and a blue-and-gray plaid scarf wrapped around her slender neck. *All we need now is a toboggan,* he thought, wishing they might have some fun together instead of the heavy discussion ahead.

He waved, moving toward her, wanting to help her along, even though the road was now nearly clear of snow.

She greeted him with a smile but did not

speak, and for a good portion of the drive she remained silent. He rambled, taking the opportunity to tell about his first-ever mud sale . . . the several household tools and a small phone table he had bid on and won.

Then, when he could think of nothing else to say, he brought up what Zeke had told him about his brother's strange disappearance and death. "The boy's body was dumped in an Amish field nearby," he said slowly. "Zeke told me this."

"Wha-a-t?" she gasped, covering her mouth. "Oh, surely not. When did this happen?"

He looked at her, realizing their conversation would be less askward if he pulled over somewhere—at a fast food place, perhaps . . . anywhere.

As he drove, eyeing the various options for parking the car, he summarized what Zeke had told him about the shocking discovery of a child's body and the hushed-up burial. It seemed to drive Zeke mad.

"I can't believe it. Zeke's brother is actually dead?" Annie whispered, pressing her hand against her chest. "I always worried it was so, but now . . ."

It was all he could do not to reach over

and pull her into his arms. She was shaking now, trembling from head to toe.

"This is the most terrible thing," she said. "Knowing Zeke and Esther as I do, it's doubly difficult."

She began to cry, unable to speak.

He turned into the nearest parking spot, leaving the engine running to provide heat. Then, reaching for her hand, he held it firmly in his own, glad she did not pull away. "This information is not to be disclosed, Annie. For some reason it is to be kept secret, known only by your church brethren."

"My father knows of this?" A look of horror crossed her face. "Oh, Ben!" She struggled further, letting go his hand to look for a handkerchief in her coat pocket.

Wiping her eyes, she sighed. "Why wasn't this announced from the housetops? The People would want to know. They would!"

He explained that the only reason he had told her was to solicit her advice. "Since I don't know the inner workings of your community. . . . I don't want to sound selfish, but I don't know what to do about a request Zeke made of me."

"Well, what's that?"

He wanted to hold her hand again but would not use her emotional state as an excuse. "Zeke wants me to go to the police. He's anxious for the murderer to be found . . . and every day that passes makes it harder."

"But if the death happened all those years ago, what's it matter?"

"That may be precisely the thinking behind keeping the death quiet, I don't know." He told her he was in favor of making the call to the police. "But there is the problem of Zeke's being shunned, too, if this gets out . . . and how difficult would the news be for your church folk if it should be known that Zeke was behind my reporting to the local authorities?"

Suddenly he thought of detectives combing the quiet farmland for clues, disturbing the peace. "What should I do, Annie?"

"I'm glad you came to me with this." She turned completely in the passenger's seat, studying his face, her eyes lingering. She had warmed to him; he was sure of it. "You must follow my father's wishes, Ben. Tell Zeke no."

"Can you explain?"

"The will of the Lord God and heavenly

Father of us all, is the only explanation I can offer," she began, going on to say it was imperative for the People to revere and obey the church leaders.

"Even when it goes against the legal system?"

"The People aren't obligated to answer to the world. When the brethren deem things ought to be a particular way, then it's best to follow." She shook her head slowly, and there was a catch in her throat. "And Zeke knows better than to pull you in on this."

"Does his temper often get the better of him?"

"Sadly so. I've heard bits and pieces from Esther." Annie looked down at her folded hands.

"Is he abusive? Cruel?"

Annie nodded slowly.

"I assumed it," he said.

"Best be keepin' that quiet, too."

He looked at her fondly. Sad or not, she was absolutely beautiful. He held his breath to keep himself in check.

"I won't contact the police," he heard himself say.

"Denki, Ben. Thank you ever so much."

She touched his arm, the slight pressure sending a charge of electricity through it.

"No, it is I who must thank you, Annie." He didn't attempt to explain, but he felt she understood.

He must put his hands on the steering wheel and drive her home now that he had the direction he needed. It was unfathomable why he should be sympathetic to the wishes of these so-called brethren of Annie's. Yet he wanted to do what was best, in the long run, for his troubled friend Zeke.

During the drive back, Annie talked nearly nonstop. By the time he turned onto Frogtown Road, he practically thrilled to hear her words: "This must be our secret, Ben. Ours alone."

He readily gave his promise. He cared about Annie's People, with their confusing yet simple ways. More than anything, he wanted to soak up every aspect of the Plain life, to share in its meanings—riddles or not—and he wanted to spend as much time doing so with Annie as she would allow.

So when it was *she* who asked if they could get together and talk again, he was astounded.

"Of course," he said.

"Wonderful-good." She smiled.

And, as before, when he braked the car, she nearly leaped out, this time coming around to his side even before he could get out. "Could we . . . uh, go skatin' somewhere?" she asked when his window was down.

"Roller or ice?" He laughed.

"On the ice might be best," she said, hands on the base of the window, eyes shining. "I know a place."

"This Wednesday I can get off work a bit early."

"Just whenever you say."

He opened his car door and got out. "I'll look forward to it."

"Well, I best be headin' home now, jah?" she said, lowering her head. "I really should. . . ."

He reached out to clasp her arms, resisting the temptation to draw her near. "Teach me all you know about your life here, Annie. Everything."

She raised her eyes to his. "Well, sure. I believe I can do that."

With that, she turned to go.

He leaned against the car door, his chest pounding as he watched her walk down the left side of the road toward the two golden lights flickering in Preacher Zook's farmhouse.

Chapter 20

Annie did not ask Lou if she wanted to take a so-called journey down memory lane. She simply started pulling out boxes of Lou's letters from beneath the bed, organized by year and month.

The afternoon weather had turned dismal following the noon meal, looking nearly as miserable as Annie felt inside about Isaac's death. But she must not let on what she knew to Mamm or others. And she could not mope around. It was enough that her father was aware and had not revealed it to the People.

Whatsoever things are pure . . . lovely . . .

of a good report . . . think on these things. She remembered hearing her older brother Christian's wife, Martha, recite the Scripture. Why Martha had it memorized, Annie didn't know. But there was something about the verse that kept her from forgetting it, too.

Today being Wednesday, she was glad to have her chores caught up, content, as well, to pass the time by reading aloud the letters in the upstairs bedroom. Lou, in turn, laughed or shook her head in astonishment, or asked to see proof of a comment or phrase in her own childish handwriting.

"Here's one that might make us cry," Annie said, lowering her voice, lest she be heard by resting Mammi Zook. It was one of the letters where Lou had shared the pain of being an only child.

"Sometimes I think of you as more than my pen pal, Annie. I try to imagine that you are here . . . or that I am there with you. Do you think I'm crazy for such imaginings?

"Oh, and if you're nodding yes when you read this, then I must also

say that having a sister is the best feeling of all.

"Have you always felt as lonely as I do? I'm only asking because you sometimes write how nice it would be to have at least one sister instead of six brothers.

"Well, I don't blame you one bit if you long for a sister. And someday wouldn't it be fun if we could meet? Maybe you could visit me in Colorado. But, just between us, the most exciting thing would be for me to see you there in Amish country. I'm not kidding!"

Annie looked up from the page, reciting the letter's date. "You were only eleven and a half and already curious about Plain life."

"Hey, I remember writing that." Lou rose to look at the stationery, decorated with Beanie Baby stickers. "Good grief, does anybody write snail mail anymore?"

"Well, I do. And Mamm writes to relatives in other states, too—they pass circle letters around, which is fun. Ever hear of one of those?"

"No, but I like the sound of it. Hey, kind of like what some people do by forwarding emails. I'll have to show you sometime when we're at Julia's."

Annie nodded, but immediately her thoughts were with Esther. "Mamm whispered to me yesterday that evidently Zeke got his wish."

"Esther's home?"

Annie said it was so. "Maybe things will be better now for her and the children."

"I hope you're right," Lou said, "but typically abusive spouses continue to mistreat those they love. Patterns don't stop because of a short separation."

"Well, Daed's goin' to be overseeing Zeke now, as I understand it."

"Not Irvin?"

"Far as I know, Irvin and Julia aren't to be contacted by either Zeke or Esther . . . but, knowin' Esther, she won't be able to cut off that close friendship. They've become 'sisters in the Lord,' as she likes to refer to their newfound kinship." Annie felt a twinge of envy.

Lou walked to the window and looked out. "Julia's an amazingly special person . . . I can see why Esther would want a close connection with her, in or out of the Lord . . . whatever sort of sister she wants."

Annie changed the subject. "So . . . are we done looking through these letters?"

Returning to sit on her bed, Lou said she was. "Let's save some for another gray day."

"Wonderful-good." Annie was careful to tuck the letters back into correct order again. Then she slid the boxes out of sight. "Ever think we were s'posed to be friends?"

"Like, uh, pure out-of-the-sky luck?"

"More like providence, like the way my father looks on most everything."

Lou frowned, looking puzzled. "Which is what?"

"Some call it God's sovereignty . . . or destiny." Annie pondered that for a moment. "Ever think that 'bout Sam, too?" she asked, daring to step on Lou's toes.

"Well, I wouldn't go that far." Lou's wide smile gave her away.

"Just think of it. What if you were s'-posed to write me all that time . . . then come here and meet Sam? Like it was planned somehow."

"You really mean it, Annie?"

"Oh, I don't know. I just wondered if maybe

you're supposed to be Amish, that's all." She threw a pillow at Lou. "Ever think that?"

"Too funny." Lou held on to the pillow, not tossing it back. She clutched it to her chest, as if it were a shield. "Goodness, why would you say such a silly thing?"

"Just 'cause."

"Spit it out, Annie."

"Well . . . I guess I've gotten so used to your hair lookin' like Mamm's and mine, and the cape dresses and aprons and whatnot." She sighed, not wanting to make too much out of what she felt.

"I sometimes wonder what it would be like to revisit my modern life," Lou said unexpectedly. "My mother would love to see me . . . wants me to come home for Easter. I guess it's safe to tell you that I miss my parents."

Annie felt suddenly hollow. "You'd leave here . . . for good?"

"Not sure."

"Well, I'm sorry I brought this up." The last thing Annie wanted was to think about saying good-bye to Lou.

———

Barely two full days had passed since Esther's return home and already she was beginning to notice the cracks in Zeke's resolve. At first, he'd gone overboard being kind, even surprisingly helpful with Zach and John, which was heartening to her. But that lasted only from late Sunday afternoon through most of yesterday.

Already today there had been several pointed, even cutting remarks, mostly in regard to her required repentance. "You have no choice but to make a confession and soon," he told her when he'd marched indoors to warm up.

She handed him a mug of black coffee. "How on earth can I?"

"Stubbornness does not become you, woman."

She would not respond and risk starting something that would only escalate, especially not with Essie Ann so small and sleeping in the wooden cradle not too far from the wood stove.

"The brethren expect you to give up this nonsense about salvation within the next few weeks," Zeke said suddenly.

She remained silent, standing next to the sink, her weight pushing against it.

"I'll not have you under the Bann forever, Esther. Ya hear?"

She nodded, not in agreement but in an attempt to go along.

"It's high time you submitted." He was standing next to her now, close enough that she could smell the barn on his clothes and feel his strapping shoulder brushing against her. He squeezed her arm till she could hardly feel her fingers. "Ain't right to keep your husband waiting . . . usin' the shun against me."

She guessed he'd think as much. *But, ach, to say it!* Zeke probably didn't care one iota about shunning stipulations. Most likely he would force her to break the rules in due time . . . once Essie Ann was six weeks old.

Ten days away . . .

Their lovemaking—if it could be called that—would then become his secret, for he would not go to the brethren with such a confession. And woe unto her if *she* did.

When Essie Ann began to whimper, Esther was relieved. Zeke let go of her, and she turned quickly away, going to her newborn and plucking her tenderly out of the cradle. Without looking back, she carried her baby upstairs to nurse in the stillness of the bedroom.

Ben got his chance to ask Annie about the local trees during their long drive to the secluded pond. She was a storehouse of information, describing not only numerous leaf shapes but differing bark textures and other identifying details of the trees he pointed out on the way.

When Ben expressed how impressed he was at her knowledge, Annie had smiled self-consciously, as if he truly was making too much of it.

But it was not Annie's familiarity with local flora he wanted to focus on this night. He had made a quick trip to the Goodwill store and purchased a pair of nearly new ice skates, and was amused at Annie's ability to smuggle a pair of her own out to the car in a wicker basket, as if she were feigning a visit to a neighbor.

The hours crept up on them as they skated on the millpond, the surroundings awash in a moon-white sheen. When they held hands, zipping round and round on the ice, he felt frozen in time, though he would never have admitted it to Annie. It was as if what was happening was not real at all, but a lucid dream—a weaving together of two hearts amid the tranquility of twilight. The few other Englishers there scarcely seemed to notice them as they flew across the ice, so their secret was safe.

Annie seemed to be an open book about her life, and he felt almost too comfortable talking with her about his family in Kentucky, as well, wishing he might introduce her to them someday. *Too soon to think this way . . .*

Eagerly she told of her longtime pen-pal friendship with Louisa, formerly one of her "big secrets," which made him wonder what other secrets might be locked away from view.

After their first night of skating he had offered to store her skates in his trunk so she wouldn't have to sneak them in and out of the house again.

They met nearly every other night after that. Annie was apparently delighted to return to the same place repeatedly. There the world seemed to go still for them, like a shelter for their growing friendship. At least while they skated they could talk and laugh and enjoy the feel of the blades gliding on ice, even though Ben was concerned that Annie not get too chilled.

Sometimes they would hurry back to the car to warm up before resuming their dance, the night dissolving into a dazzling memory of hoarfrost and snow-clad trees near the pond—*their pond*.

Within two weeks, their secluded meetings began to run together in his mind. Yet he could not blur the memory of Annie's quaint remarks, her appealing smile . . . the firm touch of her small hand in his.

Never let go . . . he thought.

And in spite of the bitter cold they endured night after night, Ben was in no hurry for warmer temperatures, nor for the sweet blossoming of spring.

Chapter 21

The house felt terribly cold to Esther this Lord's Day. Hurrying to get a hot breakfast on the table, she was aware of Zeke's pushing more logs into the belly of the wood stove. The old stove was their best means of heating the house—especially the downstairs. Their two kerosene heaters often stood in the upstairs hallway, near the children's rooms. Though Zeke was proud they weren't "spoilt with central heating," like their English neighbors, he spoke of the spring thaw often, hoping it was not too far away.

Esther hoped so, too. But there was more

on her mind today than the coming of spring. The People were planning to meet following the Preaching service today—to vote on whether or not to shun her.

She was in a quandary, no doubt about that. Here she was, grateful to the Lord for her deliverance from sin and despair, from the legalism that had ensnared and dominated her for a lifetime, yet facing the dreaded shunning.

Will my own mother turn her back on me? Will Annie and my dearest friends? Will my children, in time?

Esther would not let fear overtake her. She would move only one small step forward at a time, clasping the hand of divine guidance, the precious Holy Spirit. *My comfort in this dark hour . . .*

———

The Preaching service went longer than usual and much emphasis was placed on "waywardness leading to pride," which Preachers Hochstetler and Zook adeptly wove into their sermons. Esther observed Preacher Jesse's soberness as he stood before them, beads of perspiration on his face. More than once, he paused to mop his brow, occasionally catching her eye where she sat cradling her baby with the women. All the while, she prayed silently for the Lord's will to be accomplished in her life and the lives of the dear ones here. *Thy will be done on earth, as it is in heaven. . . .*

When time came for the members' meeting, following the closing hymn and dismissal of the non-baptized youth, Esther was asked to leave the room. Annie's father would lead the discussion, after which each member would have his or her say about Esther's unwillingness to atone for her sin of pride and defiance. Very soon, the voting would take place.

The outcome is clear, she thought, surprised to hear footsteps in the hallway from the upstairs bedroom where she waited.

When she looked, there was Louisa, Annie's friend, wearing a big smile on her face. "Mind if I keep you company, Esther?"

"Why, no. Come on in."

Louisa made herself right at home, sitting on the edge of the bed. John scampered over to her right quick. "It was kind of funny," she said, looking as Amish as the rest of the women. "I think the ministers forgot I'm not one of them."

"Oh? And where's Annie?"

"She left to help watch some of the younger children during the meeting." Louisa lifted John and placed him on her lap. "Want to ride horsey?" He nodded, giggling, and she jostled him up and down. "The deacon shooed me out when they realized I was still sitting there."

"Well, you might've gotten to voice your say and voted me out of the fellowship," Esther said.

Louisa shook her head. "I doubt that. Whatever you did isn't grounds for being kicked out, is it?"

"According to our Ordnung, a person is not to embrace the assurance of salvation in any way." She wouldn't go into this now, but she did say that she knew she was saved. "It isn't only a feeling—it's the strongest knowing I've ever experienced. The Scriptures say I can claim the promise of eternal life, and this has nothin' at all to do with pride . . . and everything to do with the love shown in the ultimate sacrifice of the Lord Jesus."

"Julia talked of faith and love being interconnected, too," Louisa said suddenly.

"I don't see how you can separate them."

She wouldn't have minded talking about the verses in the Psalms she'd read earlier this morning, but Louisa rose just then and seemed to lose interest, setting John down and going to pick up Essie Ann.

Esther put her mind on what King David had written so long ago: seeking with all of your heart and finding the peace of God in troublesome times.

Such as now . . .

She almost wanted to go downstairs and hurry up the process, the inevitable result of embracing *a perverse doctrine*, as the preachers and deacon had repeatedly said when they had met with her during her stay with the Rancks.

Breathing a sigh and a prayer, she walked across the room to stand at the window while Louisa rocked Essie Ann. She contemplated her situation, married to a man who would always uphold the Ordnung and its requirements. *No doubt I'll not even be allowed to sit at the table with my family*.

Suddenly, she felt the need to look into the sweet face of her baby, soundly asleep. She bent to kiss her soft cheek. "A gift from God, I must say," Esther said softly.

"A pretty one, too," Louisa agreed, smiling. "I'll babysit for you anytime."

"Why, that's awful nice." Seeing Louisa so gentle with a babe in arms, Esther had no doubt Annie's friend would be a good option for helping, if ever necessary. She thought, too, of her widowed mother, ever willing and eager to spend time with the children, and with Esther, too. As for Zeke, Mamma had never been too keen on her son-in-law. It was no wonder.

Turning, Esther went slowly to the window and gazed out over the undisturbed fields of white. Beneath all that snow lay hardened ground and narrow hideaways where small critters hibernated from the harsh weather.

I, too, burrowed away . . . for a time.

She recalled having walked over a thin layer of soil peeking out from beneath frozen ground just this morning. And she'd slid, catching herself.

Now the sound of Deacon Byler's calling pulled her out of her reverie. She and Louisa—who was clearly enamored with Essie Ann—and the children all headed slowly down the stairs to the solemn gathering.

Had it not been for Louisa and Annie, as well as Esther's mother, young Laura and the boys might have been exposed to the bishop's straight talk directed toward Esther and in front of the entire membership. As it was, the three women and the children scurried out to the kitchen.

It turned out the fellowship of saints, of which Esther had been a part since her teenage baptism, had chosen to put teeth to her formal Bann and excommunication: They would shun her permanently. "Even unto death, until such a time when you will bow your knee and repent," Bishop Stoltz-fus decreed.

When the time came for Esther to stand before the man of God, she scarcely knew where to look. *If Zeke should happen to catch my eye . . .*

Yet she did not accept guilt. For she knew in the deep of her heart she had come to her life's crossroad and had elected that "holy and just path."

I must cling to this for always.

Meanwhile, as the bishop announced "the blemished one" would lose her status as a voting member, Esther prayed for the strength, determination, and grace to with-

stand the years of social avoidance awaiting her.

———

Zeke was clearly put out, even swearing
in Dutch, forced as he was to miss the common meal and the fellowship with the men
because of the shun slapped on Esther.
Forced to miss much more, too.

"You've shamed me! In front of all the
People, yet. You are a disgrace, woman."
He shook his head. "Ach, and Deacon's
wife brought peach cobbler, too," he belly-
ached, as though the departure from their
usual dessert fare was more important than
accompanying his family home. But he was
required to take Esther and the children
away from the meeting place and the large
gathering for the meal, where she would not
have been welcome at any table.

There were Scriptures the brethren
looked to in the case of *die Meinding*—the
shunning. One from Matthew came to mind,
that she had heard preached since her baptism: *If (the sinner) refuses to listen even to
the church, treat him as you would a pa-
gan. . . .* Verses in First Corinthians also ad-

monished believers to abstain from eating and fellowshipping with idolaters and other sinners. Esther was now considered such an offender.

Shielding her baby from the cold air blowing into the front of their old gray carriage, Esther stared at the frost clinging to every imaginable spot as they rode. Ponds, creeks, hollows in fields and on roads, where former snows had melted and now had turned to pure ice. *Perty*, she thought, attempting to keep her chin up despite the reality of the day.

Once home, Esther quickly set about laying out a lunch of cold cuts and butter bread, along with red beet eggs—all made yesterday. Zeke, meanwhile, brought in the folding table and banged it down on the kitchen floor, then got himself situated at their long table, stonily silent for a time.

At one point Zach asked timidly, "How long is Mamma gonna sit over there?"

Elbows on the table, Zeke glowered. "Forever, by the looks of it. Don't be gawkin' at her. Just eat."

So this is what it's going to be like, Esther thought. *An outcast in my own home.*

After the meal, she put the children down for naps. Then, hurrying back to the kitchen, she redd things up and headed upstairs for a bit of a rest herself.

Curling up in bed with her Bible and Essie Ann, she began to will her body to relax. Zeke had taken the team and left the house, though he hadn't said he was going anywhere in particular. *Gone visiting, probably.*

She knew she must not envy Julia's relationship with Irvin, but the memory of hearing him tell his wife fond *good-byes* and *I love yous* prior to his heading off to run errands was altogether unlike her experience. That and their many other thoughtful exchanges—verbal and otherwise—made Esther realize that Irvin and Julia's marriage was a strong and happy one . . . a witness of God's love in a couple's life.

How can I possibly have that with Zeke . . . now? Won't he always resent me for standing firm for my beliefs? She assumed he would rail against her for not giving in to the People's expectations, for not honoring the Ordnung, in the long run. In Zeke's eyes she was most disobedient.

In God's eyes . . . what am I?

The nagging thought persisted. Closing

her eyes, she asked for the Holy Spirit's protective covering over her mind. "And help me to keep my thoughts centered on you, O Lord," she whispered.

In all her days, Annie had never felt so torn. Esther had been shunned till death, or until such time as she should bend her knee in contrition. Mamm had whispered the outcome of the solemn meeting at the common meal, and now Annie felt nearly sick to her stomach. She didn't rightly know or understand Esther's stand now that she believed herself to be "saved." Annie only knew how the People looked on such a thing. Pride was the ultimate and original sin. So to excuse Esther, even in Annie's own mind, was to join her in her haughtiness.

She could only hope she might still see Esther occasionally, although that remained to be seen. Mamm would tell her one way or the other, she knew. Daed, too, would say something if Annie was so bold as to bring it up. Non-baptized folk were not to be privy to what was voted upon.

So Esther would live under Zeke's roof and covering, yet not be allowed to partake of food at the same table. She would also not be permitted to pass money or other objects from her hand to the hand of a church member in good standing. There were other, more personal stipulations regarding marriage that Annie suspected but had never been told directly.

It would be a painful life for dear Esther. No, she mustn't even be thought of as dear any longer. Not while she was in this rebellious state. And Annie knew she must attempt to follow her parents' stance on this delicate issue, hard as that would be.

While Annie was tied up with church, Ben drove over slippery roads to locate the old covered bridge on Belmont Road. He had avoided the area altogether after the creepy sensation he'd first encountered. Now he was determined to conquer the peculiar sense of disquiet by walking through to the north entrance of the old bridge.

His snow boots clunked hollowly on the wooden planks as the boards gave with each step. When a horse and carriage came rattling through—folks from another district—the vibrations shook his entire body, and he was suddenly very aware of his rib cage.

Shakin' your liver loose—an unexpected phrase came to mind.

He smiled at the recollection and kept going, staring at the back of the Amish buggy, its orange triangle reflector catching his eye as it moved on, up the steep hill and beyond.

Stopping, he uttered a sound, listening to the echo. "Hello," he said quietly, then slightly louder, "Hello-o-o-o." Then he whistled, paying attention to the muted ricochet.

Going all the way out of the bridge and around the long stone abutment on his left, he turned and headed down toward the creek.

The snow lay in great patches, and he could see where pods from the black locust trees had fallen during the recent storm. He recalled someone once saying that cows liked to chew on ground-up locust pods. Stooping, he picked up several, noticing the reddish brown color, the deep, rippled texture, and the beanlike seeds inside. He counted fourteen.

He slipped two narrow four-inch pods into his pocket, recalling how his mother had often shaken her head, offering a bemused smile as she handed back the peach stones that seemed to wind up in the laundry from time to time. Other pieces of nature had landed in the washer, too, but she hadn't ever complained. It was as if she understood his need to pick up things, investigate, and either discard or keep them in his possession. His dad had not been so keen on his collection of "junk," as he called the array of items. But, for some reason, the peach pits had remained a favorite, just as they had for his best friend, Eric, who had carried one in his pocket for as long as he could remember, too.

Slowly, Ben moved toward the grove of trees. Reveling in the tranquility of the area, he was no longer conscious of alarm, as before. He had a sudden urge to bring Annie here in the spring to stand here with him beneath the flowering branches of these beautiful, tall trees. He was impatient to see if he was right about the blossoms, eager to know if they were white as lilies, as in his dreams.

———

Esther had been reading a Bible story to the older children near the wood stove while nursing Essie Ann. All the while Zach kept glancing at the ceiling, his eyes bright with the awareness of the ticking sound of sleet on the roof. Soon Laura and John were looking up, as well.

"Does the Lord God make the snow and sleet?" Zach asked when she finished the story.

"Our heavenly Father knows just what we need—rain, sleet, snow—and we can trust Him for everything. Even for the weather." She had been cautiously yet consistently sharing with the children, ever so eager to pass along all she was learning about the standard for holiness and godliness as found in the Holy Scriptures.

"The Lord calmed the wind and the storm," Laura told her little brother. "Remember that story?"

"Jah, yesterday." Zach, soon to be four years old, smiled, not so serious now.

"And God rained down a special kind of food," Laura said, looking quite pleased with her good memory.

"Manna," said Zach, looking equally pleased.

They came and gave her a simultaneous hug. "Ach, I love you so," Esther said, kissing each sweet head.

It was evident that Laura and Zach had noticed a change in her. She was beginning to see a tenderness of spirit in them, too. Julia had counseled that the children would become "hungry for more of the Lord Jesus" as they were presented with the gospel over time. *"Laura, Zach, and little John will know instinctively what motivates your life, Esther. Even if you don't talk of it constantly . . . they'll sense God in you,"* she'd said repeatedly.

These words, which I command thee this day, shall be in thine heart: And thou shalt teach them diligently unto thy children, and shalt talk of them when thou sittest in thine house, and when thou walkest by the way, and when thou liest down, and when thou risest up.

"Who a person is—how they conduct their lives—will influence a child for righteousness," Julia had said.

Who I am is going to have more of an effect on people than what I say. At least till they can understand. If they ever do. Esther breathed a prayer for strength to carry out her responsibility as a new believer both at home and in the community. And for submitting to her husband, as unto the Lord. She felt a renewed compassion for Zeke, which she believed had been graciously given her from God.

Still, Julia had forgotten to take into account that another spirit was at work in this house. *An opposing one,* Esther thought as she patted Essie Ann, waiting for the wee burps. She pondered Zeke's resistance to her study of the Bible, before she sent Laura and the boys upstairs to get ready for bed.

Sitting quietly in the rocking chair, she stared at the day clock on the wall, wondering where Zeke had taken himself off to on such an inclement night. She cherished the nearness of her infant, realizing how much she missed Julia and Irvin—the helpful comments and their devotional times, their children and hers listening to the stories and the prayers.

Ach, I daresn't think backwards. . . .

Any minute now Zeke would return. She must brace herself emotionally and hope she would not be wounded by his piercing words. *Nor his increasingly rough treatment of me.*

Had she not been holding her baby, she might've allowed a bit of pity to seep from her soul. It was best she not give way to tears, although it was difficult to understand how one could be banned from the "fellow-ship," simply due to embracing the whole truth of the Word of God. She had already tried to argue this with the brethren and with Zeke, to no avail. Now it was time for her to live out her walk with the Lord in a non-condemning manner, hoping to win them by her witness, in word and deed. She must let her light shine before the men who wished to rule her ability to choose Jesus Christ as her Lord and Master.

Sighing, she made her way up the long staircase, weary at the thought of the sepa-rateness that awaited her. It was not easy to sleep in the cold and distant bedroom at the end of the hall, as she had been doing since returning. Separated from the darling chil-dren who'd shared the Rancks' attic with her, all of them together snug and safe. And separated from Zeke, as she would be each night for the rest of her life, though it was not what she would have chosen, given a say.

Chapter 22

Ben was surprised when Zeke appeared at the door of his apartment. "Hey," he said. "Come on in."

Zeke stepped inside and Ben asked if he wanted some coffee or something else hot to drink. "Always coffee, jah." Zeke stood in the sitting area and looked first at the couch, then the leather chair.

"Sit wherever," Ben said.

Ambling over to the chair, Zeke sat with a groan, as if older than his years.

Ben was still puzzled as to why Zeke would track him down here at home, but he didn't ask. And when the coffee had finished percolating, he chose one of his largest mugs to fill with the dark brew for Zeke. "Sugar or cream or both?" he asked.

"Always black."

Once Ben was settled on the sofa with his own coffee mug, Zeke began to talk about one injustice after another. He rambled, seemingly upset at "the liberals," and Ben found it curious that Zeke had access to current events.

Ben waited for him to bring up the death of his brother again, as blunt as he'd been at the mud sale, but Zeke didn't go there. What he seemed to be working toward was a different sort of request: a wood-splitting workday. "I'm needin' some help to clear out trees damaged in the snowstorm. You got time?"

Ben smiled, hoping his relief wasn't too evident. "I'll make the time. When?"

"Tomorrow's good—after you're done with work?"

Ben paused, knowing Annie would be waiting for him up the road from her house, as usual. "I could help you for several hours in the morning, *before* I head for work."

Zeke grinned. "Jah, 'tis even better.

Come on over for breakfast, then. That'll be your pay."

"Sounds fine. Thanks." *Anything for a home-cooked meal,* he thought.

Zeke sat and talked a bit longer, mostly about his being under the weather due to the recent cold snap. "This winter's been too long. Nearly endless, it seems."

Ben floundered for the right words. "Who knows, maybe you'll feel better when spring comes. . . ."

"I doubt that." Zeke shook his head. "Guess a body oughta get used to losin' a part of himself . . . sooner or later."

Zeke quit talking, and Ben understood he was thinking again of his long-dead brother.

———

A hunting hound barked at the hint of first light in the eastern sky, and early risers all around Paradise estimated how many bales of hay were left in the barn.

Ben drove to Zeke's place carefully, aware of ice patches on the road. *He said to come for breakfast.* But it certainly seemed like an imposition as Ben made the turn into the narrow driveway leading to the house, dark except for a light in the kitchen.

When no one answered his several knocks, he listened at the door and heard a teakettle squealing and a baby doing the same. Inching the door open, he found the kitchen in disarray. Oatmeal was boiling over from one pot on the stove, and Esther came rushing in with the howling baby in one arm and the smallest boy pulling on the hem of her apron.

"Ach, Ben . . . it's you," she said, handing him Essie Ann, still small at just two months old. "Glad you let yourself in." She leaned down to pick up John, whispered something in his ear, and then set him back down. Hurrying to the stove, she removed the pot of oatmeal. "As you can see, it's been quite a mornin'."

"I don't need to stay if—"

"No . . . no, you're here, so have yourself a nice hot breakfast." She said Zeke had been called to help the neighbor but would be back any minute.

He felt strange alone in the kitchen with Zeke's wife, but the three children lessened his uneasiness.

"Goodness me," Esther said, looking over at him holding the baby. "I daresay you've got a gentle way with little ones."

He, too, had just realized Essie Ann had stopped her wailing. "This happens at home, too, when my sister and family visit. Their baby son, well . . . does he ever have a set of lungs!"

"And you calm him, no matter his temper?" asked Esther.

He nodded. "I'm sure it's just a fluke."

Esther laughed, leaning down to swipe a washcloth across John's face, then using the same cloth on Zach's mouth. "Well, I think it's right fine that a young man should have such a soothing effect on an infant."

He grinned at Essie Ann, who was looking up at him.

"Seems she remembers you," Esther said before walking into the next room and calling up the steps, "Laura, hurry down, now."

He chuckled. "Nobody remembers much about the day of their birth."

Esther returned, fanning her face with her apron, while pointing Zach and John toward the table. "I daresay you should think 'bout

having yourself a dozen or so young'uns."
She looked over at him again. "Sit anywhere
'cept the head of the table."

"Thanks." He sat to the right of the head,
across from the boys, who were eyeing him
now.

"That's Mamma's place," Zach said. "Or
was."

Ben rose quickly.

"No . . . no. That's quite all right," Esther
said, motioning him back down. "I won't be
sittin' at all."

A curious look crossed Zach's face, and
he turned quickly to look at his mother, who
was heading across the kitchen again to call
for Laura. "Mamma sits alone ev'ry meal
now," Zach whispered.

Ben wondered what that was about.

"Dat never says why," Zach said, clam-
ming up when his mother came back into
the room.

"Here, let me put Essie Ann down for a
nap," Esther said, taking the baby from him.
"She woke up mighty early this mornin'."

"Jah, and she cried a lot in the night,
Mamma," Zach volunteered.

"Colicky some," Esther replied.

Little John sat still, just staring at him.

Ben tried to engage him by wrinkling his face into comical poses. At last John spoke. "You . . . our cousin?"

Zach laughed. "No, you *Bensel* . . . this is the harness shop man. Mr. Ranck's friend."

"I *not* silly. He's Cousin Nate," insisted John, squinting now at Ben.

Esther carried over a large bowl of oatmeal. "This here is Ben Martin, boys. You've met him before."

"Jah, Laura says he's the one with the smoothest peach stone in the whole wide world," Zach said.

Ben was amused.

"Ever see Dat's collection of old peach pits?" Zach asked.

"Boys . . . now, that's enough. Mr. Ben's not interested in suchlike."

But Ben found their chatter refreshing.

Soon Laura joined them at the table, sitting next to John and looking bright-eyed. Her parted blond hair shone beneath her white head covering, exactly like Esther's.

"Where's Dat's bag of peach stones?" Zach asked, leaning forward, directing the question to Laura.

Laura shrugged. "Guess they upped and walked off."

"Well, you've seen 'em. I haven't." Zach resumed his attention to his breakfast plate, going for the jellied toast before the oatmeal.

"Best be askin' Dat." Laura drank nearly half her milk and wiped her mouth on her sleeve. "Where is he, anyway?"

"Bessie next door was fixin' to have her calves," Esther said, coming over to survey the children's plates.

"Aw, I want to go 'n' see." Laura frowned.

"Me too," said Zach.

"Jah, and me do, too," said John, poking his chubby chest.

"Well, now, Dat can take all of you over yonder here 'fore too long." Esther poured more milk for Laura. "Now yous need to stop talkin' Ben's ear off and eat."

"Oh, I'm enjoying this," Ben piped up.

"You come from a big family?" Esther asked somewhat shyly.

"Four younger sisters."

Zach found that funny and made his eyes bug out. "All girls, puh!"

"Aw, Zach," said Esther.

"It's not so bad havin' two of us round here," Laura said, glancing over at Essie Ann in the cradle.

"Well, at least one ain't so lippy just yet,"

Zach said, smiling at Ben as if they shared a secret, man to man.

"No, but the baby's got a fierce cry," Laura said, "which means she'll be frank enough someday."

"Like Mamma?" Zach said.

Esther laughed out loud, shaking her head, then turned back to the wood stove.

What a fun-loving bunch, Ben thought, wondering what was keeping their father.

———

Ben and the children had finished off most of the oatmeal and jellied toast. Esther, never having sat once, was already frying eggs for the boys and Zeke, offering an egg or two to Ben, as well.

Ben politely declined, not accustomed to eating so heartily at dawn. He was relieved to see Zeke as he entered, and raised his chin in greeting as Zeke came in and sat down.

"Glad you went ahead," Zeke said, explaining how he'd helped his neighbor deliver a calf. "Always fascinating." Zeke looked at Esther just then, and she hurried over with a platter of freshly cooked eggs.

"I s'pose yous offered the blessing?" Zeke said, looking straight at the boys.

"I did this time," Zach said.

"Jah, he led the silent prayer," Esther said, rumpling his hair.

"My good little man," Zeke replied.

Ben accepted another cup of coffee while Zeke downed his meal, but Esther hovered between the stove, the table, and sink, even now that Zeke was here and all of them had been served.

What's up with that? Ben wondered. *And why does she sit alone at mealtime?* Everything else about the family had seemed surprisingly normal this morning. And though he knew it was none of his business, he felt glad Esther and the children had reunited with Zeke.

———

With Annie frequently disappearing to see Ben, Louisa had more time to spend with Sam. Still, she was getting antsy. Here it was already mid-March and she wanted to start making some money again, if not for the sake of paying additional room and board to Barbara Zook, then for her own sense of self-esteem. She wasn't a slacker, and she missed the income from selling her paintings through the local gallery.

She had been eyeing section B— "Local"—of the *Lancaster New Era*, the newspaper at Julia's. The Lancaster Museum of Art, downtown, was of most interest to her. Eileen Sauders, the owner of the art gallery on Route 30, had been talking about an April event—the Spring Art Walk—which was to include some of her own acquisitions in a regional show, sponsored by the museum.

Louisa was also beginning to feel the need to extend herself, to give back something to this community she had come to respect, something even more than attending quilting bees and canning frolics here in Paradise, although that was important, too. She decided to apply for a position teaching art to younger students.

By keeping her days free for delving into the Amish culture she so enjoyed, she could spare a few evenings a week, passing on her love of fine art to children. This would not impinge on her seeing Sam, either. Besides, with the plowing and planting season coming soon, he would become rather scarce, as he had already warned her.

When she really thought about it, she knew she couldn't resist putting down a few roots here. Although it was beyond her ability to imagine how her romance with Sam could possibly move forward, Louisa realized she was trying on the Plain life in her head. Not playacting, as she had been doing all these past months, but seeing how it fit her—for real.

She tried to be attentive at Preaching services, but the sermons were in Dutch. And seemed pointless. She soaked up both Annie's and Sam's perspectives, noting that neither had joined the church as of yet. She even listened more closely when Annie's grandmother, Mammi Zook, talked in the quiet of the evening. She enjoyed the quaint and interesting way Mammi's Dutch and English became mixed together while doing needlepoint and cross-stitch. Mammi seemed almost too eager to have Louisa sit with her in the small front room of the Dawdi Haus.

When a voice mail showed up on her Palm, saying the museum contact person wanted to interview her ASAP, Louisa let out a little whoop of joy. Quickly she thought better of celebrating, since she hadn't told Annie yet, waiting to first see how things went. She'd gone so far as to apply online in order to keep from having to ask to borrow Julia's car. Until now.

Louisa knew she ought to bounce the whole thing off Annie before moving ahead. It wouldn't be fair to reintroduce the world of art, not now when Annie was looking ahead to the beginning of her baptismal instruction classes next month. Annie had managed to stay away from her artistic passion to date—at least Louisa believed she had—and she didn't want to interfere in any way with the plan Annie and her father had worked out. She didn't know exactly how Ben Martin fit into *that* equation, and Annie hadn't said much lately about her love life.

That night, after playing three games of checkers with Mammi Zook, Louisa laid out the whole plan to Annie upstairs.

"You mean it, Lou? You're gonna get a job here?" Annie's eyes lit up.

"Don't get the wrong idea," she insisted. "It'll be for only six weeks this summer . . . after I get back from Denver."

Annie frowned. "You're still thinking of going home for Easter?"

"I've already told my parents, so no turning back."

"Well, jah. I can see that." Annie's mood quickly returned to elation, and she asked if Lou had called the museum back.

"I wanted you to know first," Louisa said.

"Even before Sam?"

Louisa smiled. "Anyone ever tell you you're trouble?"

"All the time."

Louisa guessed Ben had been teasing Annie. "So . . . what's new with you and your beau?"

Blushing, Annie replied, "I need to borrow some fancy clothes."

"You what?"

"Just a perty skirt or dress . . . something 'specially modest."

Louisa pounced. "Well, let's get you out on the town, girl. Time for some new threads? I say we go shopping!"

Annie grimaced. "Now listen . . . I'm not askin' for attention. I just need to have something to wear out . . . well, in the modern world every so often."

"In *Ben's* world, you mean?"

A poignant silence filled the room, and Annie sat there on her bed like a stone statue, unflinching, looking down at her hands.

"Listen, you don't have to tell me anything if you don't want to." There. She'd released her friend to protect her private thoughts and plans. But the silence was telling.

We've both lost our heads . . . and our hearts.

Annie's request for a modern outfit came because Ben had purchased tickets to the musical *Behold the Lamb* at the Sight and Sound Millennium Theatre for the Saturday afternoon following Easter. "I haven't decided yet if I'll take down my hair, though. And I don't know 'bout my Kapp, either," Annie said a few days later.

Louisa found it interesting that Annie would even consider going out dressed fancy but still looking very Amish from the neck up. "I think it would be better to wear your cape dress and apron if you aren't going to do something cool and different with your hair."

Oops, did I say that?

But either Annie didn't catch on or she chose to ignore it. Her argument for wearing English clothes was that the weather was getting nicer, and she was beginning to feel strange about being seen with a fancy fellow when she looked so Plain herself.

"So . . . maybe Ben's influencing you?"

"Only a little."

"A little? Come on, Annie. Listen to yourself!"

Annie moseyed over to her bureau and opened the middle drawer. "Truth is, I'm crazy 'bout him, Lou."

"I think I know the feeling."

Annie turned. "You?" She broke into a smile. "Does this mean . . . ?"

"I have no idea what it means, but I'm going to find out." Louisa felt half empty without Sam, and when he held her near, she forgot every other guy she'd ever dated. **What comes over me when I'm with him?**

She had tried on many scenarios in her head, including one in which Sam finally decided to join the Amish church. Would she still want to be with him?

"You and I . . . we'll know better when you're away for Easter," he had said, which made her wonder how that could be. *"Absence makes the heart grow fonder,"* he'd added.

"Yeah, and sometimes fonder of another." She hadn't meant to be glib, but she knew this firsthand. One case in point: Trey's leaving for London had made her susceptible to Michael's attention. And the last thing she wanted was to view Sam's affection, in any way, as a replacement for that of her former fiancé.

"I'll be true to you, Louisa," Sam had promised. *"No matter how long you're away."*

His words had thrilled her and made her want to celebrate every moment they had together, yet she feared the very thing that would eventually keep Annie and Ben apart would one day tear Sam from her, too.

The revered Ordnung.

———

Footsteps in the hallway. Esther sensed them first in her subconscious, half bracing even as she dreamed. Dread filled her veins, and her legs tensed.

Now came the slow creak of boards outside her room. Hazily she attempted to open her eyes. Only slightly awake, she was aware of the darkness . . . of the crib in the corner. The unfamiliar movement in the room.

"Esther . . ."

Zeke's voice.

She attempted to make a sound. But her words got lost in the mist of drowsiness, and she wondered if she ought to remain silent. Or was she actually dreaming?

She felt the bed give way beneath his weight. Her husband was not waiting for her answer.

Moving her arm, she pulled the covers up.

"Ach, good . . . you ain't sleepin' this time."

"Well, I was. Truly, I was."

"I've been without you too long." His lips brushed her temple, her hair.

"But . . . the Bann," she said, quickly becoming alert.

"Well, then, God help us both." He stroked her hair, caressed her face.

She felt a distant yearning within, surprised by it . . . and soon with his persistent kisses, she was unable to resist his ever-tightening embrace. *Such tenderness tonight. Does he love me after all?*

Torn between her apprehension and her own latent desire, she said no more. She remembered the Scripture about an unbelieving husband being sanctified through his wife, and the thought gave her a smidgen of hope.

Later, when Zeke had fallen asleep, she slipped her arm from beneath his. Zeke started and gasped in his sleep.

Esther froze.

"I'm sorry . . ." he moaned hoarsely. "So sorry."

Esther's heart began to pound. *Can it be? Is he finally repentant for the way he treats me?*

But before she could open her mouth to respond, Zeke moaned again. "Oh, Isaac, I've wronged you so. I'm ever so sorry. . . ."

Chapter 23

Julia wouldn't hear of it; she insisted Louisa take her car.

"No need to offer money for gas!" she admonished and said she'd be praying for Louisa, too.

Appreciative of her generosity, but not surprised by it, Louisa took the offered keys and waved good-bye to Annie, as well as to little Molly and James. "I won't be gone long," she told Julia, who smiled and said to take all the time she needed.

There should be more people like her, Louisa thought, heading out the side door of the house to the detached garage. She literally felt strange wearing slacks again—chic black dress pants and a soft pink top—business casual. Her dress boots were easier to get used to again, because she often wore Yonie's or Omar's sloppy ones out in the peacock pen with Annie or when helping with barn chores. She had grown accustomed to seeing her feet in black.

Julia had been nice enough to volunteer one of the children's bedrooms, where Louisa had changed clothes, getting some assistance with her hair from Annie. The middle part hadn't seemed to want to disappear, so Louisa remedied that by brushing all of it over to the side and scrunching it up a bit. She sprayed it lightly, pleased with the flowing, mussed-up look.

Downtown, she parked in the lot adjacent to the museum, glad for her trusty MapQuest directions. The woman she was to meet, a Janet Blake, ushered her into a small yet well-furnished office. Within twenty minutes, Louisa had not only secured the teaching slot for the summer ArtSmart classes for seven- to twelve-year-olds, but she was told she could possibly be filling in for a pregnant teacher, as soon as next week.

"I can't tell you how excited we are to have you on board here, Louisa," the well-coiffed woman said. "We like to employ young people with art degrees. Too many artists hole up in their studios, disinterested in teaching." Janet seemed intrigued when Louisa mentioned her address in Paradise.

"I'm staying with an Amish family," Louisa explained.

"How remarkable. Is this a particular study—the Plain life, perhaps?"

"I'm visiting a friend."

"Well, I've seen some fine work by an Amish artist . . . and not so long ago. Also from the Paradise area, I believe."

That caught Louisa's attention. "Where was that? At a gallery?"

"As a matter of fact, my friend Eileen Sauder owns one on Route 30. She often speaks of a young Amishwoman, about your age, who has brought paintings to be framed . . . and soon are sold. More recently, though, the artist has not been supplying any new work."

Louisa realized Janet was most likely talking about her. "I know that gallery," she admitted.

"Eileen has been getting requests for

more paintings. She phoned last week, inquiring if I knew anyone among the Amish community . . . in Paradise, in hopes of locating the artist."

I need to let Miss Sauder know I'm limiting my output, thought Louisa, wondering if at some point, once she was well established, she might want to begin accepting work on commission.

She realized her thinking was askew. She was behaving as if she were going to continue to live here.

Janet reminded her to pick up a parking permit before leaving and thanked Louisa once again for applying. "I think you'll enjoy teaching here," she said, pushing back from her desk.

Louisa thanked her for her time. "I hope to see you next week." She smiled and headed out the door, willing herself not to linger at the walls filled with fine art.

Outside, she decided to walk a while, since her interview had been rather short. Taken by the lovely historic buildings along the tree-lined street, she walked up East Marion and turned on North Cherry, wondering what it might be like to lease a small downtown apartment. She breathed in the air, filling her lungs as she wandered the cobblestone streets, enjoying herself immensely. She caught herself doing a double take when glancing down at her clothing.

How strange I look to myself. . . .

When she turned onto North Duke Street, she spotted the public library and hurried to cross the busy street. Upon entering the stately old building, she noticed the lofty ceilings and impressive crown molding, thinking again how wonderful it might be to live in such a neighborhood.

Discarding the notion as pure fantasy, she strolled through the rows of bookshelves and located the magazine section. She picked up several of her favorite art-related magazines and scanned through feature articles, deciding she missed this world and should start a subscription promptly. *When I decide how long I'm staying. . . .*

When her cell rang, she checked the ID and grinned. Sam was calling from the barn phone his family shared with a neighbor. "Hey," she answered softly, having received one other call from him at this number. "Can you wait just a minute?"

Not wishing to disturb the other patrons,

she promptly made her way to the entrance. "Okay, I can talk now."

"I had to hear your voice, Louisa. My day isn't complete unless I do."

"Oh, you're sweet. Well, guess what I did today?" She didn't wait; she told him of her new teaching job. "I wish you could see the museum where I'll be working. It's just magnificent," she said. "The current art exhibit is so amazing."

"I've wandered around downtown some," he said. "I even took the walking tour with a group of tourists once."

"Really, when was this?"

"After class one day. I was dressed for the occasion, too," he said, chuckling into the phone. "Fancy, ya know."

She smiled. "I've got some mighty fine wheels today."

He admitted having had a car not so long ago, which didn't surprise her.

"You really must have pushed the limits during your teen years."

"More than you know. And I don't mean to say I'm proud of it . . . well, only of my community college degree."

Louisa wondered if he had dated other English girls, perhaps. "I need to return Julia's car," she said, checking her watch. "And change back into my Amish clothes for supper at the Zooks'."

"Dr. Jekyll and Miss Hyde, jah?"

Louisa chuckled.

"When will I see you again?" he asked.

"I think I'd better hang out with Annie this week."

"Oh." He sounded glum. "That's no fun."

"How about sometime over the weekend?"

"Saturday night?" he asked. "Wear your English clothes and we'll go somewhere as fancy folk."

She wondered how she'd pull that off. "I may have to change somewhere, after I meet you." She was thinking of not offending Annie's parents again.

"That's plenty easy. It's done all the time."

These were strange remarks coming from Sam, and she could hardly wait to hear more. When he said, "I'm sendin' a fond good-bye to you," she knew she missed him terribly, too. "Till Saturday, Louisa. Take good care, ya hear?"

"You, too. Bye for now."

———

Julia had emphasized the fact that children will absorb the spirit of God in their parents' lives, but Esther sat quite alone at a folding table in the kitchen, as Zeke and the children ate their supper together. Zeke did not speak either to the children or to her during the meal of veal ring, tomato zucchini casserole, and mashed potatoes. She had labored tirelessly to please him, although she knew how fond Laura and Zach were of the zucchini dish, too.

The past few days, Laura and the boys had witnessed, yet again, the rage simmering within their father. And for all the nights Zeke made his way into Esther's bedroom, he was not at all a placid man by day. Nothing seemed to put a permanent smile on Zeke's face.

How will our children soak up the love and acceptance of their heavenly Father if they don't see it in Zeke?

She brooded during the meal, only glancing at her family twice before Zeke called out his desire for pie and more coffee. She leaped up, responding as she knew he wished her to. She was careful not to allow tears in front of the children, although once

Laura had caught her off guard as she read her Bible alone.

Laura, more than Zach or John, had been curious upon their return home, asking why she slept alone in the bedroom, "so far away from Dat."

Because she did not wish to expose Laura to a needless fear of the Bann and shunning, she told her daughter, "You'll understand better one day, when you're lots older." She had not said a thing about joining the Amish church or committing one's entire life to a kneeling vow. A first-grader need not know what lay ahead. Esther pondered how she might steer her little ones toward the grace of the Lord Jesus. *Live out the life of faith before them,* Julia had instructed, but Julia's words and the life she lived with her thoughtful Irvin were fast becoming a distant memory.

I need the fellowship of believers, thought Esther. But it was foolish to even consider, given she'd heard tell of women losing their children if certain brethren got wind of Sunday school and church attendance at a worldly meetinghouse. Such things could be grounds for a husband to separate from the wife and take custody of the children.

Surely Zeke will not go that far.

Sighing, she wondered what was to become of her darling children over time.

Lest she create a nervous stomach as she ate, she began to count their mutual blessings, one of which was Zeke's growing friendship with Englischer Ben Martin. A most unlikely person, to be sure. Even so, Ben's coming to help Zeke chop and stack wood had been nothing less than an act of kindness—something that had put a short-lived spring in her husband's step. The sound of wood giving way to axes and chain saws had been comforting that morning, as was Ben's holding and effortlessly quieting Essie Ann.

Zeke had long declared that wood cut and stacked and put in the woodshed in late winter would burn far better in late autumn. He was smart that way, and now he had a sidekick of sorts, or so it had seemed from Ben's and Zeke's cheerful banter as they left the house together, axes slung over their shoulders.

Finished with her meal, Esther rose and cleared her table. Zeke excused himself to head outdoors, leaving the children and their places messy, but Esther didn't mind.

She often felt something of a reprieve when her husband opened the back door and exited, as if the contentious spirit followed out, right behind him.

———

Sam leaned forward, close enough to kiss her again. Louisa flinched; they'd kissed enough. "Sam, can we talk for a while?"

She leaned against the door of the car he'd borrowed from a cousin for the evening. "We *need* to talk." She wanted to be near him, sure. Her heart beat crazily when he looked at her that way, his dearest eyes . . . filled with love.

"I wish you'd stay." He reached for her hand. "In Paradise, ya know."

She yearned for his embrace, his amazing kisses, but an inner voice cautioned her.

He sighed, releasing her hand. "I have an idea . . . a place I want to take you very soon. A kind of celebration."

She wished she couldn't guess what was coming, though part of her was eager for it. What girl didn't long to be cherished? Proposed to? But Sam was enmeshed in the Amish world . . . and she was a hindrance to him.

"I want you to understand something." He folded his hands as if in prayer. "I'm in love with you, Louisa."

She held her breath. Oh, the power . . . the impact of such a declaration. Hadn't she wanted to hear this? Hadn't she suspected as much?

His eyes were earnest, as if waiting for an answer in kind.

"Oh, Sam. I love what we have . . . yes. But I'm far from being Plain. Farther, perhaps, than you know." She was thinking of her eagerness to paint and draw again . . . to teach, to earn money . . . and more.

She touched her blouse collar and glanced down at her pretty new skirt.

"This is the real me. *This,*" she said softly.

"Ach, I wouldn't change a thing 'bout you." He said no more. And all during the drive home, she resisted the urge to look at him for fear she might change her mind about what she knew she must do.

———

"I'm freaked," Louisa told Annie upstairs, in the privacy of their room.

Annie perched on her bed, peaceful as a dove. "Well, I can see that."

Louisa paced the length of the long room as Muffin poked his kitty head out from beneath Louisa's bed and watched.

"Sam wants more than I can give." Louisa groaned. "I should have listened to my head instead of thinking I could just have fun without either of us getting hurt." She stopped pacing. "Now he's in love with me."

"You're just so lovable—could that be it?"

Louisa felt like crying. "Oh, Annie, what'll I do?"

"Tell him the truth."

"Which is . . . ?"

A train whistle sounded in the distance, and Louisa flopped onto the bed. Muffin leaped up and snuggled his head into the crook of her arm.

"Tell Sam how you feel 'bout him." Annie went to her, eyes sympathetic.

Louisa shook her head. "Don't you realize what that means? I'd have to leave my life for good. If I were to follow through . . ."

"Ach, what's so wrong with that?"

"Well, you didn't leave your art for Rudy."

"No," agreed Annie quietly. "Not for Rudy." She reached over Louisa and stroked her cat. "But Sam . . . Sam makes you smile like nobody's business. You should see how your eyes shine like stars when he walks toward you. He's all you've been livin' for here lately. Ain't so?"

"You don't get it." Louisa leaned her head back on a pillow. "I don't *really* belong here. I thought maybe I did, but I don't."

"How can you say that?" Annie blinked her eyes and a frown crossed her brow. "Don't be too hasty to decide. Besides, I like havin' you here. You're my sister."

Lying there, staring at the high ceiling, Louisa wondered how she had ever fallen asleep to the sound of beeping taxis instead of the call of barn swallows. How would she ever find such peace anywhere again? But Sam . . . where did he fit in?

"People do crazy things for love," Annie said softly. "Things even harder than changing a lifestyle, I daresay."

Louisa looked at her and nodded, scarcely able to speak. Could she ever really belong to Sam, give up her art? Live under the Ordnung? But on the other hand, how hard would it be to leave him behind? Give up the chance to journey toward Julia's remarkable faith? And dear Annie—how could she say good-bye to her?

Funny, she thought. *A man brought me here . . . and a man's sending me back.*

"Annie," she said suddenly, "I don't know how I'll pull this off, but I think I need to go home."

"Aw . . . Lou."

"No, really. I should have admitted this before. To you . . . and to myself."

"Admitted what?"

Louisa sighed. "Courtney's visit stirred up a bunch of unresolved issues. At first they pushed me toward Sam, but now, well, I just don't know where I should be."

The two dressed for bed, saying no more.

Chapter 24

Annie searched for her slippers in the darkness. When her feet found them, she pulled on her long bathrobe.

"Lou?" she whispered.

Lighting the lantern, she was suddenly quite aware of her friend's absence. A quick search—beneath the other bed and in the bureau drawers—confirmed that Lou had taken her belongings. Her luggage was gone, too.

Sighing, Annie sat on the edge of the already made bed, where Lou had sat and giggled and cuddled Muffin and said the most hilarious things.

Here, on this bed, Lou had sketched drawings of two-story barns and haughty peacocks. Here Annie had found Lou's art hidden beneath the pillows when first they'd moved to this room.

She smiled wistfully, remembering all the happy days. "A wonderful, sisterly, good time."

Then, just as she rose to make her own bed, she spied Lou's soft tan skirt and creamy blouse hanging on the wooden wall pegs next to the cape dresses and aprons. "Ach, she remembered!" Annie laughed out loud, hastening to the pretty English outfit and pressing it to her face.

She noticed Lou's fashionable tan suede boots on the floor, and a sand-colored silky pair of hosiery rolled up in a small plastic bag. A pretty gold barrette was nestled in a white box atop two envelopes. One marked *To Annie*, the other addressed to Sam Glick.

Sighing, she sat near the lantern's light and opened her letter.

Dear Annie,

It's 2:30 AM and I'm writing this downstairs in Mammi Zook's little kitchen by candlelight. Can you be-

lieve it, I'm actually up before anyone in this house? Muffin is already
snoozing in his carrier, ready to fly
(stand-by) with me, and all my stuff
is gathered around me. But I
couldn't leave without writing to
you, my dearest friend.

I'm calling a cab as soon as I sign
my name here. I'm not sure if there is
enough power left, but I think there
is. (I figure if my smart phone is
dead, then maybe I wasn't supposed
to leave. Our talk about providence
still sticks in my head, you see.)

I really wanted to say good-bye in
person, but I knew if I did, you'd talk
me out of going. I also wanted to tell
your wonderful family thank you, especially your mom, who was like a
second mother to me all these
months. But I couldn't wait till the
dawn, because I would've changed
my mind in a heartbeat. And if I'd
stayed and gone to Preaching today,
well, seeing Sam again would definitely mess with my head. I really
can't go there now, Annie. Maybe
someday I'll explain, if I can.

**Thanks for everything. I mean that.
I wish I might have stayed here in
your paradise longer. Maybe forever.**
With love,
Louisa

Annie couldn't help but lament cell
phones and Palms and fancy whatnots,
wishing they'd never been invented. She
wished Lou were still here, too.

Staring at the letter, Annie noticed the
handwriting looked a bit shaky and wondered if Lou might've been crying.

**She loved being here. And she loves
Sam. . . .**

———

While frying eggs, Mamm shook her
head, saying she could not fathom why on
earth Louisa just upped and left. "Never
even said good-bye."

"She wished she could have thanked the
whole family, but her leaving had nothing to
do with any of us." Annie couldn't say any
more lest she start to cry.

"Well, dear, why don't you think of moving back to your old room?" Mamm suggested.

Annie gathered her composure. "S'pose I could, but maybe I'll just stay put for the time being."

When Daed heard the news, the lines around his mouth showed signs of relaxing. *Obvious relief . . . and no wonder.* But Mammi Zook sighed and patted her chest, her eyes moist.

They all sat down together—Annie, her brothers, Mamm, Daed, and Mammi and Dawdi—terribly conscious of the now-vacant spot where Louisa had always sat.

"That Lou was somethin', jah?" Yonie spoke up at last.

"That's the truth," Annie replied.

"I'll miss her, too," Mamm said.

Daed frowned and cut them off by signaling it was time for the blessing.

They bowed their heads in unison. But instead of offering gratitude to the Lord God heavenly Father for the provision of food, Annie skipped over the rote prayer in her head. This day she was most thankful for Lou's visit—the whole of it—and how an English pen pal had radically changed her life for the better.

———

Preaching service went longer than Annie ever remembered it lasting. During the membership meeting that followed, she sat in the far corner of the kitchen, entertaining Esther's children by tying knots in her linen hankie.

"Where's your friend?" Laura asked, her arms folded across her chest like she was a miniature lady.

"Heading home now, I 'spect." Coming right out with it was far better than fudging. Truth be known, Annie wished Lou hadn't chosen her to deliver the message to Sam. *She might've mailed it to him*, she thought. But if he were observant at all, he would have noticed Lou was missing, for she'd never once skipped a Sunday gathering here.

Annie felt for the sealed envelope deep in her pocket.

"Why'd Louisa leave?" asked Laura.

"Well, she knew she couldn't stay for good."

Laura turned to look out the window. "Too bad, *jah*?"

Annie nodded.

"I liked her a lot. She was nice to me and my brothers . . . and to Molly and James, too."

Annie nodded. "She sure was."

"Will she come see us again?"

"Anything's possible, I guess."

Laura turned away from the window, a big smile on her wee face. "That's what Mamma says a lot. 'All things are possible.'"

A wonderful-good thing.

"Believin' is ever so important," Annie said, starting a game of peekaboo with little John.

"Ach, Mamma says that, too."

When the membership meeting was finished, and the food for the common meal was brought up from the cold cellar, Annie took John, Zach, and Laura back to find Esther, who'd gone for a short walk, as she was not welcome at the meeting. On the way Annie spotted Sam, who looked as dejected as Lou had last night.

When Annie caught Sam's attention, she was glad the Hochstetler children were in tow, or she might have been tempted to stand and chat with him a while, to offer a comforting word or two.

Silently she pulled out the envelope and slipped it into his hand.

"From Louisa?" he asked.

She nodded. Taking the envelope, he walked quickly away.

———

Annie was glad Mamm was so willing to go visiting during the next few weeks. Nearly every day they dropped in on either Sarah Mae, Martha, Priscilla, or other womenfolk.

The house seemed topsy-turvy without Louisa in it, and even Dawdi agreed with Mammi when she said how much she missed Louisa spending time with her in the evenings, doing their needlework by the fire. "She was starting to understand some Dutch, too," Mammi said, shaking her head sadly.

One morning, while enjoying chamomile tea and cinnamon rolls at Martha's, Annie heard the happy news that her sister-in-law was expecting again. "The more babies in the family, the more fun we'll have, ain't?" Annie said, wishing Lou might be on hand to celebrate.

All the crocheting of booties and blankets ahead!

When not going visiting, Annie counted hay bales with Yonie. There was also some talk that Daed and Luke were planning to drive fence posts in the southeast pasture.

And Omar mentioned some of the loggers were eyeing the woods up yonder.

Winter's fading, she thought, wishing Louisa were here to see the pussy willow buds soon to appear.

With the warmer days came the anticipation of Good Friday's fast day. The membership would contemplate the Ordnung prayerfully, and, if all were in one accord, they would rejoice by taking communion as a group, followed by their twice-yearly foot washing. Shortly after that would come the start of baptismal instruction. Annie found herself looking often at the calendar, counting the days till she and the other applicants would meet with the ministers. She knew she had to be certain of her resolve before making the commitment to study, a thought which kept her awake at night.

She and Ben were still seeing each other every week, and as wonderful as it was spending time together, she also worried she was replacing one vice for another—trading her art for her forbidden beau. She knew she must decide to join church. Or, better yet, as Julia often said, seek to know the will and purpose of God.

Truth was, she had a hard time thinking the Lord could be bothered with what she did or didn't do. *With so many folk in the world, with oodles of needs, why on earth would He care one way or the other?*

Esther continued to grasp hold of hope, but what was happening between her and Zeke had nothing to do with goodness or godliness. She made tiny dots on the calendar for each time her husband dishonored her shunning, not for the purpose of reporting him, but for her own sake—if she should become pregnant again. And what a revelation to the brethren that would be!

She'd known of spouses who did not heed the Bann, disobeying the ministers; they soon ended up shunned themselves. Gently she reminded Zeke of this, yet it was impossible to thwart him. A pattern had been set, and she was helpless to stop it. But she would not allow her interrupted sleep or any of his violent outbursts during the day to rob her of the peace she carried silently within. Her greatest joy came both from the Lord and her children, in that order.

The days marched swiftly into April, and

Esther realized she had not visited her mother for quite some time. Eager to get out of the house, and missing her talks with Julia, she bundled up the baby and the boys, while Laura was at school, and took the team several miles up the road.

When she arrived at her brother's place and the small Dawdi Haus built for her mother, Esther was met with an unexpected reaction. Mamma scarcely looked at her and would not invite them in, though she eyed Essie Ann, whose bright little eyes blinked up at her grandmother. "Are ya busy, then?" Esther managed to ask, her heart heavy.

"Well, jah . . . I am."

Esther looked down at Zach and John, both shivering a bit. "I s'pose we could come another time."

Her mother stood as rigid and silent as the glass figurines Esther had seen in Julia's curio cabinet. They caught each other's gaze, and slowly but surely Esther came to understand the full meaning of rejection as she waited on the back stoop.

The shun . . .

But something powerful, even bold, rose

up in her. "The children are awful cold," she whispered, leaning forward. "Mayn't *they* come in?"

Tears sprang into Mamma's eyes, and she opened the door wider. "Hullo, Zach . . . John," she said, not bending down to kiss them. She rather ignored Essie Ann, and for this Esther felt even stronger pangs of sadness.

This isn't about the children. She must not treat them so!

As she watched her children standing in Mamma's small front room with their wraps still on, Esther realized suddenly that the social avoidance meant for her would take its toll on her offspring. This made her feel even more isolated in the face of Zeke's mistreatment of her and their little ones.

"Come, play with the blocks," her mother said, placing a large box on the floor near the small cookstove.

The boys hurried to begin their play, coats still buttoned up. Eventually Zach shed his, but it lay on the floor where he left it. Never before would Mamma have allowed that. She would have asked her grandson to hand it up to her, lest she hurt her bad back bending low. And when tiny Essie Ann became fussy, Mamma did not offer to take her and walk about the room, whispering softly in Dutch, as she had done countless times with her other grandchildren.

Esther had heard of staunch folk who insisted on placing the infant of a shunned church member on a table or other surface before the baby could be passed to another's arms, but she had not expected such from her mother.

She was surprised when, after a time, Mamma offered some hot tea. Eager for something warm, Esther asked if she could help. But she was denied that, being told to sit and wait till the teakettle whistled.

"Ach, Mamma, this is silly."

"No . . . no, the wisdom of the ages, Esther," her mother said with a severe look. "Our church leaders are to be honored."

"Above one's own flesh and blood?" Esther asked, though the answer was within her.

"The brethren are ordained of the most high God," Mamma said. "Always remember this, truly."

Is this what I must endure for all my days?

———

Leaning forward in the carriage, Jesse made his way to Al Fisher's farm. Al, who had never known of the alarming discovery on his land, needed help seeding his oats crop, and a few of the neighboring men had volunteered to put in a half day over there, after finishing up their own chores.

Barbara had asked, sweetly as always, if Jesse would be home for supper, and he had smiled and said he would. Her chicken and homemade dumplings were the best, by far, of any he had ever eaten. A big incentive . . . that, and her sweet kisses, still offered after all these years.

Jesse let his mind wander to Annie's English friend, who had surprised all of them by disappearing in the night. He realized anew how fond Barbara had been of Louisa, and it annoyed him.

Long past time for her to head on home, he decided. *Besides, Annie will soon meet with the brethren about her baptism.*

He would've patted himself on the back if he weren't out here on the road.

"Annie's goin' to make it to her kneelin' vow, sure looks like," he mumbled, enjoying the ride alone while counting his blessings. It seemed like Preacher Moses had known what he was talking about, as always.

Louisa was a godsend, after all.

He contemplated Annie's recent attitude, which seemed to have improved some since Louisa's exit back into the modern world. Barbara suggested with a smile that maybe their Annie had herself a new beau. They both had heard the soft thump of footsteps on the stairs after midnight, though Annie had not stayed out till the dawn with this new fellow, like she had with Rudy Esh, which made Jesse wonder. And none of the fathers were whispering that one of their own was seeing the preacher's daughter.

Whoever it is, he's surely keeping tight-lipped on it.

He almost chuckled at the enduring spunk of his daughter.

Chapter 25

Louisa had hardly recognized her mother upon first arriving home. *She's had a face lift or something drastic. Trying to look twenty-one again?*

But Louisa hadn't said a word, trying to ease herself back into the lives of her stiff and cautious parents. They seemed to walk on eggshells with her, too. Neither her dad nor her mother asked even once about her decision to return, which was a relief, because all Louisa could think about was Sam . . . and Annie. *Paradise.*

Settled once again in her apartment, she wished she might have waited at least until the morning—perhaps after breakfast that final Sunday—to announce her leaving. She had wanted to give Barbara Zook a hug, maybe even a little kiss on her rosy cheeks for being a stand-in mom. But she'd observed how physically reserved the Amish women were upon greeting or saying good-bye. They scarcely ever touched, but their generous spirits were like a bighearted embrace.

Easter dinner at her parents' was an all-out gala, festive in every way, with Daddy's favorite traditional roast lamb dinner, all five courses perfectly paired with five wine options. The entire time she sat at the elegant table Louisa thought of Amish country, wondering what foods Annie and her family were enjoying. Had they left a vacant seat for her, where she'd always sat at the long table? What funny antic had Yonie pulled? In her mind she could see Jesse Zook bow his head, offering thanks, which was the farthest thing from anyone's mind here at *this* table.

Relatives from out of state, as well as local friends, came for the afternoon. Mother was literally shimmering in her new orchid cocktail dress ... and triumphant smile. She had purchased a new set of fine china just for the occasion. All the expensive niceties of her parents' life did not bother Louisa as before, and she recognized what had made the difference.

"People are anxious to see you, dear," Mother had informed Louisa prior to the grand meal, as if to say: You've been out of your mind long enough. . . .

In some ways Louisa realized she *had* lost it, but certainly not mentally. She had lost something of herself, sure ... but she hadn't lost her way. She had found a new approach to living, coupled with the abandonment of self. Everything within her cried out to utilize what she'd learned here and now, in part through a strange yearning to extend herself to her domineering mother. This awareness alarmed her at first, so strikingly different it was from the old way of managing their relationship, but she no longer minded if her mom called the shots. As long as it didn't step on anyone's toes, who cared? She was suddenly seeing the world through her parents' eyes—the need to hold on to a daughter, their one and only child—whom they loved and had been deprived of having around for nearly five months. They had genuinely missed her.

And Louisa had missed them.

Soon, though, she wanted to begin sending letters to Pennsylvania—a long one to Annie and one to Mammi Zook, maybe with a few Dutch words included just for fun. And, sometime later, when she truly knew how to express what was most important, she would write to Sam again.

Back in the full swing of teaching her art students, she was already planning the next exhibit. It wasn't as if she had given up too much back in Lancaster. She had called Janet Blake on her cell to apologize for any inconveniences her leaving had caused the museum. She had merely traded one locale for another. Paradise for Denver. The People for the modern rat race.

With all of her heart, she hoped Sam— most of all—would forgive her. If only he could know how his love had given her a fresh perspective on nearly everything. She hoped something of her fondness for him had opened a door on his future, as well.

I won't forget you, Sam, she often

thought while driving to and from her art studio, her heart full with the memory of him.

I won't. . . .

The afternoon sun twinkled through new green needles on the tall white pine tree as Annie happily settled herself into Ben's car, more excited than she wished to let on. *A play based on Christ's final days on earth . . . on an enormous stage, and set to music!*

She had already shared her disappointment with Ben over Lou's leaving. So she decided not to mention it again, at least not during *this* special day.

"Your hair's different," Ben said, winking at her. "I like it."

She couldn't help but smile. She had pinned it up just long enough to get out of the house. Then, on the walk to meet Ben she'd removed her bonnet and let her hair down, clipping the side back with Lou's gold barrette. "If you think this is different, wait till you see my English clothes." Her long black coat covered up the skirt and blouse Lou had so kindly left for her.

"I'm sure they're lovely." He looked at

her. "Just like you, Annie. You're always my beautiful girl. . . ."

My girl.

"Maybe I'd better show you now, so you're not too awful embarrassed . . . later on at the theater, I mean." The car was plenty warm enough. Still she was glad for the blouse's long sleeves, sheer though they were. Her fingers found the top coat button.

She wondered if he would be surprised at the length of this skirt, only two inches below her knees. *Not that an Englischer should mind. . . .*

Slipping her heavy coat off her shoulders a bit, she said, "What do you think?"

The car swerved ever so slightly. "You look . . . very pretty."

She felt she ought to tell him "thank you," but she didn't. She was almost scared he might prefer such fancy clothes to what she usually wore.

"Did you buy this just for tonight?"

She explained that Lou had purchased the clothes when Courtney was visiting but had graciously left them for her.

He reached for her hand and she thrilled

to his touch, glancing down at their en-
twined fingers.

Then, while still holding her hand, he
lifted it to his face and kissed it. The sweet
sensation lingered all during the ride down
Route 30, to the turnoff toward Strasburg.
Secretly she was glad she hadn't worn
gloves.

The grand well-lit entrance to the Sight
and Sound Millennium Theatre appeared on
the right, and he released her hand before
making the turn. Reaching into his jacket,
he pulled out two tickets.

"Julia said it was awful hard to get a
reservation," she said, eyeing them.

"The guy at the box office said they're
usually sold out weeks, even months ahead.
Of course, this presentation only runs another week."

"Oh, I can hardly wait." She felt giddy.

Ben agreed, breaking into a grin. "It's an
enormous tourist draw—busloads come
from all different states, even from other
countries." He pointed toward several large
buses in the vast parking lot. "From what I
hear, it's one of the biggest local attractions,
next to the Amish themselves."

There was an awkward pause.

"Uh . . . I hope that didn't come out wrong," he said.

"'Course not. We both know how interested outsiders are."

They both had a good laugh over his blunder, and he seemed relieved.

He pulled into a parking spot far from the main entrance and turned to face her, his eyes shining. "About what you said earlier. I want you to know I would never, ever be embarrassed of you. Please remember that."

"All right," she replied and was not startled when he leaned forward to kiss her cheek.

Still, she wondered what he would think when he saw her wearing fashionable suede boots and this relatively short skirt. Her thoroughly English appearance would be revealed when she removed her coat in the bright theater lobby.

Slowly, happily, they made their way to the enormous theater, hand in hand.

Ben had trouble keeping his eyes off Annie as they mingled with the intermission crowd in the vast theater lobby. She had seemed struck by the drama and music as well as the colorful costumes. Having observed Annie's nearly childlike wonderment, her face alight, he wanted to open even more experiential doors for her.

When the lights blinked off and on to alert the attendees to find their seats, he reached for her hand. "Ready for the grand finale?"

"This is just so surprisingly real, ain't so? It makes the Bible characters seem like they're livin' right there on the stage . . . the Last Supper, the Lord's death . . . all of it."

Christ . . . beloved and betrayed. He couldn't stop thinking about the theme of the play. The music, the words—it was as if he had never heard this ancient story told quite so effectively. He had attended many movies and dinner theaters, but he agreed with Annie that this production was presented on a magnificent scale. He felt he was almost witnessing the show through Annie's eyes, which made it all the more memorable.

Taking their seats again, he wondered how he could ever ask her to leave the Plain community, if that time should ever come. *If* was the operative thought. Such a thing smacked of pure selfishness. He would be upsetting the apple cart in more than one way, and wasn't it presumptuous of him to think he could threaten the stability of Annie's church district? Of course, her father's church wasn't really Annie's yet in the truest sense. Still, he wondered how Annie and he could ever really be together.

He looked at her, smiling as they waited for the next act to begin. He had been more than surprised by her long hair, now parted on the side, a pretty gold barrette securing its shimmering golden thickness. She looked totally different without the white head covering he'd come to expect.

He hadn't asked her to dress differently for tonight. *Did she do this for me? And if so, why?*

She must have wanted to blend in with the thousands of people in the audience, but he'd had no intention of putting such expectations on her. With or without her prayer cap, she was exceptionally lovely.

Too warm for his sports coat, he removed it, placing it behind him on the seat. Settling back, he ran his fingers up and down his suspenders, wondering what Annie would think of these, his most recent purchase. Funny, he'd worn something Plain for the occasion, hoping to please her, and here she was sitting next to him dressed in contemporary clothes.

Annie leaned toward him. "Your suspenders . . . they look like Yonie's," she said softly.

"You like?"

"Every male I know wears them." Her eyes twinkled.

He reached for her hand. "You don't mind, do you?"

She glanced down. "You mean . . . ?"

"No . . . the suspenders."

" 'Course not." She smiled. "You do look a bit Amish, though."

He squeezed her hand, eager to watch the second half as the wide stage curtains whisked open.

How can I continue seeing her and not endanger her good standing in her community? he wondered as the house lights dimmed. He certainly did not want to appear reckless by anyone who might discover their secret. Yet reckless he was.

Chapter 26

The sky was still bright as they drove toward Route 340. Ben asked if she wanted to stop for dinner, and Annie liked the idea. Together they decided on the Family Cupboard restaurant and buffet. *Maybe I'll blend in there . . . not be so recognizable in my fancy clothes,* she thought.

She could not stop thinking about the grandeur of the biblical drama and neither, it seemed, could Ben. They talked about the healings and miracles Christ had performed while on earth. And Judas' betrayal of his Master—what had pushed him over the edge, so to speak? Was it truly Satan entering into his thinking, controlling Judas' actions?

By the time they had finished their salads and were ready to go through the buffet line for the main course, Annie had Zeke and Esther on her mind. The children, too. "Have you seen Zeke lately?" she asked.

"He comes around now and then," Ben replied.

She paused, wondering how much to say. "I go 'n' see Essie every chance I can," Annie said, but she then quickly covered her mouth. "Ach, I shouldn't be admitting it . . . well, 'tis all right for you to know, Ben. She's under the shun, ya know. So I must limit my visits. But . . ." Her lower lip trembled. "It's hard to see her treated so."

Ben reached for her hand. "I think she's a wonderful person."

Annie nodded, unable to respond.

"Friendship . . . and family, don't they count for anything?" he said.

Annie forced a smile. "Some folk observe the Bann to the hilt; others just do their best to try 'n' stay involved quietly. I, for one, might not follow the rules so well."

"When it comes to Esther, you mean?"

She nodded. " 'Tis a knotty problem for the brethren. For all of us, really."

"Once you told me there were devils and angels in those beards. Did you mean this sort of thing?" he asked quietly.

"Jah. Heart-wrenching, it is." She sighed, but she wouldn't allow the Hochstetlers' issues to spoil the happiness she'd experienced with her dear beau today. And beau he surely was, although they had never discussed the subject, nor the decisions to be made for the future.

For the time being, she was content to secretly meet him. There was no doubt in her mind he was fond of her . . . and she knew precisely how she felt in her heart toward him.

We mustn't let our feelings rule, Annie thought.

Even with baptismal classes soon approaching, she dismissed her quandary, having allowed her relationship with Ben to progress this far. *Guess I'm not much for planning ahead,* she thought, justifying wavering between what she *should* do and the joyful time spent with Ben.

Back in the car, she turned the conversation to commonplace things such as spring plowing and planting—how hard at work she and her brothers would be. From time to time Ben glanced at her in the passenger seat. His gaze seemed to question her comments, as if to say, *Do you mean you'll be too busy for me?*

She couldn't be sure on that, of course, and she had no way of knowing what was to become of their rapidly growing closeness, truly.

As they took the long drive home, Annie stared at Ben's car radio. Soon she would hold back no longer and asked if she might press the seek button. Ben smiled and encouraged her to find whatever music she liked. She was surprised to recognize the song on the first station she found.

"I think Julia listens to this station," she said. "But I can't be sure."

"Ask her next time you see her."

She smiled. Ben had no urgency in his approach to life. He seemed to take things as they came, she realized, as they waited for several cars to cross at a stop sign farther up on Harvest Drive.

But as they did, she noticed a horse and buggy on the shoulder of the road, right where they planned to turn. "Ach, lookee there," she said. "It's my father . . . broken down on the road."

"How can you tell?"

"By the horse . . . it's definitely ours."

They shared a knowing and tender look of momentary indecision, although Annie knew immediately, yet painfully, what they surely must do. Ben seemed to have arrived at the same conclusion, for he made the turn and pulled in slowly behind the parked carriage.

Ben told her to stay in the car, and he jumped out to see what he could do to help. Fiddling with her hands, Annie knew too well what would happen if her father needed a ride home. She wished she might slip out and hide in the trunk, along with her ice skates.

"Puh! I'm to be found out," she muttered, her heart racing with worry. She thought of winding up her hair right quick and finding her bonnet, and she was looking for it even as Ben came walking toward the car . . . with Daed.

Oh, I'm a cooked goose! She put her head down quickly, hoping he might not recognize her. The way she was dressed—

with her hair down—was a true disgrace to God and the People.

"Mighty kind of you," her father was saying to Ben as he got in the seat directly behind her. "I'll give ya money for gas and your time, too. Oh, looks like I'm interrupting somethin'. . . ."

Ben promptly declined any need for payment as her father had offered, and the two of them talked a blue streak, mostly about the Rawlinsville Fire Company mud sale coming up.

Maybe, just maybe, he won't recognize me, Annie hoped, holding her breath nearly all the way home.

As they drove along, Daed indicated he was looking into buying another mule since one of his was ailing and old. Evidently Ben was on chummy enough terms to engage Daed in a lighthearted manner, and she was rather surprised at the camaraderie between them.

How did this happen . . . when?

For fun, she let her mind wander. What if she and Ben were husband and wife? What a right fine relationship Ben and her father would enjoy, without any of the *Schtreit—*

strife—that was common between some fathers and their sons-in-law.

Imagining Ben dressed as an Amish farmer was not at all hard. A light brown beard, with golden strands that matched his hair, and soft to the touch. Jah, he would fit in right quick. Their baby boys would be as handsome and strong as Ben himself, and oh, their little girls. . . .

She was startled from her musing by Ben looking over at her. She had not been fidgeting, she didn't think. But here they were, where Queen Road became Frogtown Road, and Ben's confident glance said volumes: *Trust me, Annie, this will turn out all right*.

She shuddered at the prospects of being found out—face-to-face with her furious preacher-father. She had folded her hands in her lap so tightly her fingers ached.

Not until Daed climbed out of the backseat and closed the car door, waving his thanks to them, did she begin to relax.

Neither she nor Ben said a word as he backed up and turned onto the main road again, creeping forward toward their usual parting place.

When he pulled over and stopped, she let out a loud sigh. "Ach, Ben, I was beside myself."

He grinned. "No, you were right here, Annie." He reached for her hand. "With me."

Then suddenly she realized she could not simply march back into the house anytime soon, not dressed the way she was. She could put her hair into a bun, if need be, and pull on the outer bonnet, too. But going inside on the heels of her father's return home was too risky. He might put two and two together. "Oh, Ben. What a terrible close call!"

They began to laugh—nearly giggles from her—and he nuzzled her cheek. "What a wonderful-good day, Annie," he said.

"I can hardly believe my father didn't know it was me right here in the front seat."

"Saved by your new look . . . and Lou's clothes," Ben said, obviously relieved.

She was pleasingly aware of him. His eyes, his dear, dear face . . . his mouth. He reached for her hand, eyes searching hers.

No, no . . . say something—anything!

Oh, how she wanted to feel snug in his strong arms tonight, but the lovely thrill might lead them to hug and kiss. Rudy's affectionate courting had taught her that. Yet they had remained pure, which was her truest hope now, too. Besides, one lingering kiss, coupled with all the wonderful things she knew and loved about Ben, and she might not be able to put the nix on their relationship as she must. She might end up going away with this handsome man, leaving the People, and breaking her parents' hearts.

No, impossible, she thought, leaning away from him, against the door. *I could never do that.*

"I guess you're stuck with me for a while—at least long enough for your father to get some help with his broken-down buggy and turn in for the night," Ben said. "Unless you want to try to slip into the house in a few minutes."

He had a good point. "No, for the sake of not getting caught, I best wait a bit."

"Well, what would you like to do?" he asked.

"Let's go walkin' somewhere."

"We could drive over to Park City Center . . . have ice cream, ride the carousel. How's that sound?"

"I like your idea, Ben."

"I like *you,* Annie." The echo of his words and the emotion behind them was quickly imprinted on her heart.

Chapter 27

Annie was almost grateful for the unexpected turn of events, happening upon Daed as she and Ben had earlier, because Ben treated her to a most exciting evening. She noticed only a handful of Mennonite women the entire time they walked the corridors of the pretty mall.

Later, when it was time to return home, Ben waited till there was not a single light flickering from her father's house before turning off the car's headlights and creeping halfway up the drive. Then he caught her off guard and gently reached for her hand.

After his tender good-bye kiss, she pulled

her hairpins out of her pocket and began to pin up her long locks. "I had such a good time," she said. Quickly she opened the glove compartment and found her black bonnet.

"Ever ride on a carousel before?" he asked.

"Never, but it was wonderful, I must say."

"We can do it again." His eyes were drawing her back to his arms.

"Jah, that'd be right nice sometime," she said, resisting her feelings. "Well, I'd better go in." She offered a smile, then opened the door and stepped out of the car. "Good night, Ben."

Heart pounding now, she hoped against hope her parents were soundly asleep. She made her way around to the back of the house, heading quickly for the kitchen door of the Dawdi Haus. She let herself in and inched her way through the kitchen silently, then to the stairs.

If I can just make it to my room without anything creaking. She held her breath and removed Lou's fancy boots. Cautiously she tiptoed up the steps.

She might've missed him altogether had

she not glanced toward the small sitting area between her room and Dawdi and Mammi's. A rustle in the darkness—not a sound, but a feeling. Someone was definitely sitting near the window.

"Annie . . ."

Her heart caught in her throat. She was less than a yard from her own room. Pulling her long coat closed, she wished to hide the suede boots in her hand . . . her feet and legs nearly bare in Lou's flesh-colored hosiery.

Dare she dart into her room, close the door, simply refuse to talk?

Daed must not see me this way. . . .

"Annie," her father said again stiffly. "You will begin your baptismal instruction, as planned." Then a glimmer of light from a match as he lit a lantern.

The single beam revealed her treachery. *If only I'd worn my dark stockings. . . .*

But there was something terribly amiss. Why was he waiting for her?

"Come here to me, daughter."

Now she could see him, sitting tall in the old cane chair, a quilt folded on the slats behind him. He was fully dressed, and, no doubt, put out at having to wait up for so long. An early riser, he preferred to go to bed not long after sundown most evenings.

She made her feet move forward, holding the beautiful boots behind her back, ever so glad for her long coat, though it was not fully buttoned.

"I saw you today . . . with Ben Martin."

"When?" she asked, feeling stupid.

He rose suddenly. "Do not continue your pretense!" His voice boomed over her, filling the room. "And without your Kapp yet . . . your hair down—a disgrace! If it's not one thing with you, it's another."

She froze in place, biting her lip.

"I order you never to see the Englischer again!" With that he picked up the lantern and carried it out of the room. Down the stairs he went, with no effort to restrain his footsteps.

Never see Ben?

She breathed in and held it, till her lungs nearly gave out. She remained standing there with locked knees in the blackened room, aware of Mammi Zook's muttering to Dawdi in the next room now, asking him in Dutch, "What the world is goin' on?"

Quickly, lest she encounter yet another

fuming relative, she dashed into her room and closed the door.

———

Too ill and forlorn to attend Preaching service, Annie stayed in bed, covers piled over her head, lifting them every so often to breathe a bit before relishing the darkness beneath yet again.

She did not care to see the light of the day, nor did she wish to eat breakfast with the family. Her barn chores could be done by one of her brothers. Or Daed, for that matter. If he was going to cut her off from Ben, then she would simply lie here till it was time for them to come and bury her. That's how she felt, but she knew, eventually, she would get up, wash, and dress. But not for the Lord's day, and not for any particular reason except to be up and combed and wearing her clothes. Plain once again.

She waited till the house was hushed and drained of people to make a hasty search for any stray brothers. Then she returned to the Dawdi Haus, to Mammi's little gas-run refrigerator. Hungry in spite of her grief, she made two pieces of toast and a cup of hot tea.

Sitting at her grandparents' small table, she realized not a soul had come to either check on or inquire of her. *Well, maybe they had.* Hiding beneath the covers had worked, apparently. Or had Daed already told them what she had done? And now she was alone with the place to herself till mid-afternoon, when they'd all return for milking.

She recalled Ben's wonderful smile and the adoring way he looked at her, his consideration in helping her into the car and the careful way he drove. She felt so protected with him. She could still feel the press of his lips on hers, the tickle in her stomach even now at the thought of being nestled in his warm embrace. *Is this love . . . when you long to be with someone beyond any good sense?*

"Oh, Ben . . . I already miss you," she whispered into her warm tea.

She finished eating, then cleared off the table. She quickly washed and dried her plate and utensils, few as there were, and put them away for Mammi Zook.

Then she went to her room again, found some stationery, and curled up in bed. "This is for you, Daed," she muttered angrily. "And for all the People."

She began to write her farewell letter.

Dear Ben,

I will make this short, since it is a waste of time and paper to write something that doesn't make sense to me. Yet I should've seen this coming. (How could I have expected anything different?)

My father did recognize me with you yesterday and has demanded that I not see you ever again. It pains me so. I never wanted to think this day would come. Truly, I didn't! I wanted only to think of you . . . of us.

So long, Ben. It seems impossible to say good-bye. Yet for the sake of my family . . . and my future . . . I know I must.

Yours,
Annie Zook

Ben was overjoyed to receive his mom's phone call the following Tuesday, saying she'd located his birth certificate. "Here it is," she said into the phone. "Benjamin David Martin . . ."

"That's great, Mom. Send it by overnight mail."

"Well, it would be nice if you came home," his mother said. "You could pick it up then."

"Sure, I'd love to come home—for a visit. But I'm not sure when that'll be. So just pop it in the mail . . . I still need it to get a Pennsylvania driver's license. Then I can finally open a checking account here, get a bit more established." He didn't know why it pleased him, this phone call from home.

My birth certificate, at long last . . .

After he hung up, he wandered outside to pick up his mail. The day was warm, and the faint scent of spring wafted on the breeze.

He did not recognize the handwriting on the single letter mixed in with the usual junk mail. He was tired, having stayed up late both Saturday night, after dropping Annie off, and then again last evening, burning the midnight oil online with his sister, Patrice.

Then he'd stared into the darkness, lying awake and weighing plans, ways to attempt, at least, to make things work with Annie and her family, unable as he was to discard his deep affection for her.

When it came down to reality versus hope, he guessed he was on the losing side. To be audacious enough to think Annie would leave behind all that she knew, and seemingly enjoyed, to be with him? He assumed he was treading on very thin ice.

But our love . . . it's real. We can make it work.

He grabbed the remote and switched to Fox News, ready to catch up on the world. He had begun to feel incredibly isolated here. At times he loved the area—particularly when with Annie—yet at others he barely tolerated its smallness.

Reaching for the letter, he tore it open with his finger, not bothering to use the opener in his desk drawer. He saw his name and began to read the first line, only to scan down to see Annie's signature at the bottom.

No! he groaned inwardly.

He read the entire letter, brief as it was, then pressed it to his forehead.

Impossible to say good-bye. Yet she had written those very words.

Reading it again, he shook his head. Torn and hurt as she obviously was, he would not fight her decision. He'd caused Annie Zook enough trouble.

Standing, he walked to the window and

back, running his hand through his hair. "I'll bow out and give her time—some space—to figure out what she wants."

He could only imagine what was going on at the preacher's house . . . and in dear Annie's heart.

———

The next day, after locking up the tack shop, Ben drove to Irvin's, hoping to catch him before he left to visit a supplier. But upon arriving, Julia said he'd just missed him and invited him in for coffee. "You look pale, Ben. Are you ill?" she asked, treating him like a big sister might.

He assured her he was fine.

"Well, would you like some chicken soup?" She seemed to think food could fix anything.

"No, I really shouldn't stay." But he was already in the door and moving toward the kitchen in a fog. He sensed Julia's ability to calm his nerves, although he was not the sort of person to tell just anyone his problems.

He sat down at her table, and soon James and Molly came to show him a favorite book. When they scampered back to the living room, he said, "I know this may be sudden . . . well, it is." He paused, gathering his wits. "I don't want to spring this on Irvin, but I do need to return home. Very soon." He stopped again, wishing this weren't so difficult. He would miss his work and the good pay. "I need to give my notice today, Julia."

She tilted her head in the usual way, eyes filled with understanding, giving him the benefit of the doubt. Maybe that was why folk liked to be around her. Julia seemed to know how to let you off the hook and wasn't into the control thing like so many women seemed to be.

"Irvin would want to say good-bye and wish you well," she said. "I know I speak for him on this." She took the portable phone out of its cradle and offered it to Ben. "Would you care to tell him yourself? He has his cell phone with him, I believe."

He accepted the portable phone, though he might have used his own cell. There was no turning back. He would exit Annie's life and spare her any further pain. *The best thing for all concerned.*

Irvin answered his call promptly, and Ben felt as though he were going through the motions. Swimming in a haze of lost causes, lost dreams.

Irvin asked him to stay on at the tack shop for at least two weeks, so he would have time to hire someone to take his place. Ben understood and agreed, not wanting to shirk his duty. He was thankful Irvin had given him the excellent job in the first place, entrusting him with a lot of responsibility.

"All right. I'll stay until you find a replacement," Ben agreed.

When he hung up, he accepted a second cup of coffee, glad for the nice distraction of Julia's children. He enjoyed their playful expressions, their need to push their own interests—books, toys—into his lap or onto the table before him.

Julia cooked supper, seeming to take care not to disturb him. Every now and then she reminded the children that "Ben isn't a playmate." He might have been amused were he not so immobile. He felt unable to push through the blur of where he and Annie had been and where they were now. In a short time, they'd gone from enjoying many hours in each other's company to absolutely zero.

Julia asked if he would like to stay for supper, but he declined gratefully. He must figure out how to get out of his lease, if possible. If not, he'd have to make arrangements to sublet.

He remembered his manners. "Is there anything I can help you with before I go?"

"As a matter of fact, there is." Julia said there were a few things Esther Hochstetler had left in the attic room. "Would you mind bringing them downstairs for me?"

"I'll do you one better," he replied. "I'll haul them over to Zeke and Esther."

"Well, I appreciate that," Julia said, returning to the stove. "And I know Esther will be glad for them."

Upstairs in the small room, he stood in the center of the attic space and struggled with his loss of Annie. *Buck up,* he told himself, realizing he would miss not only her, but also Irvin and Julia and their children . . . not to mention the good men coming and going at the harness shop.

I made a foolish mistake, falling in love. . . .

He sat on the only chair in the room, head bowed. After a time, he straightened and noticed a long, rectangular item in the corner, propped up between the wall and the bureau.

Getting up to look, he saw that it was a

frame, tightly wrapped in brown packing paper. The name *Zook* was written in the corner with a felt-tip pen. Curiosity tugged at him, and he found himself opening a loose corner. He peered inside, intrigued to see part of a painting. He knew he was snooping, yet he removed the small strip of tape and saved it, then carefully unwrapped the entire large piece.

He stared at the painting inside—a haunting, yet remarkable rendering of the covered bridge on Belmont Road . . . the cluster of trees, and the stream below. "This is the very image. . . ." He could not believe how perfect a likeness the artist had created as he scrutinized the beauty of brush stroke on canvas. *Unbelievable!*

Opening his wallet, he extracted the folded copy he'd carried since Christmas. Smoothing it out, he studied it closely. "They're identical," he murmured.

Wondering who the artist was, he searched for a signature in the bottom right-hand corner. Finding it, his mouth dropped open. He ran his hand through his hair. "Annie Zook . . . you do have your secrets."

No wonder her eyes saw all things beautiful.

"She's really good," he said, wondering why Annie had never told him of her talent.

Wanting to stare longer at the superb work, yet knowing Julia might wonder what was keeping him, he began to wrap the paper around the frame again, even placing the tape exactly where it had been before.

Satisfied the painting was positioned just as he'd first found it, he stepped back and shook his head. "No wonder . . ." He turned to look out the window, at the fading sky. "Annie, it was *you*. You brought me here."

Chapter 28

Soon after morning milking, but before breakfast was served, Esther went to check on Essie Ann, down the hall in her crib, when she thought she heard weeping. But how could that be? Laura was out feeding the pigs just now, while Zach watched over John in the kitchen, the two playing quietly together. Not another soul was in the house, except for her sleeping baby.

Or so she thought.

The nearly eerie sound continued and she felt compelled to go and stand by Zeke's bedroom, the door slightly ajar. Inside, Zeke was muttering and whining to

himself like a child fussing over having been
harshly disciplined.

Well, for goodness' sake, she thought,
wondering what was troubling him.

Listening in on the peculiar exchange—in
essence, what it was—Esther was stunned.
Zeke was saying he most certainly de-
served to be shunned now, just as his wife
was. "If the men of God knew my sins, they
wouldn't think twice on it." Here he
stopped, and a kind of sad and despairing
wail poured out of him. "I know now what
happened. . . ."

She swallowed hard, and it was all she
could do to stand still and not let her feet
take her right in there, right now, and comfort the poor man.

Zeke continued his odd dialog, switching
to take the side of one of the preachers.
"What do you have to say for yourself,
Ezekiel? You pray more . . . nothin'
changes. You can't keep strikin' Esther, frail
thing."

Zeke moaned again. "It's rippin' out my
insides . . . who I am. Who I've always
been . . ." He paused. "Nothin's as it seems.
Nothin' at all."

Trembling, she moved closer to the door

and peeked through the sliver of an opening. There Zeke sat, on the bed they had always shared before her shunning, rocking back and forth, his big hands covering his face and part of his beard. "With pride comes shame," he said. "Ach, one wretched sin begets another and another. Ain't so, Lord God?"

Esther hadn't the slightest notion what he meant, and she inched back, afraid. She took in a slow, long breath. *O Lord in heaven, help us!*

Zeke had been strangely quiet the past few weeks, so Jesse thought it might do them both good to stand out in the barn and talk, now that spring was in the air.

Too early for straw hats yet. However he had seen a horde of bees droning over some dried-out wood at the neighbors' yesterday. Birds, including a few barn swallows, were back in the neighborhood, starting with the first robins two weeks ago, and the finches just today.

But it was the stubborn way the new grass had begun to shove its way up through old thatch that told him warmer weather was near.

He clicked his cheek as Betsy trotted down Belmont Road, heading north. His noontime dinner of fried chicken sat heavy on his stomach as he made his way to Hochstetlers'.

He wondered how Zeke was getting along with his headstrong woman. He figured it wouldn't be much longer and Esther would give in to the demands of the Ordnung. Whatever had gotten into her recently was clearly dangerous.

He turned his thinking now to the task that lay before him, feeling mighty responsible, considering his big push to return Esther to Zeke's precarious nest.

Zeke stared at the neighbors' barn telephone, clutching it till his knuckles turned white. He'd run all the way here, compelled by an urgency that had been mounting all day. Slowly he lifted the receiver to his ear and dialed 911.

A woman's voice came on the line, and he said right quick, "Send the police to my house at once."

"Please state your name, address, and phone number for verification, sir."

He managed to eke out the requested information, having to peer at the number printed on the telephone.

"What is the nature of your emergency?"

He began to weep. "My brother . . . Isaac Hochstetler is dead. He's . . . dead, and too young to die." He choked back heaving sobs.

The woman attempted to calm him, or at least he thought that was why she spoke in such measured tones. But he was beside himself. "So you best be gettin' the police out here, and quick."

"How did Isaac die?" came the dreaded question.

He stammered a bit, then inhaled sharply, dropping the phone and letting it dangle and sway on its cord. Wiping his face with his paisley blue handkerchief, he stumbled back up the road to his house.

Jesse spotted fresh tire tracks in a stubble-filled cornfield to the east. Curious, he followed the tracks with his eyes, craning his neck as the horse pulled the carriage past. He had occasionally given some thought to the faster, less strenuous work a tractor could offer. Even if he had the funds for that type of equipment, he couldn't justify entertaining such thoughts for longer than a few seconds, if at all. Truly, being a minister stymied much inventive thought.

For a moment he understood something of Annie's inner struggle, her desire to create. Surely that was inventive as well. He was convinced, however, once she gave her lifetime vow of submission to the church and the Lord God—once she settled into marrying, too—she would forget her foolish penchant for drawing and painting. He could not deny his daughter's *great talent,* as Barbara regarded her ability, but he would not go so far as to agree that Annie had a God-given gift.

Looking at the sky as he neared the Hochstetler farm, Jesse was in tune with the change of season. Winter was beginning to shed her long woolens for the fluttery skirts of spring. He'd thrilled to the softness of the soil in Barbara's garden plot, surprisingly ready to be spaded up and set to hand plowing. He'd even seen two earthworms already hard at work aerating the black soil.

"Gee," he commanded the horse. Zeke's black watchdog wagged his tail near the turn into Hochstetlers' driveway.

Right away Jesse spotted the police car parked near the backyard.

Now what's Zeke gone and done? He clenched his teeth, and his palms broke out in an unexpected sweat.

Debating whether or not he wanted any part in this—*Should I simply turn around and head home?*—Jesse sat there, his brain suddenly clouded. If the bishop had been the one pulling up to Zeke's place just now, this might be a different story.

What happened next made him flinch. Up ahead, coming out of the barn, was Zeke, flanked by two police officers.

"Ach, no . . ." Jesse whispered, dropping the reins.

His mind flew to Esther. Where was she? Had her husband lost all sense of control and blackened her eye this time? Slammed one of the children against a wall? Worse?

Or had Zeke told them what he knew about Isaac's remains?

Jesse climbed out of the carriage, patted his horse's rump, and walked to where the driveway ended and the sidewalk began.

"All right, then," he heard Zeke say, nodding, as he followed the man and woman in uniform to the waiting car. Zeke made eye contact with Jesse but only for a second. Then he bowed his head.

Jesse shuddered, but he removed his hat and approached the police in spite of himself. "I'm Zeke's minister, Preacher Zook," he said. "What's the trouble here?"

The tall, blond officer might have passed for one of the People, with his scruffy start of a beard. "We're taking him in for questioning," the young man replied, glancing over at Zeke, who was now sitting in the backseat of the patrol car.

Jesse scratched his head. "Well, now, you sure this isn't some mistake?" He tried to catch Zeke's eye again. "We Amish aren't at all interested in getting the outside world mixed in with our own. I'm sure you understand."

The policeman nodded. "I've heard as much." He motioned for Jesse to move away from the car with him. Then, standing near the house, he lowered his voice. "Between you and me, I'm not exactly certain what we've got here . . . but I can guarantee one thing: We'll get to the bottom of it."

"I'd be glad to take him off your hands," Jesse said.

"Meaning what?"

"I'll take him on home with me. Keep him away from the family until he cools off. . . ."

The officer looked at him sharply. "Are you implying the man is violent, sir?"

Ach, no. Now what have I said? Jesse hurried to explain. "I'm just tellin' you, I'll be responsible for him. Look after him . . . see what's what." Jesse was much too shaken to convey the sort of confidence the dismal situation required.

"I'm afraid I can't do that. When a man makes a call like Mr. Hochstetler did, my partner and I can't ignore it. He'll most likely be detained a few hours, if he cooperates fully."

Jesse frowned, wondering what Zeke had told them. Jesse knew he best be making another attempt to keep the pot from boiling over. Nothing good could come of hauling Zeke off to the English world. "I'm willin' to come along to town, for that matter, if it would help," he said, not sure what good that would do. But it sounded accommodating, and he was all for that.

"We can handle this." The policeman stepped back. "Now if you'll excuse me . . ."

No, no . . . stop him.

Helpless to do more, Jesse watched as the car pulled forward, turned around, and headed toward the road.

What a pity I didn't arrive sooner.

Suddenly it struck him—Esther might need him.

He hurried around the house and stood at the back door, leaned his forehead against it, aware of his pounding heart. He called out to Esther, "Anybody home?"

"Ach, Preacher Jesse," she said when she came to the door, babe in arms. She lowered her voice to a whisper. "They've taken my husband away."

He followed her into the kitchen, where she laid Essie Ann in her cradle and hurried Zach and John into the front room. "Don't forget your toys," she said softly, although there was an obvious unraveling to her voice. It was clear her emotions were ragged.

"Are you all right, Esther?" He saw no marks on her face, nothing to indicate a scuffle.

"This ain't what you think, Preacher. Zeke took himself down the road to the neighbors and called the police. Oh, I just don't understand."

"What did he tell them?" He led her to the table to sit.

She sighed and rested her head between her hands. After a time, she looked up. "I heard only bits and pieces." She fumbled for a handkerchief in her dress sleeve. "Something about knowing where some-one's bones are buried. I thought he said Isaac's. . . ."

Jesse groaned and stared at the table-cloth. The checked pattern made him dizzy—nauseated.

"What'll happen to him?" she whispered, eyes dull.

Once the world comes rushing in . . .

He'd heard of Plain communities wracked by such things as crime and police involvement. The Mount Hope, Ohio, shoot-ings during the harvest some years back was one case in point.

Quickly now Jesse regained his sense of duty. "I don't know a lot about the English world, Esther, and neither do you. We'll have to do the best we can, that's all." *We'll have to keep our noses clean, too,* he thought, not wanting to be mixed up with whatever things Zeke might say under interrogation.

Zeke knows I buried those bones!

"I'm awfully scared, Preacher. Honest, I am."

Looking at Esther's sorrowful face, he realized, quite unexpectedly, that he was breaking the rules of her shunning.

"I'll see if Barbara might come stay the night," he offered. This poor woman shouldn't be alone after such a day—shunned or not. He could not allow more pain to fill her eyes. "I'll go 'n' fetch her straightaway and return shortly."

"Kind of you" was all Esther said, wringing her hands.

He walked to the back door, and when he turned briefly, he saw that she was still seated like a stone, her eyes fixed in a vacant stare.

———

Later that afternoon, Esther searched outside for Laura, who had taken herself off to the outhouse but not returned in a reasonable amount of time, as Zeke always demanded of them.

When Laura was nowhere to be seen, Esther headed quickly to the barn. There, the late afternoon sun shone through slats in the wall, creating ribbons of light on beds of straw. She found Laura sitting on the edge of one of the hay holes, her little legs dangling through. "What's-a-matter that you're up there all by your lonesome?" she called gently.

"Mighty scared, Mamma."

Esther was glad to have found her. Truth was, Esther was terrified, too. Not for the reason Laura was, probably, but she felt ever so helpless, worried what might become of Zeke.

"I want us to stay with Auntie Julia again," Laura said, her voice muffled.

"Aw, honey-love, I'm right here."

"Still, can't we go back?"

Of course she misses Irvin and Julia, Esther thought sadly. The Rancks' home represented a deep and settled kind of peace for Laura. *For all of us.* Galatians referred to it as "fruit of the Spirit," and Esther longed for such a life. *With Zeke out of the house, perhaps we'll enjoy a few hours of serenity.* Yet she knew she should not relish the thought of Zeke's absence.

"Mamma?" Laura's small voice brought her back.

"Well, darlin', I don't see us goin' much of anywhere," she replied. "There's oodles to do around the house."

And there were the pigs. Zeke's herd required plenty of work, and between herself and what little help Laura could offer, especially now what she was at school most of the day, Esther felt she might have to hire some help. With what money, she didn't know. Either that or register a plea with Preacher Jesse for some assistance from amongst the menfolk. *This is awful bad timing my being shunned and all. What if Zeke is gone for a long while?*

Even her older brother would be reluctant to assist them, and she would definitely need help with the sows pregnant, or "in pig," as Zeke often said.

She assumed her mother would come to check on them—bad news traveled fast—hopefully offering smiles and hugs, at least for the children.

"I have an idea, dear one," she said. "Why don't we ask the Lord Jesus to take care of Dat?"

"Jah, let's." Laura's hair bun was coming

loose as she inched slowly down into the hay hole. "I want to jump," she said.

"Well, I may or may not catch you, depending how you fall," Esther warned her, glad the conversation was changing direction.

"Then I best not try. I wouldn't want to break my leg and be a burden to you." Laura rose quickly and walked to the door leading outside, then came around to return through the lower barn door. "There now. I'm all done bein' gloomy."

"Well, even the dear Lord was *drauerich*—sad." She began to tell Laura the story of Jesus' good friend, Lazarus, who had become sick and died. As they walked to the pigpen, preparing to water and feed the swine, she wished she could hurry through the sorrowful part to the happy ending.

Fact was, Laura would want to know what had happened to her father today. And the schoolyard grapevine might help out with that all too quickly for Esther's liking, although she wouldn't mind knowing something more herself. Whatever came, she'd not soon forget this day and Zeke's absurd muttering in the bedroom. *Oh, Lord Jesus, will you hover ever near?*

Chapter 29

The day after Zeke was taken away by the police, Jesse hurried out the back door at Bishop Andy's and climbed into his carriage. Together the ministers, including the bishop, old Preacher Moses, and the neighboring bishops, had gathered to hash over Zeke's latest attention-getting stunt. The People, as a whole, were sure to get beat up in the media, they feared. Bishop Andy did not berate Jesse for being unable to dissuade the police from taking Zeke into custody, but the disappointment was evident in his aging eyes.

The consensus among the brethren was

to lay low for the time being in the hope the police would soon realize Zeke was not in his right mind. But if the investigation spread to exhuming Isaac's remains and questioning the People . . . none of them had any idea what would happen then. The police had indicated that Zeke would be held only a few hours and released but he had yet to return. So what could have gone awry? Not even Esther had received word.

What's Zeke thinking, calling the police? Jesse wondered.

Back on the road now, the gentle, humdrum sway of the carriage up London Vale Road settled Jesse's frayed nerves, offering a sort of reassurance. A body could rest away the cares of the day, the week, and even longer perched in a horse-drawn carriage, letting the air hit his face. At once he felt sorry for the moderns who rode around in cars, completely enclosed. *'Specially this time of year when the air's fresh as a pasture filled with wild flowers,* he thought. *And Zeke, stuck in a jail, of all things!*

Suddenly he thought of Yonie, riding around in a car like an Englischer. He'd heard of the vehicle for some time but had never laid eyes on it. He hadn't let on just how upset he was, and he would continue to hold his peace. He wished Yonie would grow up and quit dabbling in the world. *Annie, too.*

For the time being, Jesse would turn a blind eye to Yonie's rumschpringe and hope Annie was altogether free of her sinning days. *Not even her mother has noticed any new artwork all these months,* he thought, and was glad of it. And word was, Irvin's tack shop employee had given notice—planned to return to Kentucky here before too long. If not for Annie, Jesse would be sorry to see Ben Martin go. *A right fine and helpful fellow.* Still, better that Ben was out of the picture for good.

Jesse reached into his pocket and pulled out a handful of salted peanuts, enjoying the snack as he headed to the smithy's for a visit. On the ride, he thought again of Barbara's remarks this morning. She had come away from spending the night with Esther and the children worried sick. The way Esther had talked, Julia Ranck might just up and fill the void by taking Esther again under her wing.

Esther's memorizing and poring over Scripture, Barbara told him.

He cringed, staring at the cows leaning their heads out of the fence by the side of the road.

You get one fire put out, and there's always another.

Truth was, he should try and stamp out this salvation message before it spread. And it could. He knew too many bishops who'd lost a good portion of their members to evangelists and Bible thumpers. He mustn't let that happen here.

———

Annie placed the suitcase on her bed and opened the lid. She couldn't believe what Mamm had whispered to her about Zeke last evening before hurrying to spend the night with Esther. *Zeke in jail?* There had to be some mistake. Still, it felt somehow providential that Esther was alone without her husband just now.

Looking up, Annie saw Mamm standing in the doorway. "I need to leave home," she said with as much determination as she could muster.

"Oh, Annie . . . no." Mamm lowered her head.

"I'm a humiliation to my family."

"Haven't we been through this before?" her mother reminded her. She came in and sat on the spare bed that had been Lou's.

No, Annie thought to herself. This time was far different. She was not leaving because of her inability to resist art. She had besmirched herself, abandoning one of their sacred symbols, her head covering, instead of wearing it as the Scriptures instructed. She'd allowed her long hair to go uncovered, revealing it fully to a man who was not her husband.

And never will be.

According to her father, there were more transgressions on the record of Annie's life than she cared to consider.

"I've made up my mind, Mamm. I'm goin' to stay with Esther . . . to help with the pig farm and all."

"Are you sure?"

"Esther can use the help, and Daed can't stand the sight of me."

Mamm didn't contradict her. "Does Esther know you're comin'?"

"Well, no . . . but—"

"Ach, you best be thinkin' this through. She's banned from the fellowship, for pity's sake."

"Well, in many ways, so am I." Annie set about packing her dresses, nightclothes, Kapps, and her small box of straight pins, as well as her best stationery and Lou's letters—all of the things she had brought with her when she and Lou moved over to the Dawdi Haus bedroom last year.

"You know Esther can't care for the children and the farm by herself for long," Annie went on, neatly folding her clothes. "You said you might even try 'n' help her some, Mamm."

"That's different, Annie, and you know it. The brethren will disapprove of you livin' there."

"But I'm not yet a baptized church member."

"And far from it, by the looks of it. Oh, Annie . . ." Her mother rose and hurried from the room, wiping tears away with her apron.

Struggling to keep her emotions in check, Annie braced herself, gritting her teeth. Now wasn't the time to let go, nor was it the place. She'd wept away nearly a week of long nights already. When it was time, weary as she was, she would ask Yonie to drive her up to Esther's. And wouldn't Esther be surprised—ever so happy? The thought gave Annie all the more reason to press onward.

She filled one suitcase and began to pack another. Yonie poked his head in the door and, seeing her there, said, "You're doin' the right thing for yourself. I'd be packin' this minute, too, if I had a place to go."

"Well, if you got yourself a job, you sure could." Her throat tightened. "But is that something a *son* should think 'bout doing?" She hoped he caught her meaning about his being favored and all.

"Aw . . . you're a feisty one."

"I best be leavin', to ponder things." Her breath caught in her throat and she feared she might cry.

"I'll walk up the road a ways . . . get my car for you." He twitched his nose. "Where ya headed? Out to Colorado?"

She hadn't considered that. Louisa needed time to sort out her own problems, so there'd be no going west. "If anyone needs to get in touch with me"—*if anyone cares to,* she thought—"I'll be hangin' with Essie."

He smiled. "You got yourself a good dose of Lou while she was here, ain't?"

"This isn't Lou's doing. I had plenty of gumption before she ever arrived."

Omar appeared in the hallway, poked his brother playfully, and offered to carry her suitcases down. Annie let him, thanking him with a sad smile. Yonie carried her bedding, quilt, and pillow down to the front porch.

Annie took another glance around the room she'd so happily shared with Louisa, then headed downstairs, through the connecting door to the main house and up to her former bedroom. She stood in the doorway eyeing her hope chest with its embroidered doilies and tablecloths. *No need to bring that along, she thought. Will I ever need it?*

Her gaze fell on the little desk her father had made, and she ran her hand lightly over its smooth maple surface. But when the image of her father's angry face flickered painfully across her mind, she raised her hand. She would leave the desk behind as well.

She thought fleetingly of her easel and art supplies, boxed up at Julia's. Perhaps she would ask Yonie to stop there first, before they headed to Esther's. But no, she'd made a promise to her father, and she intended to keep her word on that matter, if nothing else.

Reluctant to leave, she made her way downstairs, passing by Luke as she did. He only shook his head as if she'd done something too terrible to mention.

She headed for the front porch, where her belongings were gathered, assuming Daed was in the barn. But she had no interest in saying good-bye.

Mamm came right out and kept her company, the two of them taking in the springtime landscape of newly planted fields and grazing land. The birds were extra bold and boisterous today.

"Too bad the scarecrow's gone," Annie said softly.

"Jah, 'tis." Mamm reached over and pressed her hand on Annie's. "I'll miss you somethin' awful, dear."

"We'll see each other. I'm not shunned—or am I?"

"Knowin' your father . . . you'll be as good as."

The words struck a blow. "Why's that?"

"You're the preacher's daughter, Annie. Never forget." Mamm rose and walked the length of the porch, then turned, and came back. "When . . . *if* you ever return, it'll have to be on Daed's terms."

No fooling. They both knew where the brethren stood on such things as creating fine art . . . and there was no tolerance for a courtship with an Englischer either.

She sighed, watching Yonie run up the road, heading for the spot where Ben had always parked . . . where he had waited for her with such delight on his face.

"I guess this is so long for now." She looked at Mamm.

"But not forever, I hope," her mother said, coming to stand near. "I'll not be visitin' at Esther's so much, you must understand."

Annie looked up, taking her hand. "But you'll stop by now and then?"

Mamm sighed. "We'll see. . . ." Her mother's hand went still in her own. "Annie, your father showed me a magazine . . . the perty painting you did."

Annie swallowed, dreading the rebuke that was sure to come.

"'Tween you and me . . ." Mamm paused, wiping away tears. "Ach, I best be still."

"That's all right, you say what you want."

"Truth be told . . . I believe you've got yourself a gift from above. I told your father so."

Annie nodded, grateful for her mother's words, meager consolation that they were.

They both fell silent, until Yonie's shimmering silver car pulled into the drive.

"What on earth?" Mamm muttered, appalled, moving toward the porch steps.

But Annie rose, reached for her suitcases, and whispered only, "Good-bye."

Jesse hired a driver, and he and Bishop Andy rode to the Lancaster County Prison, which served as a holding place for those awaiting trial—and their own Zeke Hochstetler.

At first glance, the place was something out of an Englischer's storybook, Jesse thought, surveying the castle-like structure as they made their way beneath the high arched entrance on East King Street.

Bishop Andy, stating firmly he'd come only to offer moral support, sat in the waiting area, outside the visitation room. Both he and Jesse were nervously aware of the camera high on the wall, monitoring their every move. Jesse hoped the Good Lord might overlook it when their faces showed up on a hidden screen somewhere.

Entering the visitation room, Jesse was directed by the guard to a small cubicle. There sat Zeke, behind the glass partition, obviously pleased to see him. Jesse sat down in a folding chair.

"You're the first to come visit me," Zeke acknowledged.

Jesse doubted there would be many more visitors, but he didn't have the heart to say so. He listened while Zeke rambled on about missing Esther, becoming more aware that the thick glass window was not the only barrier between them.

But Jesse hadn't come to discuss Zeke's wife and children, though it was understandable for Zeke to want to. There were niggling questions, one in particular, and knowing they had scant time for a leisurely chat, Jesse directed the conversation to the business at hand. "Zeke, what happened?"

Zeke shook his head, pulling on his beard. His eyes were dark beads.

"I had me a whole group of tests yesterday." Zeke leaned back and laughed—too heartily for Jesse's liking. "I agreed to let them see if I'm of sound mind or not. I figure if I could strike Esther hard when she was only days from birthin' Essie Ann, then I'm a threat to my own family, ain't?"

The hair on Jesse's neck prickled. Zeke *narrisch*—crazy?

"They ain't keepin' me here against my will, if that's what you're thinking."

Jesse watched the man more closely, hesitant to judge simply with his eyes. Still, he observed the slant of Zeke's head, the clarity of his gaze, the set of his jowl, and the steadiness of his callused hands.

No obvious signs of mental illness that he could tell, but of course he was no match for worldly experts. He did know that Zeke was a man who said things he later regretted. He pressed the boundaries of the Ordnung and looked for ways to be a nuisance. He pushed folk around verbally and was no doubt dreadful to live with.

Zeke's wounds were undeniably etched on his soul. Anybody who knew him readily understood his loss as insufferable, coming at such a tender age. After all, someone had taken away his little brother—killed him— that long ago and shocking night.

Jesse leaned forward. "You must come home to the People . . . we'll help you."

Slowly Zeke's mouth parted and he began to speak. "I finally figured it out, Preacher, after all these years . . . what happened to my brother."

"And what's that?"

"I did it," he said flatly. "I killed Isaac."

Jesse was stunned at the conviction in his voice. "But, Zeke, you were just a boy yourself when Isaac was lost. You aren't thinking clearly."

"That's where you're wrong, Preacher. I'm thinkin' more clearly than I have in sixteen long years."

O Lord God, Jesse thought, sickened. *Can it be?*

Chapter 30

Esther cried. She stood at her back door and wept tears of pure joy, mixed with laughter. Annie thought it a strange yet lovely sort of sound.

Laura came running through the kitchen and out the back door to throw her slender arms around Annie's waist. "Mamma prayed somebody would come . . . and here you are!"

Esther nodded, brushing back her own tears. "I know the Lord answers our prayers, but this is ever so quick." She reached for Annie's hand and gave it a squeeze. "I'm so happy to see you!"

"Oh, me too, Essie! Me too!" She searched her friend's face, her eyes lingering long enough to see that Esther had not yet been scarred by the Bann. "I was hopin' you might take me in." Annie leaned down to pick John up, not ready to tell Esther why she was here. Even so, it was evident Esther sensed something and was gracious enough not to pry.

"Why sure, Annie. Stay as long as you like."

"Denki. This means so much to me," Annie replied.

"You've got yourself a right heavy one there," Esther said, meaning little John.

Annie and John rubbed noses playfully. "I think you've been eating pork chops again, young man." She squeezed his arm muscles.

John grinned, showing some new teeth.

"Oh, goodness, you don't know how *wunderbaar* it's goin' to be having you here, Annie."

"You sure? I don't want to be a burden."

"Not a burden . . . a blessing."

Yonie was already hauling her suitcases out of the backseat. "Just tell me where you want all this."

Zach hopped down the steps, their big black watchdog barking and wagging his tail and trailing behind him. "Follow me . . . I'll show ya," he told Yonie, then turned and marched into the house.

Esther whispered, "Zach thinks he's the man of the house now."

Yonie followed Zach inside, carrying the suitcases and talking Dutch to the boy.

Esther told Annie she'd moved back to Zeke's and her bedroom the night before, when she realized Zeke must not be returning from "you know where" in a few hours, as she'd first believed. "You can take the spare room at the end of the hall. It's nice and quiet."

"I'm grateful," Annie said. "And I'll pull my weight—you'll see."

Esther waved her hand, laughing. "No doubt in my mind."

Annie set John down and watched him toddle across the back porch, then slipped her arm through the crook of Esther's. "I'll do all I can to help you, Essie. For as long as you'll let me."

Esther's face clouded over. "Not sure how long my husband will be gone, Annie. I heard from your father, there's some sort of investigation under way. . . ." Tears threatened again.

"Aw, Essie . . . let's not fret. Surely something good will come of all this. Surely."

Esther shook her head. "I just don't see how."

The baby let out a holler, and Annie offered to go and get her. She hurried up the back steps and into the kitchen, bent down to the small playpen, and lifted Essie Ann up, resting her warm little head next to her cheek. "Your auntie's here," she cooed at her.

"Ach, I like that," Esther said, following Annie inside and mopping her face with a tissue. "We'll be sisters together."

Annie thought of Lou suddenly and caught Esther's look of cheer. "We always were, jah?"

There would be no further talk of jail or investigations or broken hearts. For today, they would dwell on friendship, laughter, and family—extended and otherwise.

Essie Ann was squirming to be fed, so Annie kissed her soft head and gave her to Esther. Looking round the kitchen, she felt right at home, seeing the clock shelf like Mamm's, the corner cupboard with a few German books and the pretty floral china teacups and saucers, and the green-checkered oilcloth on the table.

"Here, let me help," she said, taking a pillow from Yonie when he came back through the kitchen with her bedding and a bulky quilt. Then she followed him and Zach up the stairs.

In the room where she would sleep, Zach leaned against the door, smiling shyly. Annie took in the cheery light in the bedroom, which was larger than Julia's attic studio, to be sure.

Plenty of space for an easel and palette, she thought. *Well, maybe someday . . .*

Setting down her things, she went to admire the handmade quilt folded over the footboard. Immediately she recalled the many quilting frolics she'd attended with Louisa, and how she'd taught her friend the art of stitching.

I wonder how Lou's getting along. . . . She had received a birthday card from her and would probably get a long letter soon.

Zach still lingered near, eyeing her . . . seeing her in a different light, maybe. She was now his mother's houseguest, not merely a family friend. "This was Mamma's room before . . ." he began, his voice trailing off.

She nodded and gave him what she hoped was an encouraging smile.

If these walls could talk. She couldn't imagine what the bishop's shunning decree had meant for Esther and Zeke.

Going to the window, Zach pressed his hands and face against it, staring out. She looked fondly at the back of his little round head.

I'll be happy again someday, she thought, trying in vain to push thoughts of Ben from her mind. *Won't I?*

She realized suddenly, with a great sigh, how very small her own concerns were compared to the trauma in Esther's life. Yet as Esther had so confidently stated, the Lord God had chosen to respond to her desperate prayer.

Annie had not heard it expressed in quite that way before, except from Cousin Julia. But she decided, then and there, to do her very best to be just that answer.

Epilogue

There's something peculiar about time—knowing when an important event is to take place but realizing you aren't present as you had planned to be. Such a thing happened yesterday, and I brooded over it, imagining the brethren talking with the baptismal candidates while I sat in a Mennonite meetinghouse for Sunday school, of all things. It was the strangest gathering I've ever submitted myself to, but I went along for Esther and the children's sake. Whatever puts a smile on Essie's face is well worth any hesitation on my part. I just hope none of the brethren gets wind of it.

Cousins Irvin and Julia drove both their cars, meeting us here at Essie's, where we divided up, since there were too many of us to squeeze into one vehicle. And Julia, "to be extra safe," had infant seats all ready for the baby and little John, so not only did the two youngest ride in style, but we all broke yet another rule—going in a car on the Lord's Day. Seems anymore I'm breaking rules right and left.

I received a letter from Lou today, somberly delivered by Luke at Mamm's request. I'm going to write back tomorrow, letting her know where I'm staying now, so I can receive her correspondence directly. I'll also offer to send back her skirt, blouse, and pretty boots, since I won't be needing them anymore.

Louisa's letter to me was seven pages long—written on both sides of the paper. She clearly pines for Sam, and I'm not at all surprised, because I believe I know something of what she feels . . . as I think much too often of Ben. I suppose if he were to come looking for me now, I might even consider seeing him again. I've already disappointed my parents so much—what would one more thing matter?

Truth is, he's planning to return to Kentucky, according to Julia. So he must be as hurt as I am over my letter, though we had no business seeing each other, really. How could it ever have worked out?

Honestly, I think it was Ben's curiosity with Plain ways that got us together in the first place. But now? I'm ever so sure he'll be more content in his own world, just as I must smile through the storm of my life here.

And a storm it is. Esther's brother and sister-in-law, as well as her mother, came over yesterday afternoon and carried on something fierce about a magazine cover one of the farmers showed them. Pushed it right into poor Essie's face and said she was giving board and room to the Devil. She never took sides, but when they marched out to their buggy, she whispered to me, "Don't think another thing of this, Annie. You do what the Lord's called you to," and that was that.

I have no idea how almighty God calls someone, though it seems to me I was born with this insuppressible passion for art. Does that mean it's a calling, as Essie seems to think? If so, I'd be doing my heavenly Father's bidding, while defying Daed and the church. 'Tis beyond me, really.

I daresay my brother's in a similar pickle. Laura and I were out on the road Saturday, and who but Yonie came driving along, his English girlfriend sitting smack-dab next to him. He slowed the car and waved, smiling like nothing at all was wrong. I guess what Daed knows and doesn't seem to mind for now isn't an issue. As for Dory, his girl, that's another thing yet.

I'm not so sure I ought to feel sorry for Yonie, though, since he sure looks like he's leaning toward jumping the fence. If he doesn't end up English, when his running-around is through, he'll be stuck right back here with a great big hole in his heart. Like mine.

Esther and I saw Susie Esh, Rudy's bride, out hanging up wash this morning. Looked to me like she might be expecting their first wee one, but I didn't stare, just waved, watching her woeful expression as she turned slowly away. She was shunning Esther, no doubt. Or maybe news of my transgression, the painting on the cover of the *Farm and Home Journal,* has found its way to the Esh home, too.

Can't win for losing, Mamm sometimes said when the pressure cooker blew its top, or the fence around the peacock pen fell over.

All the same, the sun comes up every morning and sets each and every night. The moon and stars slide across the same sky I see here that Ben will soon see in Kentucky. The hands of time tick ever so slowly.

Essie says not to fret; seasons come and go. And I say right back to her: "Well, then, 'tis a waiting season. . . ."

Yet it's painful to think of never seeing Ben again. When I am alone in my room at day's end, tired after chores, I lie awake and rehearse his features in my mind, counting the weeks till my promise to Daed is done. Oh, how I long to take brush in hand and paint Ben's face, for fear I should forget him in due time.

Acknowledgments

Heartfelt thanks to three storytellers—Aunt Betty, "Auntie" Madge, and Cousin Dave—whose verbal brush-strokes of joy and inspiration are responsible for several anecdotes in this book.

I am grateful for brainstorming fun, which I shared with my husband, Dave, my "big-picture editor," and our bookworm daughter, Julie, who also enthusiastically read the earliest chapters. Also, I offer my deep appreciation to our daughter Janie, our son, Jonathan, and to my parents, Herb and Jane Jones, for endless prayer support and practical encouragement (such as unexpected goodies and brain food).

Although I have mentioned my superb editors numerous times, I cannot repeat too often my gratitude for the insight of: Julie Klassen, Carol Johnson, David Horton, and Rochelle Glöege. Also, my thanks to Ann Parrish, who reviewed the manuscript.

A special note of thanks to John and Ada Reba Bachman, remarkably kind to help with ongoing research, and to Rev. James Hagan for expert advice. Much appreciation also goes to my praying partners in various parts of the planet, as well as to regional and cultural assistants and proofreaders who have asked to remain nameless.

Thank you, as well, to my mother's dear cousins for allowing me to refer to and use scene settings from their beautiful colonial inn (Maple Lane Farm B&B) on Paradise Lane in Lancaster County, Pennsylvania.

Thanks, as always, to my devoted readers. In countless ways, these books belong to you . . . and always to God.